A DIFFERENT
KIND OF DEAD

THE "PERSONAL CRIMES" MYSTERY SERIES

A DIFFERENT KIND OF DEAD

PERSONAL CRIMES MYSTERIES, VOL. 4

TONY GLEESON

WILDSIDE PRESS

To Lily and Bill, who found time for my questions.

1.

Newspapers are dying.

Frank Vandegraf couldn't help telling himself that one more time as he sat on the stone park bench, staring idly at the copy of the Blade-Courier folded on his lap: just one more reminder that the world in which he felt comfortable was disappearing. He pulled out his new smart phone and laid it on top of the paper. He opened the screen for the internet news site he'd tried accessing earlier. It still just wasn't the same to him.

He'd heard the expression many times: adapt or die. He wasn't sure which one seemed more palatable; it depended on the day.

He saw Ben Martinez approaching up the walk, head down, looking deep in thought. He looked older and wearier since the last time they'd met. Then he raised his head, smiled, and waved to Frank. Briefly it was the Ben that he remembered.

"Thanks for coming," he said in his deep soft voice as he plopped himself down on the bench next to Frank.

"How are things, Ben?"

"Another round of layoffs last week. Looks like I survived again. Time will tell." He looked down at Frank's phone. "So you finally got rid of that old flip phone."

"World's changing fast. My partner's trying to get me up to speed with it. No easy task for her."

"You've got a partner now? You were solo when I did that story on your case, the murdered college professor."

"Yeah. Her name's Athena Pardo. She was a very capable patrol officer not long ago. You might have run into her at some crime scene."

"Pardo? Sounds vaguely familiar, but I haven't covered a lot of crime stories of late. They've got me doing investigative journalism now."

"How's that working out?"

Ben shrugged. "Better than if they'd put me on animal adoption stories. Now and then I get something I can sink my teeth into. They ran my three-part series on Highway Department kickbacks not long ago."

"Oh yeah. I saw that. Good stuff…"

Frank liked Ben, but they were not exactly close friends and he felt a bit awkward right now. After a long uncomfortable silence, each of them staring off into space so as not to look at the other, he finally asked, "So, why'd you want to see me?"

The reporter spoke very quietly, occasionally looking around to see if anyone else in the park might be approaching them. "I got this call the other day from a guy named Orrin Lattimer. Heard the name?"

"I don't think so."

"He's a tech guy, high up in a recent startup called Humbletech. You must have heard of them, right?"

"Yeah, vaguely. Self-driving smart cars or something like that? Run by some kind of eccentric tech wizard?"

"You're thinking of another company and another eccentric tech wizard that's always in the news. There's no lack of them. Smart cars, people movers, smart trains. I wouldn't be surprised these days if they're doing smart pogo sticks. But no, this company deals in scooters actually. Those urban electric scooter things? You know, the kind the hipster kids can pick up on some corner, rent on their phones and then leave anywhere?"

"Oh yeah. You can't avoid them. Someone almost ran me down on the sidewalk with one of them the other day. Obnoxious things. Don't think they're even supposed to be on the sidewalks. Can't twentysomethings, like, walk?"

"You are ancient, aren't you? Gonna come join me shaking our canes at the damned kids on our lawns one of these days? Anyway, Humbletech's front guy is Lane Dembeau, who definitely fits the eccentric label in my opinion. Flamboyant promoter, loves publicity, travels extensively, makes outrageous pronouncements. The news media love him because he's full of sound bites."

"Uh huh, now I know who you're talking about. He's certainly full of something."

"Some people call him a visionary, but as far as I can see, he's the head of a small company that rents scooters. All the rest of his pronouncements about how he's going to improve the world with wonderful technology is like tilting at windmills. He likes to see himself as a globe trotter and a world saver. I suspect he's a wizard who's all hat and no magic."

"That so? You can't help but hear about him, and from what I've read, he certainly talks a good game."

"But to my point...which is not Mr. Dembeau but his associate Mr. Lattimer. He contacted me on the strength of my kickback articles. He wanted to meet with me to talk about...stuff."

"Stuff?"

"He was vague, said he couldn't talk much on the phone. He said he had inside information about something in his company; he called it a blockbuster. Okay, Humbletech is a small company, but it's pretty high profile these days, definitely of interest to my editor, and the potential for a blockbuster is certainly there. It sounded promising, at very least worth checking out. So I asked when he could come talk to me. He was adamant that he couldn't just meet me in the open. He said he was sure he was being watched, and that it was remotely possible that his life was even in danger. So we arranged to meet last night in a clandestine locale out near the wharf. Real spy fiction stuff: prearranged signals, the whole bit."

"Wow. Like the journalists in the movies. But why are you telling me all this? I don't deal with corporate crimes; the Department's got a special division for that. And even if there are crimes involved, I'd think you'd be looking to protect your sources."

"That's the thing, Frank. The meeting never came off last night. He never showed. I waited around until almost midnight and then got back in my car. When I turned on the radio for the drive back, that's when I found out what had happened."

"What happened?"

"You heard about the light rail accident yesterday evening, the guy that got killed at the Northcote station right where the train goes underground?"

"Sure. It was all over the news. The guy slipped and fell in front of the train just as it was coming into the stop."

"That was Lattimer."

"Really? Everything I read and heard said it was an accident. There was a witness, the station was pretty empty, and nobody seemed close to him."

"And maybe it was an accident. But if so, quite a coincidence, don't you think? The guy's paranoid he's being followed, feels that he's got something sufficiently explosive that his life is on the line. And this happens an hour before he's supposed to meet with me, probably on his way to that meeting. That very train has a stop about a five-minute walk to where we were supposed to meet."

Frank found himself furtively glancing around like Ben was doing now and then. "Why tell me in this hush-hush manner?"

"Frank, whatever the circumstances of his death, if he was right and there's really something going on, and I blew a whistle loud and clear, there'd be a coverup. I don't want this guy to have died in vain."

"Uh huh. Not to mention you might still be able to pull a story out of all this."

Ben raised his unkempt eyebrows and spread his hands. "This I cannot deny. The point is, I felt discretion would be the better part of valor."

"So you called me."

"I remembered that murder case of yours that I wrote about, how you ran down the leads. Now that was great stuff. You even traveled a hundred miles upstate to personally dig up the information that broke the case. You're hands-on, old school, like me. I can tell you're trustworthy. You've got integrity. And you care about finding the truth."

"You're not planning to nominate me for sainthood in the near future, are you? Because I'm not even Catholic."

"You can laugh, but you know what I'm talking about. I'm old enough that I don't trust too many people anymore. The young ones aren't bright and the older ones lost their ideals. The moral compasses are spinning like crazy these days. And none of them care. I get the feeling you still do. So are you willing to look into this?"

Frank sighed. "You know, I've been told what a dinosaur I am lots of times, but that was just the *noblest* way anybody ever put it." He shook his head and pursed his lips. "All right. But I can't promise anything, Ben."

"All I'm asking is that you seek. And give me an exclusive if you find."

Frank shook his head. "I'll look into the possibility of a wrongful death, and that's it. I can't spend too much time on this. It's likely a snipe hunt, and Athena and I have our hands full. But I can ask around and let you know."

"Understood." Ben stood up and offered his hand to shake. Frank followed suit. As the reporter trudged away, head down, Frank couldn't help but think that they were both men that had found themselves in a new and increasingly unfamiliar era.

If you're in a situation, he mused, it's nice to know you're not alone.

Frank was able to catch up with the two patrol officers who had first arrived at the scene of Lattimer's death. He knew them both well: experienced veterans who approached a scene with care and skepticism. If there was anything to Ben's suspicions, these two were a good place to begin. They were grabbing a quick bite at a popular taco stand; he joined them around a small round sidewalk counter.

Alonzo Mabern, the older of the two, short-cropped hair receding back on his high dark forehead, paused in anticipation of the meeting of his mouth with an entire *al pastor* street taco. "So you got a partner now; how's Athena doing?"

"Don't tell her I said so, but she's coming along great. I'd say she's a natural."

"Kinda miss her on the street. She's one smart cop, good instincts, confident but not cocky. Always knew she'd be a detective one day. And Personal Crimes, no less!" Mabern could wait no longer and plunged into the meat and onion laden taco.

"Glad to have her, too, especially with the Creep case lately."

"Oh, you pulled that one. How's it going?"

Frank shrugged. "Hoping to catch a break. It's a bear."

"And how's Dan Lee doing?" asked Sandra Kovetsky, Mabern's partner.

"Oh yeah, I heard you and he had a thing for each other. He and his partner, Detective Garvey, are keeping quite busy." Mabern, even with a mouth full, couldn't suppress a guffaw and almost choked. Kovetsky was unamused.

"Oh come on, Frank! We don't have a *thing!* He's just a good guy, that's all! Who's been telling stories up there, anyway?"

Frank shrugged and took the opportunity to bite into his own carne asada taco.

Everybody paused to enjoy their lunch for a minute. Then Mabern asked, "So what's up? What brings you out here with cops who actually work for a living?"

"Heard you two were first responders last night, along with the paramedics, at the Northcote train station."

Mabern shook his head. "Oh yeah. Lattimer. That was a bad one."

"Guy looked like hamburger," Kovetsky added. She looked at her own salsa-laden taco plate. "Or carne asada."

"What's the story on that?"

"The platform was pretty empty when it happened," Kovetsky said. "Only one witness. He said the guy just pitched forward off the platform onto the tracks as the train was coming in. There was no way the train could've stopped. He thought he might have tripped and fell, or maybe he was leaning too far forward."

"So it's not like there were people nearby that might have shoved him or anything?"

"Doesn't seem like it. Sunday evening, there were maybe four people spread out over the entire platform."

"Until the incident," said Mabern. "Then the rubberneckers just appeared out of nowhere. Weird how that happens, huh? We happened to be nearby when we got the call; we arrived right behind the EMTs and at the same time as the transit cops."

Kovetsky nodded. "When they saw we had the witness interview under control, the transit guys weren't even interested in talking to him. They just devoted themselves to taping off the area and clearing out the thrill seekers."

"So, only the one witness who saw anything?"

"Only one willing to say he did, yeah."

"Who is this guy? Did he know Lattimer?"

"He said no, he'd never seen him before. He was a kid, on his way home to meet some friends or something." She looked down at her plate.

Frank looked at Kovetsky for a long time. "You're being tentative. Like maybe you didn't totally believe him?"

She shrugged. "Got nothing solid to base that on. He just seemed a little shifty."

Mabern chimed in. "It's just that he was a little weird. Kinda nerdy. And private. Not exactly forthcoming with his personal information. He was more or less willing to describe what he saw happen– and when he got going, the kid had a good memory for detail, I'll give him that. Then he wanted to take off right away."

"Usually nobody wants to get involved, especially if they have something to hide, like your guy might have."

"Ain't that the truth. But in the end, we had nothing tangible to base our doubts on, so we took his statement. Maybe he just had one of those photographic memories. When the coroner showed up, he found nothing inconsistent with the story we had gotten, and there was no other testimony to confirm or deny the witness. In the end it seems like everyone was happy to accept that the whole thing was an accident."

Kovetsky swallowed the last of her taco and licked her fingers. "And it probably was. Just one of those odd vibes you get sometimes from a wit, you know?"

Frank nodded. "Who was the medical examiner?"

"Mickey Kendrick."

"You got the best, and on a Sunday night. And what was the name of your sketchy witness?" He had his notebook open on the counter, a drop of hot sauce staining a corner of a page.

Kovetsky pulled out her own notebook and flipped a page. "His name was Zone. Lucas Zone. Right out of Central Casting for 'Millennial on train platform': flannel shirt, soul patch, and a wool hat pulled over his head. Carrying one of those typical shoulder bags. Said he was some kind of internet blogger. An 'influencer,' as he put it."

Mabern smiled wryly. "The kid probably had something in the bag he didn't want us to find. He just wanted to give his story and get out of there. Not like we were going to search him or anything."

"But he was agreeable enough to tell us how Lattimer died."

"Where'd he go?" asked Frank. "After you talked with him, I mean."

"Well, it looked as if the track wouldn't be cleared for some time, so I guess he left to go find a bus or an Uber or something."

"Or a scooter," muttered Frank. "I hear they're everywhere."

"I do not like those damned things," Kovetsky said. "We see too many accidents involving idiots riding them, especially on the sidewalk, where they're not supposed to be."

"I'm with you there. I presume you got contact info for this Zone. Can I get that from you?"

"Sure. It might even turn out to be legit. I had two potential wits give me fake numbers last month."

Mabern shook his head. "This job is not getting any easier."

"Any next of kin or friends of the victim, anything like that?"

"It's been turned over to the Metro Transit Accident Investigation Team. They'll be looking into all that. You could try them. Why the interest?"

"I've just been asked to check out a few things. It's probably like you say, just an accident."

"If you talk to that Zone guy," Kovetsky said, "you'll see what I mean. There was just something off about him. But that doesn't mean he wasn't telling the truth."

"Out here these days," muttered Mabern, "they're all off."

2.

Frank had learned from the officers that the Metro Transit investigator who'd taken the report was an ex-police officer named Russ Payne. The guy was well named. He preferred to avoid talking to Payne, and he didn't want to be perceived as stepping on any interagency toes if there was another way to do this. He figured it couldn't hurt to try giving Lucas Zone a quick call to ask a few innocent questions. Maybe everything was just what it seemed and he could let this rest. He sat in his car and dialed the number on his cell phone. It rang several times before it went to a generic voice mail, an androgynous robotic voice telling him to leave a message. He thought it best to simply hang up and try again later. He might as well continue his inquiry from back at his desk.

Frank returned to Personal Crimes to find the unit's common room alive with activity everywhere; every member of the squad was overloaded. His partner, Athena Pardo, was no exception, busily working her phone and computer simultaneously.

Years earlier, the unit had officially been called Special Crimes and before that had gone by the prosaic but accurate title Robbery-Homicide. At some point, the Department had decided the name Personal Crimes bore more solemnity. The unit still dealt with basically the same types of crime, almost entirely felonies: homicides, severe assaults, robberies, hate crimes. Simultaneously, the unit that handled burglaries and similar non-violent crimes, currently housed in a similar squad room one flight up from them, had gained the moniker Property Crimes. The veterans of either group would likely have remarked that there had been little difference beyond the name changes.

Athena, phone receiver to ear, looked up at Frank as he approached her desk, raising her eyebrows as if to ask how his interview had gone. Frank shrugged and headed to his own desk. She'd get caught up soon enough. Another call to Zone went through to the same disembodied voicemail and once again he hung up. It looked like he couldn't avoid the call to Payne.

Frank remembered Russ Payne from back in his days as a uniformed police officer, when he was already being referred to behind his back as "Major" and other, less repeatable plays on his surname. His transfer to accident investigation at Metro Transit must have felt like heaven: a limited number of colleagues with whom he needed to get along and a limited number of hours he needed to put in. Overtime and sociability were not hugely important to him.

Frank considered that he hadn't had any contact with Russ in a few years now. Perhaps he had mellowed. People do change.

"What the fuck do you want, Vandegraf?" That opener doused Frank's unusual optimism.

"Nice to hear your voice too, Russ. Just had a question about a case you picked up. Orrin Lattimer. The guy who fell in front of the train?"

"Oh yeah. The Northcote station. He made quite a splatter. I tell you, this job is not for the faint of heart or weak of stomach. What about him?"

"It's going down as an accident, is that right?"

"Of course it is. Why else would it have been given to us? The guy tripped over his own two feet and fell in front of the train. What a lamebrain."

"My understanding is there was only one witness to what happened on the platform."

"Yeah. And he was pretty clear about what happened."

"So you spoke to him?"

"First thing this morning. Why are you interested in any of this?"

"I happened to be talking with the unis who were on the scene and I got the impression the witness might have been a little dubious about what went on."

"Nope. When he called me this morning he was crystal clear about everything. He was maybe ten feet from the guy, who was keeping too close to the edge of the platform. The guy seemed like he wasn't paying attention. He was off in the ozone somewhere, pacing back and forth. He lost his balance and slipped onto the tracks just as the train was coming in. What are you doing interrogating the unis about my case?"

"Nothing like that, Russ. Remember Mabern and Kovetsky? I was taking a break at a taco stand and encountered them, we got to talking, and it came up. I asked what was new and interesting. That was pretty interesting, you've got to admit."

"Best one I've seen in a while, for sure. Might even get the Federal Transportation Safety people involved before we're through. So why call me about it?"

"Just curious. Sounds like a good story. I wanted to get it from the horse's mouth."

"Sounds like you got too much free time over there at Personal Crimes, Frank."

"Actually it's crunched as usual… wait. You said the witness called you? That's unusual. I usually have to chase the wits down with a net."

"Yeah, well, I left the guy a message earlier and he got right back to me. He was very eager to help. A regular solid citizen."

Frank had a sudden brainstorm. "Actually I do have an ulterior motive for calling, Russ."

"Uh huh. I figured."

"I have an informant named Lattimer. Don't pass that around, okay? I hope this guy wasn't related to them. Do you know if he had family?"

"His wife, Meryl. You know a Meryl Lattimer?"

"I don't think so, but I better check just to be sure if there's a connection. Is she here in the city?"

"I don't know. I'm trying to find her. There's nobody at the Lattimer household up in the hills; at least nobody's answering the phone number I got."

"Hopefully they're no relation. Thanks, Russ. Nice to talk with you."

"Wasn't it, though. Can't wait to talk to you in another few years."

Frank hung up, absent-mindedly rubbing the back of his neck and shaking his head. That was about the best he could have expected to get from Russ Payne.

"You're doing that again. The neck rub thing. So is this a live one you walked into?"

He looked up at Athena, standing over him, her arms folded, eyebrows raised in a quizzical smile.

"I really don't know. Likely it's nothing. Pull up a chair and I'll tell you the story."

"Forget the chair. I'll stand. So tell me."

It took less than ten minutes to lay out the entire tale.

Athena shook her head. "It seems pretty straightforward. Is this even worth pursuing?"

"I honestly don't know. If it weren't for Ben Martinez's misgivings, my answer to you would have been no, it isn't. But Ben's no alarmist and this really seemed to worry him, so I promised I'd sniff it out."

"Maybe it was just a tragic coincidence. Maybe the guy was so distracted by what he was planning to tell Martinez that he wasn't paying attention."

"Maybe. I'm just going to look into one or two more things and then, if nothing looks promising, drop it. We've still got our hands full with the Creep."

"I hate that name. It's the only way the news will refer to the case. This is somebody killing innocent people, not a media star. Anyway, I've been checking out a lot of stuff on the victims. I still think there are connections; I just have to find them."

When Athena got hold of something, she did not let go easily. Frank had come to admire that about her. "My time would be better spent joining you on that. Give me an hour or so and I'll be back."

Back on his phone, Frank called Lucas Zone's number back once again, and this time he left a message identifying himself and asking for a callback. He figured there wasn't much chance of any complaint now from Russ. The only other avenue that seemed open to him was Lattimer's wife, Meryl. Payne had stated that the Lattimers had a house in the hills, but that it was presently unoccupied. He wasn't sure how Payne could have been so sure of that. It was an easy matter to trace an address for an Orrin Lattimer in that area. It couldn't hurt to drive out and see if Mrs. Lattimer were available now.

The eastern part of the city rose into a set of verdant hills with often breathtaking views of the shore to the west. It was a high rent district with a lot of expensive neighborhoods. The Lattimer house was on a secluded street, modest by comparison to others in the vicinity but still very comfortable. The tech industry seemed to have its rewards. Frank parked in front of the property, which was surrounded by a high iron fence through which he could see trees and lush shrubbery around a ranch-style home. A gardener was just opening the gate and carrying out a plastic can of yard cuttings. He looked up as Frank approached him with his ID already out.

"I'm looking for Mrs. Lattimer. Do you know if she's around?"

The gardener peered at the badge and ID card in the folder, then shook his head. "Don't think any of them have been here in a couple weeks."

"How can you be so sure?"

"I come every Monday, and for the last two weeks nobody's around and nothing's moved or changed around the yard or house."

"So, somebody's usually on the premises when you come here?"

"A lot of times, yeah. Sometimes the kid is home. Mrs. Lattimer is around a lot and leaves the gate open for me. She comes out and waves and says hello. Very polite lady. Or she might come out and talk to me about something she wants done around the yard. When she's not here she leaves a key for the gate under one of the stone figures around the side. The key was there the last two weeks."

"So there's a daughter? How old would you say she is?"

"Maybe twelve, thirteen. I have a sixteen year old daughter myself, and the Lattimer girl looks a little younger."

"What about the husband, Mr. Lattimer? Ever see him around here?"

The gardener shook his head. "Almost never. Once or twice I saw him coming or going, that's it."

"Has she ever left contact information for you when she's not here? Maybe she mentioned she was going somewhere?"

"She once mentioned the family's got a cabin or something up north. That's about all I remember."

"You always deal with Mrs. Lattimer, I take it?"

"Uh huh. She's the one who keeps the yard and the garden, and she pays me, always right away."

"How's she pay you…cash? A check?"

"She makes an automatic monthly payment online from their bank account to mine."

Of course, Frank thought, the wife of a tech wizard would have digital payments set up. "And she's been up to date? When was the last payment?"

"Three weeks ago. Right on time."

"But nobody's been here for a couple of weeks now? Are you sure?"

"I can tell. Nothing's been touched anywhere around the property."

"But there's been no mail in the mailbox?" Frank pointed to the large brass decorative letter box along the gate.

"You got a point there. I don't look in the box when I come by, but after a couple weeks, you'd figure it might be stuffed. Someone must be coming around to pick it up." The gardener, hefting the can of clippings, looked impatient. "Mind if I get on with my work here?"

Frank nodded and waved the man on. He spent a minute staring at the house and then turned to head back to his car.

He was about halfway there when his phone started chiming like a bell. He still hadn't found a ringtone on his new phone that he liked; this one was kind of annoying.

"Vandegraf."

"Is this the detective that left a message for me? This is Lucas Zone." It was a young voice, a little on the whiny side.

"Yes, Mr. Zone, that's me. Thanks for getting back to me."

"I already answered a bunch of questions for the other detective this morning."

"Inspector Payne, you mean. I'm following up on another aspect of the incident and had a few more questions, if you don't mind." Frank didn't stress the distinction between his agency and Russ's. The less complicated he kept this, the better.

"Like what?"

"Can you just run through what you saw happened last night?"

"It's like I told the other guy. I was coming down the stairs to the front of the platform. The guy was maybe ten, fifteen feet from me. He wasn't paying a lot of attention, kind of pacing back and forth, fidgeting around. He seemed nervous. He had walked really close to the edge, maybe to look out to see if the train was coming. It was just pulling through the tunnel before the station. Then he kind of doubled up forward, and his feet sort of went out from under him, and he fell off the platform right into the path of the train. The guy landed on the tracks just as the train got to him. There was nothing the guy driving the train could have done. It was pretty awful."

"And there was nobody else closer to the victim?"

"Nope. There were only a few people on the whole platform, waiting for the train. They were down at the other end, moving to where the doors would open when the train pulled all the way in."

"And nobody touched him. Nobody had any contact with him?"

"Uh-uh. Nobody was anywhere close enough to touch him. He was alone."

"Was he carrying a briefcase or a bag or anything?"

"I don't remember seeing anything like that. I wasn't, like, really staring at him. My attention was drawn to him when he started to fall."

"And you say he just pitched forward, like he bent over? You say his feet went out from under him? Are you saying he might have purposely jumped in front of the train?"

"Oh, no. No…it just didn't look like that at all. It was like he wasn't paying attention and stumbled over his own feet. That made it even more horrible. I could see the shock in his face as he fell. It was, like, totally out of nowhere. One second he was there and the next…"

"You say your attention was drawn to him as he started to fall. Why was that?"

"I don't really know. I had just come down the stairs to the platform, kinda looking around the station at stuff. You know how you do that when you enter a train station so you know what's going on, stay alert, to be safe and all? And I happened to look in his direction just a few seconds before it happened. His fidgeting, maybe, kind of caught my attention, and then… aw jeez. That's really all I saw. It was totally messed up. I wish I hadn't seen it."

"I'm sure, Mr. Zone. I appreciate your being so cooperative. Just for background, what were you doing there at that time?"

"I was on my way home to meet some friends, from some research and interviews I'd been doing for my gaming review blog. I'm an internet influencer."

Frank wasn't quite sure what a gaming review blog might be, or an influencer. And he wasn't particularly interested to digress sufficiently to find out.

"And you remained there to tell the officers what you had seen?"

"That's right."

"Nobody else seems to have seen anything?"

"Guess not. I wouldn't know."

"I appreciate that you stayed and gave them the information. Anything else you can remember about what happened?"

"Not really. It all happened so fast."

"But you seem very sure that it was an accident."

"It had to be. He just fell, you know?"

Frank asked one or two more questions, noting that Zone seemed to be losing patience. He finally thanked him and ended the call.

Now he understood what the officers had been talking about. Zone was a squirrelly, uneasy sort, but not necessarily a liar. Frank had encountered more than a few people of that age group that seemed to have a problem concentrating like that.

At best he had come to a dead end, and at worst he was on a total wild goose chase. There were pressing matters requiring his attention. He needed to put this matter on the back burner or, preferably, close it down.

So…what was bugging him about this?

There was one last thing he might be able to do before returning to the squad room. He looked at the phone in his hand and started tapping the screen. He still wasn't very good at navigating around on his phone browser, but he finally brought up the information he wanted. Humbletech was, surprisingly, not that far away, in the heart of the city. He could make one more stop on his way back to Personal Crimes.

More surprises awaited Frank, who was expecting some kind of spacious campus like the tech companies he read about. Instead he found himself walking up to a two-story building on busy Goff Boulevard and into a high-ceilinged lobby, visually clean and modern but comparatively modest. A large sign at the entry proclaimed SMALL STEPS TO SOLVE BIG PROBLEMS; that and two large graphics of attractive twentysomethings, happily riding brightly-colored scooters, orange and purple versions, with logos reading HUMM, were the only adornments on the white walls.

He only had to cool his heels for about ten minutes before a serious young woman dressed entirely in black trotted down the open spiral staircase from the second floor and introduced herself as Sharon Brooks, Orrin Lattimer's personal assistant. She escorted him to a small conference room, pointed to a chair and sat down across from him. He could feel a vibe of alert energy from her; this was a person who didn't like to stop their forward motion, even in the midst of derailment by tragedy. It was likely how she dealt with the shock of loss, in fact.

"This is a terrible thing. Orrin's death has knocked us all for a loop, Detective Vandegraf."

She got his name right. It was a small thing, but Frank was impressed. He could recite a long litany of mispronunciations of his name over his years. Almost nobody ever seemed to get it right the first, or the fourth, time. He'd heard them all: Van de Camp, Vanderbilt, Vanderpump, even Vanna White. Not this time.

Apparently there were some sharp tools in this shed.

"I'm a little confused," she said. "I had a very extensive telephone conversation this morning with the person in charge of investigating the accident. I gave him all the information I could."

"That would be the investigator for Metro Transit, Inspector Payne. I'm just following up on some details for my own department."

"And how may I help you?"

"Can you tell me a little about Mr. Lattimer's role here?"

"Orrin was one of the founders of the company. In fact, he was the lead developer."

Apparently it was *de rigeur* to use first names here. Frank wasn't sure if that was a function of the modern tech industry, or Miss Brooks' generation, or both.

"Just how big a company is this?" he said.

"We're still quite small, about a hundred employees," she said. "But we're growing."

"I'm not sure what a lead developer is," Frank continued. "What did Mr. Lattimer do here, exactly?"

"Officially, his title was Chief Innovation Officer," Sharon Brooks said. "He oversaw the development of new concepts and directions."

"So Humbletech plans to branch out into other things besides the scooters?" Frank was beginning to get the picture.

"Oh, definitely." She warmed to her subject. "That was always the vision of the founders, Orrin, Lane and Collis."

"Lane would be Lane Dembeau, I assume? And Collis…?"

"Collis Westermark is our Chief Financial Officer," she said. "The three of them started Humbletech. The scooters are just the opening project. There are several other sustainable transportation concepts in development."

"Mr. Lattimer sounds pretty important in the scheme of things. This is all very interesting to me. I was under the impression that Lane Dembeau had been the whole show here. He's certainly the person you always hear about when the company is in the news."

"Yes, Lane is the face of Humbletech, as we like to say." She smiled. "His official title is Lead Designer—he hates old-thought titles like Chief Executive Officer—but he's so much more. He's always been the engine that drives the organization. He's absolutely tireless; right now he's on an international tour to negotiate and promote new projects."

The entire description was given with the level tone of someone who had given the same speech many times before. There was a long pause. She sat, hands laced on the table, staring at Frank, eyes wide, awaiting his next question. She showed no sense of impatience but that internal energy was clearly bubbling under the calm surface, sending a subtle message to get to the point and let her get back to things that mattered. Frank sensed that she was a lot more agitated under the serene facade.

Cool customer. This is a lot harder for her than she wants me to know.

"I understand you must be extremely busy at the moment, running things in Mr. Lattimer's absence," he said. "What kinds of projects was he working on?"

She hesitated. "Well, much of what he was involved with is confidential, of course."

"Of course," he said. "I just mean in general. Whatever you feel comfortable in telling me."

"Orrin was developing several ground-breaking transportation concepts that were in different stages, including some things the company hopes to be introducing in the near future."

Again she paused. "Beyond that, I can't really tell you anything."

Frank rubbed his neck, figuring how to pose his next questions.

"Had Mr. Lattimer been involved in any…controversies recently—any personal conflict with anybody in or out of the company?"

"Controversies? Not at all. Why do you ask?"

Frank spread his hands, as if to repeat that it was all just routine. "What kind of guy was he? I mean, his temperament, how he got along with everyone?"

"He tended to be very reserved, stayed in the background. He could be distracted; his mind was always racing with ideas. He was a brilliant man. But he was certainly not combative or aggressive. He didn't argue with anyone."

"Did he seem in an unusual state in recent times, in an odd mood, maybe bothered by something?"

She thought it over and slowly shook her head. "I wouldn't say so. But he wasn't a demonstrative sort. It was hard to read his mood. He could pour out ideas or instructions but never in an emotional fashion. He was always on the same level."

"What about his family? Do you know them very well?"

"I've met Mrs. Lattimer and their daughter, of course, but don't know them well at all."

"So Mr. Lattimer had no domestic problems to your knowledge?"

"Those wouldn't have been my business, Detective Vandegraf. But I certainly saw nothing that would have indicated anything like that."

"Have you seen his wife or daughter recently? I was unable to locate them."

"It's been a long time since I've even spoken with Mrs. Lattimer. I'd assume they were home. I'm afraid I can't help you with that one."

"How long have you worked here, Ms. Brooks?"

"For not quite a year now; I joined right after the company began."

"And for all that time you've been Mr. Lattimer's aide?"

"Yes. He is– I guess I need to say he *was*– a great boss." Her manner considerably brightened as she spoke of him. "He demanded a lot but he was always fair and considerate. He gave me a lot of responsibility, valued my input, and even got me a raise after my probationary period had ended."

Frank sat back in his chair and pinched his nose, trying to figure out where to go with this. He wasn't even really sure what he was looking for. If trouble had been brewing for Orrin Lattimer, there didn't seem to have been any sign of it at work.

Or was it just being kept in the family?

Sharon Brooks dropped the energy level back, resumed her noncommittal expression, and stared patiently at him while she let another silence settle. For the remainder of the interview, the momentarily-glimpsed perky sprite did not re-emerge out of the cool administrative assistant. Frank asked a few more questions but nothing seemed to lead anywhere. The silences between his questions grew more awkward. Finally he thanked her and ended the interview.

Walking back to his car down Goff, stepping around two bright orange HUMM scooters, abandoned tipped over on the sidewalk for pick-up, Frank tried to decide if he had just totally wasted his morning. There were odd things that didn't totally gel but none of them added up to tangible evidence of a murder. Maybe Ben Martinez was right and Orrin Lattimer had been involved with something questionable, but that didn't necessarily translate to his death being other than accidental.

The edgy witness? Might not mean anything whatsoever. Frank had met a lot of sketchy millennials. He might just chalk that up to the generation gap and his own cranky nature.

The disappearance of Lattimer's family? He knew better than to immediately presume foul play. He had seen too many sudden absences for too many reasons.

For the moment, at least, there were other matters requiring his attention. Foremost was the assailant that had become known as the Creep.

Their salient case at the moment involved a series of violent assaults near local parks. Over the past two months, three individuals had been the victims of especially brutal stabbing attacks; the circumstances logically dictated the same perpetrator in each case. Two of the victims, a man and a woman, had been killed. The third and most recent victim, just the past Friday, had barely survived and remained in intensive care. She had been attacked and pursued in darkness; she owed her life to the fact that she ran to an area where other people happened to be walking. They heard her cries and the assailant fled. She had dropped to the ground but, before lapsing into unconsciousness, had been able to pant out a rudimentary description of her assailant. "Man. Big... creepy." There was a public uproar and resultant departmental pressure to find the assailant– whom the media had of course gleefully dubbed the Creep– before he could strike again.

A search for other witnesses and a painstaking canvas of the neighborhoods for security cameras had both proven futile. Given the current proliferation of surveillance equipment on banks, stores, and even apartment houses, they were surprised to come up empty and had begun to suspect that the assailant had chosen and scouted his areas carefully before his crimes.

All three attacks had occurred evenings around park areas, where a certain amount of seclusion existed. One theory was that that they were crimes of opportunity, where the attacker had lain in wait for a victim in an environment he judged to be safe. But Athena had come to believe that might not be the case. For one thing, there were no signs of robbery or sexual assault; the attacks seemed to be the goal in themselves. The victims had been stabbed repeatedly with a force that suggested it was personal. They had decided to look for any connections among the victims, a lead to someone they had in common. At first, there did not seem to be such a connection but Frank noted that Athena showed a devoted tenacity, continuing to delve ever more deeply into their backgrounds.

At the unit, she had created a schematic across a portable standing board, which she had rolled to her desk. She was pointing to various items pinned on it as she brought Frank up to date on her research, recapping information they already knew and adding anything new she had uncovered.

"I still don't know if there's anything to the fact that there were exactly twenty-eight days between the first and second assaults, and again between the second and third, but it's something to think about." Going through the familiar ritual still once more, she pointed with her pen to the name and photo on the first sheet. "First victim, Blanche Liwicki, age sixty. Spent her early life in Albuquerque, New Mexico. Lived here for thirty years. Retired as of last year from her longtime job at the Department of Water and Power. Found dead in Sunset Park, six stab wounds." She moved to the next pinned item. "Second victim, Ephraim Coates, age forty-three. Supervisor at the central storehouse for the Clips office-supply company. Originally from Detroit, Michigan; moved here six years ago. Stabbed nine times. He was killed in the dog park a block from his home. His dog was recovered three days later. And then... most recently, Natalie Riemer, age twenty-nine. She's a registered nurse at City Hospital and has an apartment within walking distance. Her family is in Oak Creek, not too far away. She grew up and went to school in the area. She was assaulted on a jogging trail in the foothills but managed to fight off the attacker. He chased her and continued to stab her before her shouts attracted attention and he got scared away, but in the meantime her wounds got the better of her and she's been in intensive care ever since. Her rescuers didn't get a good look at the guy and all we've got are her last words while still conscious.

"So we know it's a guy, acting alone. We know he's 'big'– possibly over six feet since Riemer herself is five-ten– and 'creepy' in some way that she didn't specify." Athena sighed. "As far as we can tell, the victims were strangers to one another. I can't find any employment history, any family or friends where they intersect. I'm not seeing a connection, but I can't lose the nagging feeling there's a pattern."

"The only pattern I see so far," Frank said, "is that his victims are getting younger."

"I thought about that. I think that's coincidence. There's some other connection that's just not clear yet."

"The twenty-eight day thing… she was attacked, what, three days ago? Possibly we're going to need to worry again in another twenty-five days?"

"Unless we catch him first," Athena replied, deep in thought. "What happens every twenty-eight days?"

Frank shrugged. "New moon?"

"Looked into that. The moon cycle is twenty-nine and a half days, and these have happened mid-cycle, nothing overly remarkable."

"Speaking of cycles. Female cycle?"

Athena shot him a look. "For some women, maybe. I don't see that being relevant here."

"Just brainstorming with whatever blurts out. That's all that comes to mind."

Athena shook her head. "Well, thank you for that different perspective. That was definitely something that just blurted out. Oh, by the way, we got a letter this time." She reached into her desk and pulled out a Manila envelope. In block letters it had been addressed to the station, no return address, and had been opened at mail stop and passed on to them just a short time ago.

She carefully pulled out a single sheet of paper by its corner and laid it on the desk so Frank could see it. He leaned over the desk, staring down at it.

It wasn't unusual to receive mail, phone calls and even emails claiming to be a current serial killer. The correspondents almost always were sick wannabes desperately seeking attention; it was a major reason that details of killings were routinely withheld, to weed out the fakes. After the second fatality, Frank and Athena had fielded a handful of crank calls purporting to be the Creep and had quickly ascertained every one of them was bogus. They were sure there would be more claiming responsibility for Natalie

Riemer soon enough. But this was the first piece of physical mail they had received that apparently was connected to the case.

Frank nodded. "I'm sure we won't have any better luck on prints on this one than we usually do. It's been handled by too many people by now. Probably some generic paper that can be bought at office supply stores all over town."

They stared down at the sheet, upon which the message had been printed with a broad felt marker in large block letters.

THE CREEP
THERE WILL BE MORE

3.

"This reminds me of something," Frank said as he gazed down at the page. Finally he shook his head. "It'll come back to me. So this was mailed to the Department?"

Athena nodded and held up the envelope, which was covered with stamps. "It was mailed to our unit. Postmarked from the University station."

He lowered his head in thought for a long time.

"What is it, Frank?"

"There's something. I can't place it yet. This is ringing a bell somewhere. Give me some time and I'll think of it."

Athena had learned that Frank had a deep detailed archive in his memory but that sometimes it took some time for it to become accessible. His method was, as he put it, to shift mental gears while the search worked in the background. Changing the subject seemed to help; several times, the "aha" would happen. He'd suddenly come up with what he had been trying to remember. She found it a weird way to process, but everybody had a different method of working through a problem. She dropped the letter back into her desk drawer. Maybe changing the subject for the moment would help.

"So… are you giving up on the train guy? Satisfied he fell, or could he have been pushed?"

Frank shook his head. "There's that one witness, Lucas Zone. He's pretty clear that it was an accident. He says he was ten feet away from Lattimer and nobody else was nearby, and the guy just slipped and fell off the platform. But there's something about what he told me that's odd."

"What do you mean?"

"I don't know. It all seems too glib. He's got the story down pat. It was like he was reciting it by rote."

"This is, what, at least the third time he's been called upon to give the whole story to an investigator? Wouldn't that account for his having it down so well?"

"Maybe. It's just the smallest bit odd. Maybe I'm reading too much into it."

"Possibly there were other witnesses that will come forward?"

"It doesn't sound as if there were any others. Even if there were, I don't get the feeling that Russ Payne is going to go to any effort to find them. He's convinced of an accidental death."

"Some investigator," Athena smirked. "Starts with a conclusion and works forward to the evidence?"

"Russ is a clear cut example of the Peter Principle. What can I tell you? And then there's the disappearance of Lattimer's family."

"Wait. His family is gone?"

"Wife and daughter; they haven't been at the house in two weeks, according to the gardener. He said something about a vacation cottage up north or something like that…"

"Couldn't that explain their absence? Maybe it was just a good time for a break. Maybe Lattimer was busy and had planned to join them later."

"So they took the daughter out of school? She's like twelve. And they haven't come back yet after he got killed? Conceivably he sent them there to be out of harm's way while he blew the whistle, if Ben is to be believed. Maybe they're just so out of contact that they don't even know what's happened to Lattimer. It's tempting to conjure up foul-play fantasies, but it's all empty conjecture. So far I have no evidence to back up anything. I can't work from feelings and blue-sky theory. That's dangerous."

"So what are you going to do?"

"Just to do right by Ben, I'll look into this a little further, just so I can tell him I did what I could. But I'm not seeing anything tangible. I can do it on my own and not distract us from the Creep."

"Would you stop calling him that? Actually I'd like to be in on this with you. I'm interested in Humbletech and if this means we might get a chance to take a peek inside…"

"Don't tell me you drive those damn scooters."

"The HUMMs? Now and then on a day off. They're fun, and they got me out of my car for a while last month."

"Really? I sincerely hope you didn't run down any pedestrians on the sidewalk. That would be embarrassing."

"I obeyed the law and observed safety precaution. I even wore a helmet. Anyway, count me in, at least until we can rule out any possibility of a wrongful death. I guess we better clear this with the Lou?"

The "Lou" was their Lieutenant, Hank Castillo, a man with personal presence and bearing that tended to give the initial impression of arrogance. The veteran detectives of the unit had decided from day one of his arrival to test him with the nickname, and it had stuck. To his credit, Castillo had taken it all with straight-faced humor from the outset without ever relinquishing an ounce of his considerable authority on the unit. Frank shook his head.

"Not just yet. He's going to discourage us from any distractions from our major case. If we uncover anything, then we can bring it to his attention. If not, he doesn't need to know."

"Okay. How do you suggest we proceed?"

"Well… maybe this Zone character. Think you could find anything on him with an internet search?"

"Let's find out." Athena swiveled around in her chair and began to hit keys on her computer. Frank marveled at how fast she started bringing up things on the monitor. He was getting better at digital tech but he still didn't feel comfortable with much of it.

"This guy told you he's some kind of blogger, right?"

"Yeah, and he called himself an *influencer,* whatever that is."

"That's kind of self-glossary, wishful thinking that you have some sway over people's buying habits. There are actually people who make decent money off spouting their opinions. Sometimes it's a rationale for not really having a job."

"That wouldn't surprise me in this guy's case. He said something about gaming or whatever. A gaming review blog. That was how he described it."

"This might be our man then. The Ultimate Zone: Games and gamers, reviewed by Luc Zone."

She turned the monitor towards Frank and he bent closer to peruse the screen. It was cluttered with an assaultive rainbow of garish graphic images. He was no artist but it struck him that there was way too much going on and everything was fighting for his attention with everything else.

"Are we supposed to be able to read this?"

"Some of these sites get pretty loud, but this one's particularly bad. He could definitely use a good web designer."

"Any info on the guy himself? Maybe a photo?"

Athena moved the cursor across the screen and clicked multiple times, bringing up one new page after another, with titles like "About" and "FAQs."

"Doesn't look like there's anything about our host. He's a mystery. Wait, what's this?" She brought up a new page bearing only a short paragraph in all caps superimposed over another explosion of garish color. It was difficult to read despite being in a large type size.

STAY TUNED FOR BIG NEWS!!!!! BIG PLANS IN THE MAKING!!! COMING SOON: ORIGINAL NEW GAMES AND EXCITING CONTENT FROM THE ULTIMATE ZONE!!!!!!!

"What do you make of that," asked Frank, squinting his eyes, "aside from the fact he loves exclamation points?"

"Whoever our Mr. Zone might be, he's got big plans. Sounds like he's anticipating starting up his own gaming company."

"He sounded like a teenager on the phone. Or maybe a twentysomething at best."

"I hate to tell you, Frank, but there are a lot of people that age who are millionaires these days."

"I guess I picked the wrong business."

Athena gave him a sly sideways look. "When you were a twentysomething, did they even have personal computers or smartphones?"

"*Touché*, wiseass. Could there be a connection between this guy and Humbletech? I mean, they're both into tech stuff."

"Kind of a stretch, Frank. Humbletech deals solely with transportation. Zone is a gamer—or more accurately, a reviewer of games, and not a very sophisticated one, it would seem. You can't get much farther apart than that."

"Do you think there's anything else to be found on Zone?"

"Let's take a look."

Athena continued to tap the keys and navigate the mouse.

"While you do that, I'm going to make a quick call to someone I know in Financial Crimes, just a chance that maybe there's something to Ben's claim that Lattimer had what he called a 'blockbuster' for him. It's a long shot."

"Humbletech's legal problems are pretty well known, but they're from injury and liability lawsuits about their scooters. Some people, including some politicians, consider them a public nuisance and are outright trying to get them banned."

"So I understand, and I could agree. But I don't see any of that as something Lattimer would have wanted to meet with a reporter about."

"Unless he had information about some kind of bribes to officials to make the trouble go away?"

"That seems kind of small time. I don't get the feeling that was what it was about. He was acting all cloak and dagger with Ben. I'm going to try that long shot with Financial."

Frank's call confirmed his assumption: neither Financial Crimes nor the District Attorney's office had current investigations into Humbletech for any type of financial malfeasance, or for any suspected criminal activity, to the knowledge of his contact. Within a matter of minutes he was back at Athena's desk, where she sat frowning at her monitor.

"There's next to nothing else on Luc or Lucas Zone," she said, "just a few sites that refer back to the Ultimate Zone website. No photos. This guy's a cipher. Clearly it's a screen name. I can't even be sure this is the same guy as your witness."

"He said he was a game reviewer so he's got to be the same guy."

"Well, he's done a good job of divorcing his online persona from his private life. Maybe with some time I could pull up some connection but at first shot, he's a mystery man. And from the look on your face, I assume Financial Crimes was a bust as well."

Frank nodded.

"So is there a next move on this?"

Frank waved his hand. "For the moment, no. But I let myself get sidetracked. If we brainstorm some more on the Creep…"

"Would you *please* stop calling him that? Uh…Frank? What's the matter?"

Frank had frozen in his tracks and brought his hand up to his temple, his eyes widening. For a moment, Athena was afraid her partner was having a stroke or seizure.

"Rackham," he said quietly.

"Rack 'em? What are you talking about?"

"Not *rack 'em*. Rackham." He raised his head, staring wide-eyed at her. "I remember. I remember what I was trying to think of earlier."

4.

"Ronnie Rackham," he said.

"What in God's name are you talking about, Frank?"

"A case. It's what the note reminded me of."

"You think there's a connection with one of your old cases?"

"Maybe. Maybe my memory is faulty. Let's see, that would have been…" he lowered his head again for a long moment. "They should still have it in Records here. If we're lucky, it hasn't reached the point yet where it would have been sent over to P&E. Come on, take a trip with me downstairs."

The basement of the building housed the immediate Records Department, where collected evidence and records from closed or cold cases, and other records pertaining to case files of the units in the building, were stored until a certain time had been passed, when they were sent to the central Property and Evidence location. It didn't take long for a clerk to locate and unseal the box requested by Frank, the one labelled RACKHAM along with an identification number. After checking it out of evidence and bringing it back to the unit, he and Athena now stood at his desk and removed items from the box. He withdrew a dark blue plastic binder and flipped it open between them.

"Here we go. It's gotta be in here."

"Okay," said Athena, "you gave me the short version on the elevator ride down and back, now give me the whole story."

"It's a sad story. Ronnie Rackham just hit a patch of real bad luck. She'd been a school counselor before she fell on hard times. She got 'riffed' from her school district…"

"Reduction in Force, you mean?"

"Yep. When the district had to trim its budget about five years back. You may remember, since all of us were concerned about the city-wide belt tightening and what dominoes were going to be knocked over. Ronnie was one of the dominoes; she lost her job and her health insurance coverage. Her husband died after a long battle with a chronic illness that depleted what savings they had, and she ultimately wound up on the street. She wasn't well equipped to deal with being homeless. One night she was murdered in an alleyway." Frank had been paging through the binder and now he stopped and pointed to a sheet in a clear plastic sleeve. "There it is."

It was a yellowing piece of cheap paper, creased twice from where it had been folded to fit into an envelope, on which was scrawled in large block letters:

RONNIE RACKHAM
THERE WILL BE MORE

"Remind you of anything?"

"Wow. It does look pretty close." Athena walked to her own desk and pulled out the recent envelope, extracting the page as she returned to Frank. She held it next to the binder and stared back and forth at the two notes for a long time.

"Where did that come from? Was it Ronnie's killer?"

Frank stared down at the page as if he was pulling the memory directly out of it.

"It was sent to the unit through the mail– the envelope's still in there as well—and turned over to me. My first reaction was that it was going to turn out to be a crank—the overwhelming percentage of the time, that's exactly what it turns out to be. But I still had to follow it up. In any case, I had very little else to go on at that point. I really hoped I wasn't dealing with a nutcase who was going to start randomly murdering street people."

"Did you find out who the sender was?"

"I did, in fact. It was a guy named Teddy Ralski."

"And he turned out to be the killer?"

Frank sighed and shook his head. "No. He was a crank."

"What?"

"He was a kind of screwed-up character. Came back from a military tour of duty with what would be diagnosed as PTSD and had an angry, threatening streak. He'd actually sent some other threatening letters to a few other people... city officials, local stores... which was how I tracked him down. He'd never actually committed any violent acts as far as I could ascertain, but he acted out a lot, screamed and threatened indiscriminately, and in the process he was seriously scaring a lot of people. I decided he was desperately looking for attention but he hadn't yet actually committed a violent physical act. I was having trouble seeing him as someone capable of an act of that level of savagery. Right around that time, I'd found my real suspect, the person I was sure had done the crime. It was a guy who preyed on homeless people in that neighborhood, and I ultimately got him. Meanwhile, I asked Ralski questions about the circumstances of Ronnie Rackham's death and his answers convinced me he didn't know crucial details. He couldn't have done it. He had read about it in the paper or seen it on the news and all he knew was what we had allowed to be released. He couldn't even tell me the exact manner in which she was killed."

"Which was?"

"She was stabbed in the back. Four times."

Athena stared quietly at Frank.

"Yeah, another coincidence. And there's at least one more, if I'm not mistaken."

"Which is?"

Frank turned the plastic sheet over in the ring binder and pointed to the legal-size envelope inserted behind the letter.

"There it is. Ralski mailed his letter from the University Station."

"What happened to Ralski, anyway?"

"I tried to get him some help. He couldn't stay on the street. He'd been living alone, with nobody able to offer him any kind of support or treatment. He was a veteran and he deserved better. He hadn't done anything worse than acting out in angry letters and phone calls, but if he was allowed to descend any deeper, he could have ultimately become a danger to himself if not to someone else. I found him a facility that worked with vets, where he could safely stay and they could work with him, get him professional psychological attention."

"So…Ralski was no killer; he was just sending letters. Who did you decide was good for the murder?"

"A guy named Leland. Several of the homeless people that knew Ronnie told me about him. Nasty character. A total predator. He routinely beat, cut and robbed people on the street that he sensed to be weaker. Over time his attacks got increasingly brutal and it was just sheer luck that some of his more recent prey had actually, barely survived. Ronnie was the first out-and-out death but it made sense. It fit his pattern."

"So you apprehended this Leland guy and he got put away?"

"In short order. We found a scarf of Ronnie's, with her name written in the tag, in among his stuff."

"Sounds like a bingo to me."

"He squirted through the trial like he was oiled. He had a bad record, a lot of barbarity, and it didn't help him any to wind up with a new and inexperienced public defender. He was found guilty hands-down in record time."

"So he's still in prison, I assume?"

Frank shook his head. "He died in prison not long afterward. Ran afoul of the wrong people, apparently."

"And Ralski, you say, went into a treatment facility?"

"Last I heard, yeah. About a year after, I followed up and he seemed to be doing pretty well. He was even working at the center in return for board.

That was the last I heard, though. It's been a while. There's always other stuff."

Athena nodded; that was for sure. "So…now, several years later, you're thinking he's regressed and returned to his old habits?"

Frank shrugged. "It's one possibility."

"But let's suppose he did send us those letters and it's not just a coincidence. It just means he's mailing crank notes again and doesn't necessarily have anything to do with our real perp."

"Well, yes and no. Here's the thing…"

"What?"

"Leland never admitted to the crime. Several times he said he'd known Ronnie but had never done anything to her. He claimed he'd never actually killed anyone in his life. He admitted he might have tried, but he insisted he never succeeded."

"So? You're saying that you didn't get the right guy?"

"Not then I didn't. The evidence was there; it was open and shut to me. Later on I did wonder, just a little. But by then it was water under the bridge."

"Why the eventual doubts?"

"It wasn't until sometime later that I found out the details of how Leland had died in prison. Various predators on the weak aren't always exactly popular in prison. He got into a fight with a couple of inmates because he adamantly persisted that he hadn't killed Ronnie Rackham. He said he'd done enough in his life that he could accept being behind bars, but for some reason it was important not to be blamed for her. He was willing to go to the wall with that argument and it got him killed."

"Or maybe what got him killed was the wrong guys in a max security just didn't like him. That happens."

Frank shrugged. "Sure it does."

"But the point is, by then you didn't see any reason to go back."

"What could I have done? There'd been a clear conviction. Distant relatives of Ronnie who'd been out of touch with her for years showed up and must have felt horrible guilt. I hoped they'd achieved some closure and peace after the verdict. It was just a shadow of a doubt I had developed; it wasn't like some new piece of evidence had been found or anything. Leland was a violent sociopath who got into fights, and wouldn't have been the first guilty convict to constantly protest his innocence. Nobody behind bars is ever guilty of anything. I moved on."

"But did you ever entertain the thought that Teddy Ralski had actually killed Ronnie Rackham?"

"Not seriously." He raised his head to stare at Athena, pursing his lips. "But this is too much of a coincidence. I think I need to look into this now."

"*We* need to be looking into this. Two heads are better than one."

"Understood, partner. But let me make the initial inquiries, since I know these people." Frank tapped the back of his knuckles on the plastic sheet holding the yellowed note. "If it looks like it might be anything more than still another dead end, we can jump on it."

"Frank, I know you. Don't try to do this alone, okay?"

"Promise," Frank said with a smile. "The moment I've got something worth us both jumping on."

5.

The logical place to begin was the treatment center where Ralski had checked in two and a half years earlier: a building in the far southern part of town, almost on the border with the raucous neighbor city of Sycamore, operated by a charitable nonprofit foundation called Reboot. The center was managed by a combat veteran named Cary Wilde, and his main focus was with veterans who seemed to have hit their own particular wall.

Frank figured he should go right to the source. The person answering the phone crisply said, "Reboot," and Frank, identifying himself, immediately asked to speak to Cary. Luck was with him and he got put through.

"Detective Vandegraf," said a deep raspy voice. "It's been a long time."

"How are you, Mr. Wilde? How's everything at the Center?"

"Ups and downs. Always some new fire-fight. More shit on the street and less resources. But we fight the good fight. All things considered, we're keeping our heads above water. How can I help you?"

"I wanted to check in and get an update on Teddy Ralski, the guy who came to you as the result of my case at the time?"

"Sure, I remember Teddy. Things seemed to work out pretty good for him. I'm not sure when you last spoke with him…?"

"It was, well, some time ago."

"I figured. As you may remember, we got him into the VA for outpatient treatment: he got meds that evened out his disorder and he was being seen on regular outpatient visits to the hospital. The voices he'd been talking about had been gone for a long time."

It sounded as if Cary was speaking of Teddy in the past tense, which worried Frank. "As I recall, he was even working there as a staff member?"

"Yeah. In return for his room and board, he came on as an employee of Reboot. At first he did, like, janitorial work, sweeping and mopping, picking up the trash. He seemed to be *simpatico* with some of the residents so we started letting him do some, I guess you'd call it orderly work."

"How'd that work out?"

"Took to it like a fish to water, man. He helped the older or less mobile residents get around and like that. Since being on the meds, he was patient and considerate, even with some of the harder cases. He started moderating some of the group sessions we run here. You know, we get some real ornery types here now and then. Lotta damaged souls come through here, just like

Teddy, and he just had this knack for dealing with them. He seemed to be pretty happy with being able to help others and he liked the routine of being here at the center."

"I get the feeling that Teddy's not there anymore?"

"No, he's been gone for, must be close to a year now."

"What happened? You say he seemed to like his life there. Where'd he go?"

"He wanted to try leading an independent life again. That is, after all, the point of what we're doing here. He said some family member had come back into his life and he'd have a place to stay and a support system while he worked at getting a job. He was pretty stable and responsible. We considered him a success story here. Not everybody leaves here with as much hope as he did."

"He would have needed to keep up his meds, I assume."

"Sure. And his regular outpatient visits to the VA. That was just part of his life now. I didn't think that was going to be an issue; he liked the staff there and seemed deeply appreciative of the help he had received."

"Have you heard from him since?"

"A couple times right after he got resettled. Not in some months now."

"You said there were support group meetings. Did he still come to those?"

"For a while. Former residents are welcome to come to them. He stopped after a while. But that's not necessarily unusual. People start getting their lives together, they get busy. It's kind of the whole point of what we're doing here, to let people get normal lives back."

"So, you don't have any idea what happened to him after that, what kind of job he may have wound up with or where he ended up?"

"We respect the privacy of our 'graduates' here, Detective. I'm always real happy to hear from them if they contact me or come back to visit and fill me in or to ask a favor…but I never go looking for them. Besides which, I've got my hands more than full with the residents here."

"Any possibility he backslid, fell back into his, well, his agitated side again?"

"Anything's possible. I've seen everything happen. But I'd bet on Teddy. He'd have to go off his meds in order to re-embrace the craziness, and he was just too happy finally being sane. The VA was taking good care of him. I'd be willing to bet he'd rather cut off his own arm before he'd allow himself to go back to that hell he was living in when he came in here."

"No chance he could have been cut off, maybe caught in the system, unable to get his medical attention or meds?"

"I can't say shit like that doesn't happen, but one of the things I tell everybody who comes through here: if they have those kinds of problems, come see me. I know the system as well as anybody. I'll advocate for them. I'll go to the fucking mat for them. And they know I will."

"So you're saying that not hearing from Teddy, was like 'no news is good news'?"

"That's what I'd like to believe. Look, of course we have recidivists and backsliders, you know? I've cleaned up more than one junkie and sent them out only to have them come back strung out or turn up dead in an alley somewhere. I've had residents who seemed to have gotten their heads back, then stepped out the door and fell apart again. It's the nature of the beast, Detective. I don't understand the whys of the beast but I know it's devious as hell. I'm sure you're no stranger to that either."

"No. No, I'm not, unfortunately."

"But here's the thing: not Teddy. I've seen broken folks, too many. Like I said, I'd put money on Teddy. He's going to make it."

"I hope you're right," Frank replied.

"Why are you asking me all this about Teddy? You don't come around here to ask about him in a year or two and now all of a sudden you're very interested. That tells me Teddy's in some kind of trouble...or you suspect he is."

"I don't know for certain, Mr. Wilde. I just want to have a conversation with him. Can you tell me his last known address?"

"A conversation about what?"

This was a man fiercely protective of his charges, who took very seriously his responsibility to the damaged goods of his city. Frank wasn't going to learn anything more from Wilde unless he could win his confidence.

"Okay, look. Before Teddy came to Reboot, he got in trouble by writing a lot of threatening letters. He sent the police a letter relating to a serious crime. He was almost a suspect before I cleared him and realized he was simply acting out."

"Yeah, yeah. I remember all that. That was the old Teddy, years ago, before he got the medical attention he required."

"We just received a note, relating to another case, identical to the one he sent us back then. Identical."

"Oh, fuckin' A, so now you want to pin this new thing on him?"

"Mr. Wilde...Cary...I still don't see Teddy as a suspect. But I've got to check out every angle. If for some reason he's started sending out letters again, maybe I can get him back to some help again, before he gets himself into more serious trouble. And then I can write off the note as something that isn't going to lead me anywhere and devote my time to finding better leads. On the other hand, suppose I can be sure it was *not* him who sent the letter. That means I need to look elsewhere. Generally notes like this one aren't sent by someone who committed the crime; they're people seeking attention or help. I still have to follow up on them."

"And this crime is as serious as last time?"

"I can't talk about specifics, but yes. And what you said before, about my not checking in about Teddy…you're right. That's my bad, on me. But I cared and I still care. My feeling is that everybody out there has got to matter and I've always tried to live that, maybe less than perfectly. I tried to help Teddy by steering him to you and Reboot in the first place. You probably don't always trust the police and you've probably got reasons based on experience, but I'm telling you I'm not going to try to pin something on Teddy to make my life easier. But I need to talk to him and I'm going to find him one way or the other."

There was a long silence on the other end of the phone. Finally Wilde spoke.

"You know, I *don't* totally trust you guys, no offense."

"None taken."

"So I made a point to look into you, personally, back when you first brought Teddy to us. You've got a good rep. I heard more than once that you're righteous. One guy called you one of the good ones."

"I'd like to think that's true."

Wilde sighed. "Okay then…"

Frank filled Athena in on his conversation and said he was on his way to see Teddy Ralski. Grabbing her jacket, she answered, "Not without me, you're not."

"What do you mean? It's not necessary for both of us to spend time on this. Chances are it's a dead end. Either he's off his meds and sending crank letters again…or he's not, and we've got some other crank on our hands. And maybe two of us showing up will spook him."

"On the other hand, maybe he'll feel less threatened by a woman? And suppose, just suppose, that your only-slightly-likely scenario turns out to be true, that Ralski is a murderer who got away with it? He dropped off Wilde's radar how long ago? Just before the current killings. There's a chance, however small, that you're walking in to confront a dangerous unbalanced killer. You're not doing that alone."

"Athena, I may have my nagging doubts about how that case went down but they're tangential at best. I can't believe there's any danger here."

"Frank, don't be a jerk. You are *not* going into this alone. This is why you've got a partner. And stop rolling your eyes."

"I wasn't—damn, how did you know I was rolling my eyes? I wasn't even looking at you!"

"I could've heard them rattle from across the room. You're not going to win this argument. Case closed."

Frank sighed. "Okay, wiseass. I think I liked you better when you were still a demure rookie cop."

"I was never demure. Just had you fooled. Shall we?"

The address that Cary Wilde had given Frank was in an older neighborhood that looked ripe for gentrification. It was a street of small apartment houses and duplexes, and their destination was one of the numerous add-ons at the rear of the property, often converted garages, the kind that were sometimes called "mother-in-law apartments."

"Do you think Wilde called and warned him we were coming?" Athena asked as they walked down a narrow driveway to a newly-painted structure with large windows. Frank noted a lack of bars on the windows, though they were a common feature of ground-floor dwellings in most of the city. Apparently they hadn't experienced as much crime as other areas of the city, or maybe there were just a lot of people in denial.

"He might have. I couldn't really read how he felt about this whole thing. He seems pretty protective of his people, even after they've moved on."

They stepped up the three steps to the stoop and knocked on the long glass window of the door. Shortly thereafter, the blinds behind the window were raised and a small elderly man peered out at them through thick glasses.

"Yes?" he asked through the glass. "May I help you?"

Frank and Athena had their badges and IDs out and held up to the window.

"Very sorry to bother you, sir. I'm Detective Vandegraf and this is Detective Pardo. We're looking for Theodore Ralski. Is he in?"

"He's not here."

"When will he be back? He's not in any trouble. We just need to speak with him."

"He's not here."

Athena stepped forward. "Please, can we just come in for a minute and talk with you?"

"He doesn't live here anymore. He hasn't been here for some time."

"It would be a lot easier if you'd just let us in. We won't take much of your time. It might be important to Mr Ralski."

The man's eyes, looking huge through the lenses, shifted back and forth at them, settling on Athena for a long moment. Finally he said, "Just a moment."

He reached up and unlatched two door locks, opening the door.

"Come on in then." He gestured to the cluttered but sunny parlor behind him. There were spacious windows on three sides.

"You'll have to excuse the place; reading is my love, even as nearsighted as I've gotten. Luckily this place has a lot of light."

There were books everywhere. He swept away newspapers and magazines from the armchairs, depositing them in a pile on the coffee table that the seats surrounded, and motioned for them to sit down, then followed suit.

"So what's this all about?"

"First of all, who exactly are you, sir?" began Frank.

"I'm Phil. Phil Wozniak. Teddy's my nephew."

"He was living here with you, is that correct?"

"Yes. He contacted me in Lake Havasu City, where I own a condo. I moved here and rented this apartment to give him a place to stay while he got on his feet. That was about a year ago."

"Up until then, had you been in touch with him at all?"

Wozniak shook his head sadly. "After Teddy came back from the service, he was…disturbed. He didn't want anything to do with me or anybody. Well, there really wasn't anybody else in the way of family remaining anyway. His mother, my sister, died a while back, as did his father. My own wife passed away as well. I'm all that's left. When we used to have contact, he was so angry and…not quite right. He would go on about a lot of things: he'd gotten a bad deal, people had it in for him and so on. Honestly, he scared me. He needed some kind of help but I had no idea what, or where to begin, so I stayed away from him. I was honestly relieved to not be hearing from him for quite a long time. And I suppose that gave me a certain sense of guilt. When sometime later he finally did call me up, he sounded so different. He told me how much Mr. Wilde had helped him and that he had gotten the proper medical attention and even some support checks. Now he was ready to live on his own again and be self-supporting. He just needed a little assistance to get a leg up. I was happy to help; he sounded like he had finally gotten so much better."

"How long did he stay with you here?"

"He was here until—let's see—about three months ago, maybe? He found a job. It paid enough that he could afford a place of his own. He said he'd appreciate if I could help him get established with a little extra money, for a security deposit and things like that, but then it was important that he get out on his own and not stay dependent upon me. He told me he was grateful for my help but he needed to feel like a man again and not like a kid. That was how he put it. I still wanted to help him somehow. I wasn't able to help him move, I'm just not physically fit for that kind of activity— not that he had all that much to move. He was able to do that on his own. I told him I'd stay here in town for a while in case he needed any help. My place in Havasu is rented out for another year anyway, and I've got a lease on this apartment that runs about the same length of time, so I don't mind being here. It's an old neighborhood but it's reasonably safe and the people are nice. There's a library nearby and even a newsstand—there aren't very many of those left anymore—so I can get plenty to read. The market is a short walk and the University's not far away, where it's lovely to walk in nice weather."

Frank and Athena had politely let him continue without interruption and now Frank realized that he'd pointed out that the University was nearby… not to mention the University postal station.

"Where did Mr. Ralski move to?" asked Athena. "Is he close by? Do you speak with him often?"

"Oh yes, he moved maybe nine or ten blocks away. But I don't hear from him all that much; I haven't actually seen him since he moved out. He's never come by here, and I've never been in his place. I dropped by his new building maybe three times and he's never been home. I don't really like going over there. It's not that far but it's more marginal an area, do you know what I mean? The neighborhood changes rapidly in that direction. It's a little scarier for an older man like me. I've tried calling him but he doesn't pick up his phone. I think it might have been disconnected recently; that happens. He's got a month to month agreement and it's easy to make a payment late. I'm a bit surprised he didn't ask me to help him out if the bill was a problem but…I suppose it's important to him to solve his problems on his own now."

"You said he'd gotten a job," Frank said. "Do you know what it was?"

"He said it was for that large supermarket chain, Farlow's. He told me that once he got a driver's license, they'd move him up to an even better job."

"But he didn't tell you which store? Farlow's has a lot of them all over the city."

"What he said was that they hadn't placed him yet. He wasn't worried where they'd send him; he knew the bus system here and it could get him wherever he needed to go."

"How did he seem when he moved out?"

"Fine. He seemed fine. What are you asking?"

"He didn't seem to have changed in any way? Was he acting different? Was he unusually agitated or unhappy, for example?"

"No, in fact he was very happy, making plans for his future. He seemed to be looking forward to being on his own again. I was proud of him."

"I understand he was regularly seeing a doctor at the VA hospital."

"Yes. He kept his appointments downright religiously. He liked the doctor he was seeing there."

"The doctor—do you happen to remember his name?"

Wozniak raised his fingers to his forehead and knitted his brow. "It was a her, not a him. He mentioned her a couple of times but I can't remember... he called her by her first name...Audrey, maybe?"

"You were aware that he was also on medication, weren't you?"

"Yes. I saw him take them regularly. And he refilled the prescriptions regularly."

"So he hadn't stopped taking them recently? He didn't, say, accidentally run out?"

"I don't think so, no. That wouldn't have been like him."

"Could he have forgotten to take them with him when he left?"

"No...I cleared out anything he might have left in the medicine cabinet after he left. There were no pharmacy bottles, nothing like that."

Athena leaned forward. "Mr. Wozniak, we understand Teddy was attending support group meetings at Reboot, where he had been living. Did he stop going to them?"

"Oh, yes. He liked the meetings very much but he didn't want to lean on anybody anymore. He wanted to spend all his time getting back on his own two feet, as he put it."

"So he stopped going, and cut off all contact with the center and Cary Wilde?"

"I suppose so. After some point, I'm not sure exactly when, he just stopped talking about them anymore. It wasn't that he didn't like the place. He never said anything bad about it, except that he'd come to feel like an invalid. He didn't think he'd ever be whole again until he didn't feel dependent on it. That was how he put it."

The conversation meandered for a short time more, with Wozniak happily drifting into slight digressions and expansions. It was clear there wasn't much more he could tell them. Finally Frank nodded to Athena and said, "Have we covered everything?"

"I think so." Athena stood up and smiled at Wozniak. "Thank you for your time, sir. Oh..." Her smile turned slightly embarrassed. "...would you mind terribly if I used your powder room before we left?"

Wozniak, smiling for the first time, gestured behind him. "Certainly, young lady. Back that way, to the left. Hard to get lost; this isn't exactly a huge apartment."

"Thank you so much." She headed in the direction he had indicated.

"A couple final things, sir," said Frank. "Do you have a phone?"

"Of course. I've got a land line here. Not a fan of the smart phones. Too much to figure out and too expensive. It was enough to keep Teddy's paid up while he was here."

"And I assume you'd like to know if we hear any news of your nephew?"

"Well, certainly."

"So, if I could get your number in case we have any information for you…and also the address where you said you tried to visit Mr. Ralski…?"

He jotted both down as the elderly man recited them.

Shortly thereafter, Athena returned to the living room and both the men rose from their chairs, signaling the end of the conversation. Frank and Athena each shook Wozniak's hand, thanked him for his time, and handed him their business cards.

"Please, let us know if you hear from your nephew, Mr. Wozniak. We appreciate it."

"I'm still not sure what this is all about. You said he's not in any trouble. Why haven't I heard from him? Could something have happened to him?"

"We don't know of anything definite like that. He's probably fine. We'll find him."

Frank wasn't sure he totally believed that by now, but it was all he could say to the man who was now more concerned than ever.

As they walked back out the driveway to the street, Athena said quietly, "There are no obvious signs of Ralski still living there. Two small bedrooms. One is obviously Wozniak's: there are books and magazines everywhere. The other is empty, nothing on the shelves or the closet, the bed made. I also checked out the medicine cabinet in the bathroom. Nothing that looked like it would have been left behind by Ralski. Wozniak was likely telling us the truth."

"I figured that's why you had to suddenly go tinkle. Smooth move."

"Told you you needed me to come along. I can't imagine you getting away with that one."

"Putting one over on a sweet, myopic senior citizen. No, I never could have pulled that one off."

"Our friend is some kind of polymath."

"Polymath. Nice twenty dollar word."

"That means a guy who's well-versed in a lot of things…"

"I know what it means, thanks, Pardo."

"Anyway, he sure is a voracious reader. And he runs the gamut. I happened to quickly scan a small bookshelf in his room. It had this one bunch of hefty volumes: history, sports, even medical stuff. There's a baseball encyclopedia, an atlas of maps, and a musical dictionary. Some anatomy books. He's even got a PDR in there."

"A PDR?"

"*Physicians' Desk Reference*. Describes all kinds of drugs and pharmaceuticals."

"I actually knew that too. I guess I'm surprised that you knew it on sight."

"An aunt of mine is a nurse; when I was little I was fascinated by some of the books and instruments she had and she's always had a PDR. Lots of pictures of brightly colored pills and capsules and things, looked like jewels to a little kid. Big thick book, like a dictionary.... Wozniak had one of those too, on the floor, an unabridged one."

Frank was duly impressed by how much Athena had taken in on one quick trip around the old man's apartment. "You were quite the snoop. How does a youngster like you know what an unabridged dictionary is, anyway? Don't you just look words up online?"

"I guess I've learned a few things about ancient history, Frank…you know, the way my ancestors used to do things." As they reached the car, Athena pulled out her smart phone. "I'm going to try to reach someone at Farlow's and find out if they have employee records. Maybe we can locate him if the job Wozniak said he mentioned was for real. Shall we walk to Ralski's address?"

"Nine or ten blocks, he said? Rundown neighborhood? Let's drive."

By the time Frank had driven them to their destination, Athena had hung up her phone. "I got hold of someone in Farlow's Human Resources who's going to get back to me," she said. "They should be able to give me info on him if he's a new hire."

The distance might have only been ten blocks but Ralski's new neighborhood looked to be in a different world. As Wozniak had said, things changed rapidly heading in that direction. It was more congested and neglected. Frank realized with a start that it wasn't far from the cheap crash pad where he had first encountered Ralski.

"Definitely went to a lower rent district," Frank remarked as they locked up the car.

"Well, he did want to be on his own. This is probably the best he could do."

Frank stepped around a bright orange HUMM scooter that had been left lying on its side in the middle of the walk. "Well, the residents scooter here, too."

"Everyone scooters, Frank. Everyone under a certain age."

"You know, Pardo, I've decided, yes, I definitely liked it better when you were a young patrol officer showing some deference to her elders."

"Fake memories. Is that a symptom of getting older?"

The apartment number they had been given was a third-floor walkup, down a long dark corridor. Frank sniffed at the pungent bite in the air.

"Somebody's cooking something," Athena remarked. "Onions. Garlic. Curry maybe? Powerful stuff."

"Some kind of odd undertow to the smell. Here we are. Three-twelve."

They knocked on the door repeatedly but got no answer.

"Maybe there's a super on the premises," Athena suggested.

"That would be too much good luck," Frank muttered.

There was no sign or other indication of a manager, and there didn't seem to be anybody around at all.

Frank checked his watch. "Maybe Ralski's at work. Maybe everybody's at work, except the cook up there. Another couple hours, maybe we'll have better luck."

As they stood outside the building, Athena's ring tone sounded. She pulled out her phone to answer. The conversation was short before she rang off.

"That was Farlow's HR. They hired Ralski three months ago, just as Wozniak told us. He went to work as a stock clerk at their store on Mission Road."

"So I guess that's where we should go look for him."

* * * *

Mission Road was a busy multi-lane thoroughfare just off the freeway near the upscale north end of town. The Farlow's market was in a large outdoor mall that still appeared busy, despite the fact that about four or five stores, including one of its large anchor stores, were now closed and empty. The large parking lot still had a good number of cars in it.

"I wonder how long this one's got," Frank remarked as they walked from their car to the market. "Malls are an endangered species."

"This one seems to be hanging in though, so being in this part of the city is an advantage, I guess. The restaurants may help. Um…what are you looking for?"

"Not seeing any scooters around here."

"I think you're obsessing on those things, Frank."

The manager of the Farlow's market was named Manager…Lou Manager. He was probably tired of hearing jokes about it from the sort of people who think they're the first to come up with an observation of the obvious. Frank, being no stranger to clueless unintentional disrespect towards one's surname, understood that often the situation led to someone becoming an admirably patient soul. He considered that fate sometimes indeed has a quirky and unkind sense of humor, and he also knew to stay mercifully silent on the subject.

Manager looked like a harried man, despite a low key disposition. He was probably not yet forty but his hair was prematurely thinning, and he looked haggard. He could only spare the detectives a few minutes in the corner of the produce aisle, but that, unfortunately, was all that would be needed.

"Teddy Ralski. Sure. He started here, maybe ten or twelve weeks ago?"

"Is he here now?" asked Frank.

"No. He hasn't been here in close to a week now. He just stopped showing up for work."

"Is he sick or something?"

Manager shrugged. "I have absolutely no idea. He hasn't called or emailed or anything. He just hasn't been coming in."

A young woman in a Farlow's uniform ran up with a clipboard and asked him for several signatures, handing him a ballpoint pen.

"I try to give people leeway," he said. "But there's only so far I can go. He doesn't show up tomorrow, he's fired."

"How was he doing up until this past week?" Athena asked.

Manager handed the pen back to the woman and she moved off hurriedly.

"Up until then, great, for the most part," he said. "Smart guy. Seemed pretty motivated, picked up things quickly. Got along with his co-workers and was polite to the customers, which is crucial. I was hoping to be able to promote him after his probationary period was over. I'd say that's out the window unless he's got a really good excuse. Pardon me."

A woman with two kids pushing a cart asked Manager where to find maple syrup and he directed her to the proper aisle with a big smile.

"You said 'for the most part.' Did something change?"

"The last week he was here before he ghosted, he seemed a little, I don't know, *sullen*? He was quieter, seemed a bit distracted. Nothing I was particularly worried about at the time. New hires kind of hit a wall after a few weeks, they start getting anxious. I've learned you've got to especially keep an eye on them by the second month. They usually settle down and gain some confidence and then you really get to see if they're going to do okay or not. I figured he was just hitting his rough patch and it would pass. Then he didn't come into work."

A lanky bespectacled man in a clerical collar excused himself for interrupting and asked to be directed to the dairy case. Manager pleasantly pointed to the far corner of the store.

"So the last time you saw him here was, what, six days ago?"

"Let me think. Yep. Sounds right."

"Have you tried to contact him?"

"Oh sure. His phone never picks up, at least the number he gave us doesn't. Can't even leave him a message."

"Did anything about him seem…bothersome?" Frank asked. "Did he seem agitated, disturbed in any way?"

Manager rubbed his chin, where a literal five o'clock shadow had begun to crop up. "No, aside from that tentative quality I mentioned, he seemed okay to me. What'd this guy do, anyway, that you're looking for him? He didn't seem like any kind of, you know, criminal or anything."

"He's not wanted as a suspect. We just have some routine questions for him."

Just then the loudspeaker blared, "*Manager to checkout four! Manager, checkout four please!*"

"Gotta go," Manager said.

"One quick last question," Frank called to him as he turned away. "What hours did he work here?"

Manager wheeled around but kept backpedaling away. "We had him on a swing shift, being the new guy. Sometimes he'd come in evenings. But mostly he was here early morning to stock shelves, like four, until early afternoon. Sorry to run!"

"I gotta give it to Mr. Manager," Athena remarked. "He's handling a lot pretty well."

"Yeah, well…he was clearly trained in forbearance."

"What do you mean?"

"Never mind," said Frank. "Long story."

* * * *

"I don't get it," Athena said as they left the market. "Ralski's doing great, and all of a sudden he just drops out. What happened?"

Frank walked thoughtfully for a few seconds then picked up his head.

"Sit down."

"What? Now what are you talking about?"

"I'm talking about that bench over there. Fancy that. Nice that they still think of pedestrians, even in a mall. I could stand to take a breather. Let's sit down for a minute and hash this out."

The concrete bench wasn't exactly inviting—Frank wryly noted that malls now seemed designed to keep people moving, not to encourage them to idle—but Athena followed him over and plopped down beside him. He paged through the notes he had taken that afternoon. She grew a bit impatient.

"So I ask you again: what happened to Teddy Ralski?"

Frank shrugged. "Whatever it was started about two weeks ago. Something got him out of sorts and knocked him off his game. Then it continued to get worse."

"It would seem, whatever it was, he didn't want to confide in anybody. He didn't talk to Cary Wilde or to his uncle. He apparently turned his phone off. If he's still in that apartment, he doesn't answer the door."

"And then we get that note," Frank mused. "I really think he sent it to us. But why?"

"You don't think he's our killer, do you?"

"It doesn't make sense. But his schedule wouldn't rule him out. If he worked a lot of early mornings, he could have had the opportunity. I just don't see the why or how of it."

"What happened that first time? Was he able to explain to you why he sent you the note? Why 'There will be more'?"

"He wasn't exactly linear; he was pretty confounded by the time we brought him in and I sat down with him. Best I could figure, he meant there would be more letters. Or maybe he meant that things would just get worse."

"I'm not sure I follow you."

"He had written three other letters before sending me the note about Ronnie Rackham. The first was to the Department of Animal Control, a short rant complaining about stray dogs around his building. He said he knew nobody would do anything about the problem and there'd be more of them. The second was to a fast food joint near where he lived, complaining of how he had been treated there, and he wouldn't be the only one to experience that…again, just a couple of sentences, saying he'd make sure nobody would go there anymore. The third was to the Department of Sanitation and said simply, 'No trash pickup today! This neighborhood is a sewer! It will get worse!' With each note, he was getting angrier and briefer. It was getting harder and harder for him to articulate his concern. In every case he would write it neatly and carefully—and in every case, he'd say 'There will be more!' or something to that effect. By the time he got to the letter I saw, he was down to six words, pretty much nothing *but* 'There will be more.' It seemed that he was actually losing his ability to articulate, as if the mental noise and chaos was growing. When I talked with him, he would slowly blurt out a handful of words and then stop as if he couldn't find any more words for a few seconds, like there was an actual bottleneck in his mind."

"How strange."

"We kept him for twenty-four hours while I checked out his background and found out about the other letters. I talked with him several times. At first he'd get frustrated and angry but in general I got the feeling he just wasn't violent. It was more like he was terribly frightened. As we progressed, he seemed to calm down a little. As he could relax, he became more communicative. I figured out that he was isolated, living with his own demons with nowhere to go for support, nobody to talk to; writing the letters seemed to be his only outlet. That was also when I got the first inkling about Leland. Talk had spread rapidly among the street folk in that area that Leland had killed Ronnie. I figured for a lot of reasons the best move would be to get Teddy into some kind of facility where he could get some help and I could keep tabs on him. I had learned about his service experience and that's when I found Cary Wilde and Reboot."

"And over time you decided you'd made the right moves."

Frank nodded. "At the time, I was one hundred percent on that."

"But then you developed doubts?"

"Not strong ones. Maybe that certainty dropped to ninety percent. It was negligible. I was still pretty clear that I'd gotten the right guy and that Teddy wasn't capable of murdering Ronnie Rackham."

"And yet you were sufficiently worried to come back now and follow up on Teddy. I can tell this bothered you more than a little."

"Well, the coincidence took me by surprise. At very least I needed to take the new letter off the table as a crank note. And this was an obvious way to start."

"You mentioned that Ronnie Rackham was killed in a similar way to our recent victims, stabbed in the back multiple times?"

"I can't overlook it, as big a stretch as it seems." Frank shook his head. "Maybe this is just me starting to worry that I'm losing it."

"I wouldn't say that you're losing anything. You saw an important connection. I think you're right. Odds are that the new note was written by Teddy. It's sad to think he's fallen back into his illness, but we'll find him and try to get him back into the center, and in the process I bet we'll learn he's just sending crazy notes again."

She stood up. "Come on, let's go back. I'll try giving the VA a call and see if he's still keeping his appointments."

Frank also rose from his seat. "Have fun navigating the bureaucracy while I'm driving."

By the time they had returned to the Department parking lot, Athena was ringing off on a call after being transferred several times.

"That was Ralski's doctor, Audrey Chen."

"Awfully short conversation. Don't tell me, stonewalled you, right? Patient confidentiality, that kind of thing?"

"Actually I did a little better than that. She said she'll have a conference call with us in an hour. She was very tentative about what she might tell us, but at least she's not shutting us down completely."

The "conference call" turned out to be Frank and Athena sitting at a table in a commandeered interview room on speaker phone. Dr. Chen sounded fairly young but extremely officious. She seemed to have been under the impression they were calling with information on Teddy Ralski for her, and seemed both relieved and disappointed they had nothing to tell her about him. It was clear, when she understood they were actually calling with questions of their own, that she was not going to be forthcoming with very much information about her patient.

"The one thing I can tell you is that he missed his last appointment. Your call, frankly, had me a bit concerned because of that. If I understand properly, there's no indication that anything has happened to him, and your inquiry was not provoked by anything happening to him, all of which I am happy to hear."

"Have you contacted any authorities about your concerns, Doctor?" Frank asked.

"Not outside the department here, no. I've had our aide trying to reach him by phone. So far she's been unsuccessful."

"What was the last time you saw him?"

"The last appointment he kept was…let me see…not quite a month ago. He's missed one appointment, as I said, and has another one coming up shortly."

"He hasn't showed up and you can't seem to reach him. Isn't that sufficient concern to contact the police?"

Chen audibly sighed. "This isn't all that unusual an occurrence. People miss their appointments. Do you have any idea the number of patients we have here, Detective?"

"So you aren't concerned that Ralski might have, say, stopped his medications and lapsed back into his previous condition?"

Chen hesitated for a long time, as if in thought as to what she could or couldn't say. "I have no clear indication that has happened."

Athena chimed in. "Doctor, has Theodore Ralski continued to fill his prescriptions?"

"That's an area of patient confidentiality, Detective. I can't talk about that."

"For the sake of discussion, let's say he had discontinued his meds. Would it take long for his disorder to return?"

"I can't talk to you about the nature of his medication. That's patient confidentiality."

Frank, unable to totally hide his growing frustration, said, "Doctor Chen, we need to locate Theodore Ralski. Isn't there *anything* you can tell us that can help us?"

"Has he committed a crime?"

"At this time he's not a viable suspect of having committed a crime, no. He might be a person of interest, but…"

"Is there any proof that his life in danger?"

"No. We think he might have contacted the police regarding a crime that's being investigated."

"How do you mean? Did he call you, email you? Did he identify himself?"

Frank slapped a hand on his forehead and bent forward at the table. It was a great big game: nobody wanted to divulge their privileged information. "No. We received an anonymous note in the mail."

"And it had information about this crime to which you refer?"

"Well, not exactly. But we have reason to believe…"

"So just why, exactly, do you think that you have cause for me to violate patient confidentiality?"

Athena broke in. "Doctor, the note we received was very similar to one that Mr. Ralski sent this department a few years ago, before he sought medical help. He sent several letters at that time to different agencies. Perhaps he told you about that."

"Detective, I am not going to talk about any conversations I've had with my patient. Not on the basis of something as flimsy as this. You received an amorphous letter that seems to refer to nothing specific, and you have no real indication it came from my patient. What I will tell you is that it makes little to no sense that he would have written such a thing."

"It said, *there will be more*," blurted Frank.

"I beg your pardon?"

"The letter. It referred to a recent death and said *there will be more*. Is that sufficient enough for you?"

Chen hesitated briefly before replying. "No. I'm sorry, it doesn't. I believe in helping the police and supporting them, but…no, you need more. When you have that, talk to me again."

"You said he's gone missing!" Frank sighed, his head still buried in his hand.

"No, what I said is that he's missed an appointment or two. That is not at all unusual. As I said, if you have something more substantial, please contact me again."

For some time after they had rung off, Frank simply sat at the table in quiet thought.

"Well," Athena finally said, more to break the silence than anything else, "she wasn't much help."

"She told us more than she wanted."

"I'm not following."

"First of all, she knows about the old letters. She has to know about them. But she's not worried about him, it would seem. She's pretty confident it's not him that started writing them again. I'm guessing that means she's sure Teddy hasn't stopped filling his prescriptions, at least not for long. I'd bet she looked into that and knows that. If he had, I'm betting she'd be a lot more concerned."

He looked up at Athena, his eyes wide. "There's something about Teddy that's inspired hope and confidence in the people who care for him. They aren't ready to believe he isn't going to make it. The doc's money is still on Teddy, just like Cary Wilde's. She's figuring he's taking a vacation or sloughing off or something."

Athena nodded. "It comes down to the question of the meds. I guess we have to try the pharmacy and ask them. But I'm guessing they'll be as tight-lipped as Doctor Chen."

Athena's suspicions were correct. They ended their shift with no better handle on Teddy Ralski or his whereabouts. Frank was still mulling everything over in his head as they prepared to leave.

"I'm guessing," Athena told him, "that you're not ready to give up on this Ralski thing yet"

"Do I think he's the Creep? I just don't know, Athena. It seems a long shot. But what else have we got right now?"

"Then we come back tomorrow and see what else we can come up with. We'll find him."

"Maybe," muttered Frank. "Maybe."

6.

Frank was surprised, when he got off the elevator early Tuesday morning, to find Lieutenant Hank Castillo waiting for him, arms folded, his mustached mouth screwed up into one of his typically inscrutable expressions.

"You've got a visitor in Interview Three waiting on you, Frank."

"What? I didn't have anybody scheduled for this morning."

"She's a walk-in. Pardo is babysitting her but she said she wanted to speak with you specifically."

"Who the hell is *she,* Lou?"

"Collis Westermark. She says she's the CFO of Humbletech. I'd really like to hear more about this one later. You're running in some rarefied circles these days, Detective."

Castillo raised his thick salt-and-pepper eyebrows momentarily, then turned in the direction of his office.

"By the way," he said over his shoulder, "she got your name right."

Frank shook his head and headed for Interview Three.

The best that could be said for Interview Room Three was that it was the *least* dingy of the array offered by the unit. It had received the most recent paint job, the lights all worked, and none of the chairs that surrounded the metal table were in need of repair.

Collis Westermark still seemed out of place, sitting across from Athena, a fit forty-something woman projecting quiet authority with her tinted glasses, platinum-silver hair, and expensive but understated blazer and sweater. The two women interrupted what had apparently been small talk to turn to look at Frank as he entered.

"Ms. Westermark, this is my partner, Detective Frank Vandegraf. Frank, Collis Westermark of Humbletech."

The visitor extended a hand to Frank and actually began to rise. Frank asked her to please sit down as he shook her hand. He plopped himself into a chair next to Athena.

"Ms. Westermark, this is a surprise."

Athena gave him a glance as if to ask if she should stay or leave. Frank simply gave her a nod to remain.

"I assume you have no problem if my partner stays."

"Not a bit. We've just been getting to know each other. I was delighted to learn that Detective Pardo seems to be a big fan of our HUMM urban scooters. It's nice that our mission to reduce congestion and pollution is appreciated by law enforcement."

"Is that so," said Frank, shooting a sideways glance at Athena. "So what brings you to us here at Personal Crimes?"

"It's my understanding that you came to our offices yesterday and spoke with Sharon Brooks about the terrible death of Orrin Lattimer. I saw the card you left her and noted you were from Personal Crimes, which means you are investigating a serious crime; perhaps you even suspect Orrin was murdered."

"We can't comment on an ongoing investigation."

"Of course not, Detective Vandegraf," she smiled briefly. "But the very possibility that Orrin's death could be considered the result of—does *foul play* sound overly dramatic?—came as a shock to me."

"So you don't believe Orrin Lattimer's death was anything but an accident?"

"Of course, I only have the information I've been provided"—she raised her eyebrows at Frank—"but the consensus seems to be it was a tragic, freak accident."

"Forgive me, but…may I assume you didn't come all the way down here just to tell us that, Ms. Westermark?"

She flashed that same short enigmatic smile then cleared her throat.

"The timing of this is particularly bad. We're in the midst of a very sensitive time at Humbletech, dealing with serious issues, with the potential for spurious rumors to cause great harm if they were leaked. I thought I might be of some help to you while keeping this in—shall we call it a less sensational vein? So I preferred to come see you here, away from the company, for a less *public* conversation."

Damage control, thought Frank. Corporate politics and spin and so forth. Even in times of tragic death, it all has to go on.

But he kept it to himself.

"Well, we certainly appreciate your coming in like this. I'm sure you have an extremely busy schedule. What do you feel we should be aware of?"

"This is a highly sensitive matter. May I assume this will be kept in strict confidence among us?"

"Unless there's something that applies directly to the commission of a crime. At that point, I can give no guarantees. But as background, yes, what's said in this room stays with us."

"I assure you, there's no crime involved in this. Certainly not a murder."

Collis Westermark sighed, laced her fingers on the table, and stared downward in silence for a long moment.

Finally she looked up brightly. "This is all rather troubling. Do you think it might be possible for me to get a cup of tea before I start?"

"I'll take care of that," said Athena, shooting an overly sweet smile back at Frank. He sat in awkward silence across from Westermark for what seemed forever before his partner returned.

Westermark sat in thought, staring at the plain Styrofoam cup before her, the tag of a tea bag hanging down its side. Clearly adopting a stoic attitude toward the unit's Spartan level of comforts, she took a sip and began her account.

"Orrin's terrible death was a tragic accident. Just devastating. But it comes at a particularly terrible moment for all of us—a crisis, if you will. Those of us guiding the company still need to soldier on and address this crisis."

She delicately pulled the tea bag from her cup, finally deciding to lay it on the napkin that Athena had brought along with the cup, and took another sip.

"Please," Frank said, "go on."

"I assume Sharon filled you in a little bit on the background of Humbletech and that you know who Lane Dembeau is?"

"We certainly know who Mr. Dembeau is, and something about your company."

"Perhaps you know that we're a privately held corporation. It's not precisely a secret, but not generally known, that we are planning an initial public offering in the near future. We have a number of new projects we're hoping to introduce once there's new funding in place. I'd prefer not to talk of those in any detail."

"Okay," said Frank, wondering where all this was going.

"The point here is that Orrin was a vital force behind all our project conception and development. Losing him was a catastrophic setback for the company."

As it must have been, Frank thought, for his family as well. He exchanged a look with Athena that indicated they were both thinking along the same lines. Neither of them said anything.

"But the prospect of losing Orrin had already occurred to Lane, in a much different way," she said.

"I'm sorry?" Frank looked up, confused.

"Not long ago," Westermark said, "Lane confided to me that he believed Orrin was planning to leave the company, to jump to someone else. He seemed to think Orrin was acting *disturbed* in some way. It seems that not long before Lane left on his current trip, they had some kind of confrontation. It may have had a distracting effect on Orrin. He *was* acting a little differently these past few days: it was as if he were trying to avoid engaging with many of us."

"Why do you think Mr. Dembeau thought that about Mr. Lattimer?" Athena asked. "Do you think there was anything to his suspicions?"

"I can't imagine, Detective. Orrin was so deeply invested in Humbletech and was such an important element of it, it made no sense at all to me that he'd consider leaving. Perhaps you have to understand a little bit about Orrin—and Lane—to see my point.

"Lane Dembeau is a visionary. His particular genius gave birth to Humbletech. Three of us founded the company but it wouldn't have been remotely the same were it not for Lane. But 'visionary' is an apt word for Lane in other ways as well. He sees things differently, let us say, from the rest of us. Sometimes he can be...odd. He'll think and say odd things. There's a certain sense of drama around the man. He thinks he sees things that the rest of us don't.

"But if Lane is the embodiment of our greater mission, Orrin is our conceptual mainstay. He's the spark behind every innovation, the driving force behind every idea we're currently working toward. All of the engineering of our scooters and our future products is under him. As much as Lane is the face and soul of the company, Orrin is the brain center. Humbletech was built around both of them, and created specifically to actualize their ideas, what they called 'microtechnology for macrobenefit.' It made *no* sense that Orrin would walk away, much less give his ideas to another company. Personally, there's just nothing I can imagine that could have tempted him to do that."

After a long pause, Frank jumped back in. "Let's say Lane Dembeau's suppositions were true. I'm no expert on this kind of law, but aren't there legal mechanisms at Humbletech's disposal to prevent another company from appropriating proprietary material like that?"

"Certainly, we have non-disclosure agreements, intellectual protections of all sorts."

Westermark removed her glasses and stared at Frank. "But here's the thing, Detective. Neither Lane, nor Orrin, nor I for that matter, have ever signed a contract with the company."

"What?"

"We *are* the company. As I said, it's privately held and the three of us are by far the majority shareholders. Everybody who works for us is covered by numerous agreements and contracts: everybody *else,* that is. But we three have never entered into any kind of obligatory agreement with the others."

"That's crazy. That's *insane*. Forgive me, Ms. Westermark, I didn't mean to be that blunt."

Westermark replaced her glasses, pushed back a lock of silver hair, and shrugged.

"No offense taken. It's a common reaction when someone learns a little bit about us. That's Humbletech. We're an unusual company. We're also a young one, and in the throes of growing pains. There are plans to introduce new products, new technologies. We'll need to expand in terms of location and personnel and we will require extensive resources; hence the current consideration of an IPO in the near future, so very soon we'll have to close up those loopholes. But up until now we've operated in unorthodox ways, often based on trust and confidence in our common goals. In some ways we're more of a family…a large one, but a family nonetheless. It's part of why we've been so successful so far. But yes, we're approaching a tipping point where we'll need to be exceedingly corporate if we expect to move on."

"How was Mr. Dembeau planning to deal with this issue?" Athena asked.

"I'm not sure. The days before his departure were hectic and a bit confused. I'd guess Lane planned to deal with it further upon his return."

"Then it would seem he wasn't overly concerned that Mr. Lattimer might bolt the company immediately."

Westermark's eyes grew large. "Apparently he was not. He didn't communicate anything further to us in that regard. Perhaps he spoke with Orrin and tried to put his mind to rest for the moment. If so, it didn't seem to have the hoped-for calming effect on Orrin."

"Did anything unusual happen after Mr. Dembeau left?"

"Business progressed as usual and Lane maintained the expected communications every day to me, Orrin and the others. We have great people on our staff and they are all very capable of keeping things running on an even keel whenever Lane is away."

Athena wrinkled her brow in thought. "But yet you say that there's been a certain amount of turmoil in the company and that Mr. Lattimer was acting a little strangely?"

"I wouldn't characterize it as turmoil, exactly. Definitely there was a hubbub of activity. There's a lot going on as we hammer out upcoming plans. We encourage a free flow of ideas so there was considerable vigorous discussion throughout every department, though we try to keep it all in-house.

"As I said, it's a delicate stage. Orrin, on the other hand, was even more reticent than usual, but it seemed to me that everything was moving along reasonably well. In our daily communiqués, Lane seemed satisfied that everything was in hand."

"And he didn't mention his misgivings about Mr. Lattimer to you again in your conversations?" Athena said

"No. It was just that one time."

Frank jumped back in. "You said you couldn't think of anything Lattimer would have to gain from jumping to another company with Humbletech secrets. Is it possible there was a threat to him or possibly his family if he didn't comply?"

Meryl Lattimer and their daughter had been absent for two weeks.

She looked totally shocked. "My God, I…I can't imagine such a thing. Is there any evidence of such threats?"

Frank raised his hands reassuringly. "No, I'm just trying to look at every possible angle, Ms. Westermark. Do you know his family very well? Did they come to visit him at work, or were they at social events, maybe?"

"There were no social events to speak of. That's not Humbletech's style. I've met his wife Meryl a few times and I think I met their daughter once, but I hadn't seen either of them for some time."

So much, thought Frank, for the company being like a big family.

"Personally," she said. "None of this makes any sense to me. I'm beginning to worry that Lane has been suffering from some major delusion and that he simply unnerved Orrin because of it. It's all too unbelievable."

"And yet Orrin Lattimer died Sunday night."

"Yes, and by all accounts, it was a tragic accident. The Metro authorities seem to be quite sure of that. I can't see any scenario in which he would be *killed* by anyone; I'm not sure why homicide detectives would be investigating his death. The only thing I can even conceive is that Orrin was disturbed by Lane's peculiar accusations. The poor man might have been unnecessarily troubled or distracted and that's what led him to slip and fall on that train platform."

Westermark actually slipped a fingertip under her glasses and wiped a small tear from the corner of her eye.

"I don't want to say I'd blame Lane for Orrin's death," she continued. "Absolutely not; but I think that, compounded by the pressures at work, it might have been a factor."

"Ms. Westermark, you're not suggesting, are you, that Mr. Lattimer might have had suicidal tendencies?"

"Oh good Lord, no! You think I mean that Orrin purposely stepped off that platform? Absolutely not!"

"Any idea why Lattimer was on that train platform Sunday night?" asked Athena.

"I don't have the foggiest notion. It wasn't a line that ran near his house or near Humbletech. He apparently didn't have a bag or briefcase or anything, so I assume it had nothing to do with work. But it doesn't make sense that he was running off to another company."

"How do you know he didn't have a bag of any kind?"

"The Metro investigator, Inspector Payne, told me that yesterday afternoon. We had a substantial conversation."

Athena continued. "Let's assume for just a moment that Lattimer was implicated in something…irregular, whatever that might be, and that Lane Dembeau had picked up on it. Would Ms. Brooks, his assistant, have had any knowledge of anything of the sort?"

"Sharon was his right hand. She knew everything he was involved with in the company, but after talking with her, I'm totally convinced that she knew of nothing like that. I think there *was* nothing like that. She doesn't know why he was waiting for that particular train last night either, so it couldn't have had anything to do with Humbletech business. Maybe he was going to visit a friend…I can't really speculate on his private life."

A friend, thought Frank. *Are you suggesting an affair?* But he moved on.

"His home was nowhere near that train stop. Neither are the Humbletech offices. Why would he have been catching a train there, rather than some other closer station, to begin with?"

"Again, no idea, Detective. Orrin played his personal cards close to the vest, so to speak, and this past weekend he was playing them particularly close."

Frank cleared his throat. "Ms. Westermark, if you don't mind my asking, just what was your contribution to the founding of the company?"

Westermark smiled serenely. "I don't mind at all. I brought money to the table: my own, and that of selected investors. And I set up the fiscal structure of the concern. I'm the financial face of Humbletech."

"As you suggested, it's a most unorthodox company," Athena commented. "In its organization, I mean."

"We've got everything covered," Westermark replied, holding her smile. "There's a lot of odd genius in Humbletech. Part of our mission statement has been to explore innovative organizational approaches as well as technical ones."

"Just out of curiosity, who's going to run Mr. Lattimer's side of things now?"

"It's going to be tough, but we have good people to step in and keep the course steady until we work that out and add in new leadership and resources. Our engineering department is particularly strong. Orrin was a *huge* loss. It's going to set things back, I won't deny that, and it will take some innovative thought, but Lane and I will hold steady."

"I assume Mr. Dembeau has heard about what happened and will be returning from his trip to address everything."

"In fact I spoke to him very early this morning. He's of course devastated by the loss of Orrin, like the rest of us, but he's the captain of our ship and can't neglect his responsibilities. He plans to cut his itinerary short and return in three days, on Friday. He can't get back earlier than that due to sensitive commitments."

Athena again spoke up. "Ms Westermark, just to be clear here, you are not suggesting in any way that Lane Dembeau might have had something to do with the death of Orrin Lattimer?"

Her eyes widened. "No, absolutely not. And I'll reiterate: in my opinion, Orrin Lattimer did *not* die by anything other than a tragic accident. Everything else is a confidential internal matter for the company, and it's vital that any rumors about corporate espionage or foul play not get started. To that end, I've come here to fill you in on the background and to depend upon your discretion in this matter. It could be disastrous if the wrong rumors arose."

In the brief silence that followed, Westermark took her cue and stood up. "And now, if you'll excuse me, Detectives, you can understand I have a million things to attend to. I trust that everything said here today will stay among us?"

Frank and Athena also rose and shook her hand, thanking her for coming in. Collis Westermark held Frank's grip for a beat or two beyond expectation, smiling brightly, and said, "It was a great pleasure to meet you, Detective Vandegraf."

The moment that the elevator door had closed on Collis Westermark, Athena turned to Frank and smirked. "I think you liked her."

"She was charming, in a kooky sort of way."

"*Kooky?* How quaint. Do they still use that word?"

"Well, I still do, obviously."

"She sure was giving you the eye during the interview. And quite a sense of drama, removing her glasses to look wide-eyed at you and all that. I might as well not have been there, except as a fan of her scooters."

"I think her supposed interest in me is just your imagination. Anyway, I'm not interested; that would be inappropriate at best."

"Maybe you're still quite the catch and might not be aware of it. Frank, just curious: what was the last time you went out on a date, anyway?"

"Since when is that any of your business?"

"That long, huh?" They started walking back to their desks.

"I could ask you the same question."

"You think I go out on those scooters by myself?"

"I think I liked you better when you were a staid and proper patrol officer."

"I was just hedging my bets back then. Seriously, though: what do you make of her coming in to see us? I got the distinct impression she was throwing Lane Dembeau under the bus. Or in this case, the train."

"She did go out of her way to insist she saw no wrongdoing in Lattimer's death."

"Oh, she bent over backwards to do that, all the while emphasizing how Lane harbored strange suspicions about Lattimer's disloyalty that might have rattled him, and had some unspecified plan for dealing with him. And the comment made about Lattimer going to meet a *friend*. Was she trying to send us a subtle message?"

Frank shook his head. "I don't know. I'd lean toward spin control, as she implied: to pre-empt any public gossip about Lattimer. There's nothing she told us that we can really follow up on. If there was industrial espionage going on, that's out of our realm. Maybe the message she really was trying to plant was that the company's batshit-crazy, Dembeau and Lattimer especially, and he really did die because he was distracted and clumsy."

"Or maybe it's subtle infighting. She figures the word will get out from us that Lane Dembeau is becoming unstable, his paranoia contributed to the death of Lattimer, and he shouldn't be in control of the company."

"Wow! That's pretty subtle, all right, considering it runs counter to her expressed reason for coming to see us. You've got quite the Machiavellian mind there, Pardo."

"She strikes me as a subtle individual. Despite her calculated image as a bit of a ditz, she might well be the smartest and most stable of the founders to begin with…which isn't saying a whole hell of a lot."

"Interesting assessment, Athena."

"Well, it's your call. Is there anything there? Write off *l'affaire* Lattimer or no?"

"I just don't know. Probably not, but I still can't be a hundred percent certain…maybe more like ninety. Let's keep it on the back burner for the moment. The Creep is still our focus. I think it's worth going over to talk to Natalie Riemer's family again. She's still our most viable possibility."

Athena sighed, gave Frank a look, and then decided it wasn't worth continuing to protest his use of the name.

"Sounds good to me. If only she can regain consciousness."

* * * *

Natalie Riemer's mother and sister had seldom left her side at the hospital since the night of the attack. They greeted Frank and Athena wanly, and the detectives apologized for bothering them. The sister, Thalia Riemer, gave her mother a kiss and told her she'd return, accompanying them out of the room and down the hall to a small deserted meeting room.

"How are things?" Frank asked. Thalia was younger than Natalie but right now looked considerably older. Frank wondered if she had been getting any sleep the past few days. Despite herself, she forced a smile.

"About the same. She hasn't regained consciousness for even a moment. We're with her around the clock. We want at least one of us to be with her when she comes back."

When she comes back. Frank noted the refusal to give into the possibility of any other alternative. From the outset, he had admired the grace and courage with which the two women were handling the horrible situation of Natalie Riemer.

"And how are you doing?" Thalia continued, looking back and forth at them. "Any luck finding the person who did this?"

"We're working on it," Athena replied.

"I assume you came here to ask some more questions, so please, tell me how can I help?"

If only everybody were so willing and helpful, thought Frank silently.

Athena pulled out her phone and opened up photos of the earlier victims, Liwicki and Coates, asking if it were possible that Natalie might have known either of them. Thalia shook her head at the pictures and the names. Neither was familiar to her.

"We're close. We visit each other often. She comes out to see us in Oak Creek and I come to her apartment every week. I've met a lot of her friends and co-workers and I don't ever recall either of those people."

They noted that Thalia always spoke in the present tense. Her faith and optimism were high.

"Is it possible she might have known them from the hospital?"

Athena had already interviewed numerous people at the hospital where Riemer worked and none of them could remember ever seeing either person; furthermore, there was no record of either victim having ever been admitted there.

But she had to keep trying.

Thalia shook her head. "Not to my knowledge."

Frank asked, "Ms. Riemer, has anybody else come to see Natalie here in the ICU?"

"Yes. They don't allow more than one other person in at once, and only for a brief time, and all they can do is look in on Natalie and wish us well, but several of her co-workers from the hospital have stopped by— nurses, doctors, techs. Also, there have been several of the people from her apartment complex. They've all been absolutely wonderful, and a great source of support for us."

"Was there anybody you *didn't* recognize, possibly somebody who wasn't a friend or co-worker?"

Thalia thought it over.

"No. Everybody who's been here, I'm pretty sure, was somebody I've met before or seen with Natalie. And as I said, this hospital is very sparing with who they allow to come to visit to begin with."

Her eyes flashed with alarm. "You don't think he'd come back here…?"

Frank gently shook his head. "Most likely not, but as you've seen, we've been keeping a uniformed officer on the floor at all times just to be careful. I was more wondering if there's somebody who might provide us with a connection we hadn't yet considered."

"All Natalie's connections are pretty much what you've seen already, I'd say."

Athena sighed.

That was the problem. Maybe Frank could add a fresh viewpoint now that he wasn't distracted by the Lattimer death.

That lack of distraction, though, was about to change.

7.

Frank had just returned to his desk when his phone buzzed.

"Vandegraf."

"Detective, it's Cary Wilde. I wanted to follow up and see if you've located Teddy Ralski."

"Not yet. Anything you can do to help me there, Mr. Wilde?"

"So he wasn't at the address I gave you?"

"He was staying there with the relative you mentioned, but he moved out a few months ago. I really need to find him and he's gone off the radar."

"What do you mean, off the radar?"

"Look: can you, or can't you, help me find him?"

"I can try. I probably know a lot more about him than you do. But will you tell me what's going on?"

"He's stopped going to treatment. Maybe he's off his medications. It's not clear. He'd just started a new job and he abruptly stopped going to work. Nobody has heard from him in a week. His phone seems to be turned off."

"Yeah, I tried calling it too. Sure sounds as if he's isolating again. Do you have a current address for him?"

"I've got one, but nobody seems to be home."

"Now I'm worried. Can we meet? Maybe he's home but won't answer the door for anybody. Maybe he'll answer if he knows it's me."

Frank considered the offer. He didn't have any better idea. "When?"

"You tell me. I'll make the time."

"Okay. How about an hour from now?" He gave Wilde the address where Ralski was said to be living.

"You got it."

He hung up and turned to Athena, who was tapping away at her computer.

"I'm going to give another shot to Ralski's apartment. Wilde's going to meet me there. He's thinking that Ralski is holed away and not responding. Maybe he can get him to answer. It's probably another fool's errand."

"Give me a minute and I'll join you."

"No need. I'm going to have a combat vet as a backup, not to mention someone who Ralski probably trusts more than anyone else in the world."

"I still want to come. I'm just spinning my wheels in my searches at the moment and feeling frustrated."

"Okay, sure. But first, something occurs to me. Can we find the building management so we can call and see if someone can let us into the apartment? Ordinarily I'd look at this as an opportunity to hone my computer skills but time is a factor. You can do this a lot faster than I can."

She cleared her screen. "What's the address?"

It took Athena exactly six minutes to locate the management company and ascertain that they oversaw four properties in the immediate area. She had them on the phone in short order. Frank wondered if he'd ever have those kinds of internet skills.

The person charged with the maintenance of Ralski's building lived a block away and did not seem thrilled at the prospect of meeting them on short notice, but agreed to do so. At the appointed time, a surprised Cary Wilde arrived at the building to meet not just Frank but a trio.

Cary was an imposing figure, tall and lean, arms ropy-muscled and tattooed, wearing a black T shirt and jeans despite the chilliness of the day. His long black hair was disheveled and he looked weary. He pulled his wraparound sunglasses off and stared at the little group of people waiting for him.

"I was under the impression I was meeting just you, Detective," he rasped to Frank.

"This is my partner, Detective Pardo. And this is Mr. Shoemaker, the superintendent. We might need his help to get into the apartment."

Shoemaker didn't look any happier about the situation than Wilde. "Can we get this over with, whatever it is?"

The group ascended the stairs to the third floor and had stopped at the door to 312 when they first began to notice the smell.

"I don't remember that from yesterday," Frank said.

"There was somebody cooking," Athena said. "The hall was pretty strong with it."

"They're doing that again?" Shoemaker moaned. "I've warned them about that. What in hell are they cooking now? It stinks!"

They knew this new odor all too well. It wasn't anyone's cuisine.

Frank rapped on the door loudly. "Mr. Ralski? Mr. Ralski! Are you there?"

There was no answer. Frank knocked again. "Mr. Ralski, it's Detective Vandegraf. Do you remember me? I helped you get to the treatment center!..."

Wilde wedged himself in front of Frank and banged harder on the door. "Teddy! It's me, Cary! If you're in there, man, come on, please, open up!"

Frank turned to Shoemaker. "Better open it up."

"Look, are you sure about this…?"

"Open it up."

Shoemaker pulled a huge pack of keys from his belt and began sorting through them, muttering something unintelligible. It seemed to take forever before he finally unlocked the door. Luckily there was not a latch chain to prevent entry. The door swung open.

"Both of you stay back," Frank cautioned as he and Athena stepped forward. Shoemaker seemed quite happy to do just that.

Cary more reluctantly stopped at the threshold. The smell was not unfamiliar to him either.

Three of them, at least, had a good idea of what they were about to encounter.

There were no lights on in the windowless front room…nothing but darkened stillness in the sparse little parlor with only two chairs and a beat-up wooden table.

"Mr. Ralski?" Frank called out.

The door to the back bedroom was closed; a weak sliver of light showed from a crack beneath it.

Frank pulled out a handkerchief and used it to turn the doorknob and slowly push the door open.

The smell grew stronger, erupting out to greet them.

The blinds had been pulled open on the room's small window, overlooking a narrow alleyway. It afforded sufficient ambient light for them to clearly see the figure lying supine across the bed. His head was turned to his left and his right hand, still holding the small five-chamber revolver, lay close to his temple. The blood had splattered and soaked across the pillow and bedding underneath and had caked into a dry mass of dark maroon.

"Is that…?" Athena started.

"Ralski? I think so."

"What's going on in there?" yelled Wilde from the doorway.

Frank stepped back out of the room and over to Wilde. The look in the vet's eyes told Frank he needn't explain any further.

Quietly he said, "It's bad. I could use a positive ID. Are you okay with doing this?"

Wilde nodded. Shoemaker actually stepped further back into the hall, clearly wanting no part of this.

Frank gestured to Wilde and the bedroom.

"Watch where you walk," he said. "Be careful not to touch or disturb anything. Mr. Shoemaker, I'd appreciate it if you'd stay out there in the hall and keep any passersby away."

Wilde nodded and stepped in. The stunned super just stared at them as Frank, still using his handkerchief, pushed the front door shut.

"The smell might be a problem," Frank told Wilde as he followed him back.

"I've smelled death before."

He entered the room and moved to one side to let Frank in. The three just stared silently at the scene, each trying to process it, as if none of them wanted to break the terrible stillness.

Wilde finally spoke, and the words came with difficulty. "That's Teddy. Shit." He shook his head. "Shit."

A man who had already seen too much violence and misery, and had just seen more, knew all the head shaking in the world wasn't going to clear it out of his brain.

The detectives could tell, from experience, that Ralski had probably been dead for at least a couple of days.

Athena reached for her phone, stepping back a few paces. "I'll call it in."

Frank carefully approached the bed, sweeping the area with his gaze.

Ralski was dressed in an old Army fatigue jacket, white T shirt, and jeans, socks but no shoes. The bedroom appeared to have been recently tidied up; there was almost nothing lying around. The small dresser was empty, as was the night table, except for a sheet of paper and a felt tip pen.

Ralski had left a note, written in capital letters, presumably with the black pen. Frank took out his own pen and carefully nudged the letter so he could read it without touching it.

IM SORRY I TRIED. CANT MAKE IT WORK. TOO MANY VOICES. EVERYTHING WRONG AND THERE WILL BE MORE. MIGHT AS WELL BE DEAD. LIFE IS JUST A DIFFERENT KIND OF BEING DEAD.

"There will be more." The same phrase he'd used in his earlier notes. Frank wasn't sure what it had meant. Now he'd never know.

"Jesus Christ," muttered Wilde. "Fucking damn it."

"Thanks for confirming the identification of the body, Mr. Wilde. Can I ask you to step outside? This is a crime scene and we have to secure it. Then I'd like to talk to you some more. You don't have to hang around here. If you want, I can meet you later."

"What do you mean a *crime scene*? He killed himself, for fuck's sake! Look at the note! Look, he's still got ink stains on his fingers!"

Wilde turned and pointed at Ralski's gun hand. Some black smudges could indeed be seen on the fingers that grasped the weapon, alongside the blood spatters.

"You must know that suicides are treated as crime scenes. It certainly looks like a self-inflicted wound. We still have to follow procedures." Frank placed a hand on Wilde's shoulder. "Come on, I need you to step outside with me." He walked him out carefully.

In the hallway, Wilde took a heavy breath. "Yeah, I think I need to get away from here. Call me when you need me."

"If you need a good stiff drink, I certainly get it."

"Not an option for me anymore," Wilde said over his shoulder as he trudged down the dimly-lit passage toward the stairs. "Been sober for eight years now."

A tenant two doors down had opened her door to see what the commotion in the hall was. The dazed super didn't look to be in any shape to assure her so Frank told her there was nothing to be concerned over. She peered at him for a moment and then retreated back into her apartment, slamming and locking the door.

Then he turned to a clearly agitated Shoemaker, who was nervously rubbing his hands over his forearms.

"Is someone dead in there? They are, aren't they? The company's gonna have my hide for this! When this gets out, nobody's gonna wanta rent here!"

"Good point. For that and a lot of other reasons, it'd be a good idea to not talk about this with anybody just yet."

"The company's gonna have to know!"

"Yes, they are. We'll tell them what happened. You don't have to worry about it. I'll make sure they know you were of great assistance to us in discovering the crime. Nothing that happened here could be seen as your fault, could it?"

Shoemaker shook his head violently. "No, no, no, I had nothing to do with him! I never came near the place, haven't entered the apartment since the tenant moved in!"

"What can you tell me about the man who rented this apartment?"

"I. I...I don't know. I've got four buildings I have to watch over. There's always stuff to be done. He moved in here a couple, three months back. Never had anything to do with him once I gave him the keys and explained the rules. Nobody ever complained about him and he never made any waves. It was like he wasn't here. Good quiet tenant."

"He paid his rent on time?"

"I guess so. I don't get the rents; tenants send them to the company. I only hear about the deadbeats that I gotta go collect from. He never came up on my list."

"I get the feeling you don't have much involvement with any of your tenants."

"To be honest, I try not to. Nothing but trouble when you get too close. I take care of maintenance, fix stuff when it breaks, go after rent deadbeats, that kind of thing. These aren't my friends here. I keep it strictly business."

Frank nodded. He pulled out his notebook and asked for Shoemaker's contact information, saying he might have further questions. He tried to reassure the nervous super that he was in no trouble himself and said the best thing he could do now would be to go back to his own apartment and not spread the word of what had happened. If the crime scene investigators needed him to lock up the apartment or for any other reason, they'd contact him.

Athena emerged from the apartment. "The ME and SID are on their way," she said. "I'll need to go get tape from the car so we can tape off the scene."

"Okay. Mind walking Mr. Shoemaker down? I'll hold down the fort until the teams start arriving and then I'll canvas the neighbors."

Frank had a definite feeling that Shoemaker wasn't about to go talking about what had happened; he was still trying to tell himself that it hadn't actually happened.

* * * *

The County Medical Examiner and a Scientific Investigation Division team showed up quite promptly—it must be a quiet afternoon, Frank mused—and went to work with their usual dispassionate manner.

The examiner was a young woman named Sela Hovsepian whom Athena seemed to know fairly well. She was relatively new in her department and Frank had never encountered her until now, but she was already acquiring a reputation as a fearless and scrupulous coroner.

From the stories, Frank had expected a dour and serious sort, so he was surprised to meet an outgoing, downright cheerful individual. She stepped into the apartment carefully, sidestepping the yellow tape that had been strung to limn out a path to the bedroom, wearing her Coroner's Department windbreaker and carrying her kit. She motioned to an assistant to follow her.

Several SID techs in jumpsuits were already setting up lights and pulling out cameras.

"Hello, Detectives. Show me what we've got. Hey, Athena!"

Athena introduced her to Frank and, with the formalities disposed of, they got down to business.

Hovsepian gave a preliminary estimate of death as three to four days previous but said she'd likely be better able to narrow down the time once she had performed an autopsy. Frank and Athena figured they'd best give the crime scene investigators their space in the small apartment and went out to start knocking on doors of the neighbors.

They actually found four tenants present and hesitantly willing to talk with them. None of them had ever actually met Ralski or spoken with him. Only one had actually seen him in the hallway. He apparently kept his own counsel, befriended nobody, and came and went like a veritable wraith. Nobody had even heard any sounds or noises coming from the apartment (perhaps not surprisingly: there was no television, radio, or computer to be seen therein).

Most oddly, nobody had heard the sound of shots at any point.

Frank suspected that if anybody had heard or seen anything, they weren't of a mind to talk to the police about it. It was that kind of building.

When they returned to apartment 312, Hovsepian was ready to pack and ship the body and the crime lab techs were wrapping up their work. Everything was pretty cut and dried. The SID team would seal the apartment when they were finished.

Frank and Athena were done here for now.

But the least pleasant part was yet to come. It now fell to them to inform the next of kin of the passing of Teddy Ralski.

* * * *

"Detectives! Have you come back because you have news about Teddy?"

"You'd better let us come in, Mr. Wozniak, okay?"

They sat down in the identical seats they had taken the day before. The old man sat expectantly, his eyes wide behind the thick lenses. Athena began to break the news to him that they had indeed found his nephew, and he was dead.

It took Wozniak a while to process what he had been told. It was as if they were waiting for a bomb to go off.

Finally he reacted, slowly.

"Oh my God. Are you sure?"

"Yes, sir," said Frank quietly.

"How… how did he die? What happened?"

"It looks as though he took his own life. I'm sorry."

Wozniak seemed to just stare into blank space, his eyes full of sadness but not a tear coming.

Not yet, Frank reflected. Sometimes it just didn't immediately hit home with some of them.

"Oh, my Lord," he finally said haltingly. Something came back into his eyes. He looked up, first at Frank and then to Athena. "What happened?"

They tried to spare him as much detail as possible, but there was no way to totally cushion this one. The pain was obvious in Wozniak's eyes as he absorbed the story.

"I should have made him stay here," he said. "I…I had no idea. He seemed like he was doing… he was doing so well, do you know?"

"You can't blame yourself, Mr. Wozniak," Athena said gently. "You did nothing wrong."

"He seemed so happy while he was here. So…*serene*. That's what he was, serene. He was back in the light." He buried his face in his hands and sobbed. "I should never have let him go to that terrible dark apartment. He should have stayed in the light."

"You said he was on his medication when he left here, is that right? He was making his appointments and keeping up his prescriptions?"

"Oh, yes. He made sure he knew the bus route to the hospital from his new place. He knew how important it was to keep up his medications."

Wozniak suddenly looked horrified. "Are you saying he stopped taking his medications?"

"Apparently he had stopped making his regular appointments at the VA. He may have stopped refilling his prescriptions as well. That's not clear as yet."

"I don't understand. How could this have happened?" The old man looked searchingly back and forth at them both.

They both only wished they had an answer to that for him.

* * * *

The place was called Kerrie's and it was within walking distance of the Reboot treatment center. It looked like an old school neighborhood bar, where you were welcome…just so long as you were a neighbor.

Frank got several sideways looks from some rough looking patrons as he strolled down the bar, and deposited himself on a stool next to Cary Wilde. Wilde looked up nonchalantly as if he wasn't surprised to see him.

"They told me I'd find you here."

"Yeah. Lots of my old friends here. It's someplace people can find me if they need me, and vice versa."

"I thought you weren't a drinking man anymore."

Wilde gave a mirthless smile and, with thumb and forefinger, held up a glass of clear bubbly liquid and lightly shook it. The ice cubes tinkled.

"Club soda. That's actually what it's still called here. None of that 'sparkling mineral water' shit."

Frank cast a quick glance all around him. For a Tuesday night, the place was pretty well attended, though subdued. Conversations were murmuring all around him.

"Some people in recovery would have a hard time hanging around someplace like this."

"Yeah, like they say, sit around the barbershop long enough, sooner or later you'll get a haircut. It's never bothered me. When I was done, I was done. I've actually always found a certain, I don't know, peace in this place. Helps me to calm down and think things out."

"You must like the place because of the name, huh?"

"Actually…this place is owned by my ex-wife. That's her behind the bar. Her name's Kerrie. Cary and Kerrie…that was kinda confusing back when we were together. We actually ran a sort of pet store together for a while called C&K Reptiles…great big exotic snakes and lizards and shit like that. Got into it because we had a big old anaconda of our own. Bikers loved that joint."

"What happened to the reptiles?"

"Turns out neither of us knew how to run a pet store. Well, actually we got along with the reptiles okay, but not so much with each other as partners. We sold it and then broke up."

"I guess that doesn't bother you either, being around her, huh? I'd imagine that'd be tough for some guys too."

"Same deal. When we were done, we were done. Just remember the good stuff. We drank and fought a lot, but man, the sex was great, and we had some epic adventures. She got custody of the anaconda when we split. Kerrie's great. We're still friends."

He motioned to the purple-haired woman in a leather vest behind the bar. "Hey Kerrie, see what my friend here's drinking?"

Frank decided he was signed out for the night and off duty. He wasn't much of a drinker but he noticed a couple of customers with bottles of an imported beer he sometimes liked and asked for one. When she brought it back to him, Wilde made a perfunctory introduction.

"Kerrie, meet Frank Vandegraf," he said quietly. "He's the guy who brought Teddy to Reboot back when."

Since he'd sat down to talk amicably with Cary Wilde, Frank noted the suspicious glances had subsided. They might return if his job title were to be proclaimed, which he noted had been avoided. The bar owner gave him a quick smile, said hello, left the bottle and headed back down the bar.

The two men sat in silence, staring at the bottles lined up in front of a mirrored wall behind the bar.

Finally Frank gave a sigh. "Long day."

"I bet. Have you informed the uncle?"

"Yeah. A while ago."

"How'd that go?"

"About like you'd expect. Not good. The old man seemed a bit muddled but he took it pretty hard."

"I never met him. Don't really know anything about him, but I guess he sure came through for Teddy."

"He was planning to return to Arizona once he was sure Teddy was settled. He was there for him, all right. Rented out his own condo and took on an apartment here where Teddy could have a home."

Wilde kept looking straight ahead as he talked. "I wish I knew what happened. Why'd he do this? Why do any of them do it?"

"Do you see this a lot? Suicides, I mean?"

"Wish I could tell you it was my first rodeo, but I see too many of them."

Wilde finally turned and stared at Frank. "And not a fucking one of them ever makes sense."

"This one doesn't make sense to me either. From everything I've heard, he was a downright miracle recovery. What pushed him back to the darkness?"

Frank thought of how Wozniak had contrasted the sunlit home that he'd provided and the dank place that served as Ralski's final address.

Ralski had quite literally returned to the darkness from the light.

"I don't know, Frank. Can I call you Frank?"

"Sure."

"You know, you see guys who come through the center, you just know somehow they're not going to stay. They go out and get loaded again, isolate, go back to the street or their demons, whatever they might be. It's not a huge surprise after a while. Sometimes working the center is like trying to hold back the sea. You can show them hope and they go back out anyhow.

"What you call the darkness is a pretty powerful place, Frank. I've looked into it myself."

He held up an index finger. "Then you get the *one* who chooses hope. What you called a miracle. That's why we do what we do, for that one out of a dozen or a hundred or a thousand who chooses hope. That was Teddy. He got his mind back. He got his soul back. Of everyone who's come through Reboot in the last few years, if you asked me to single out one guy I'd put my money on to make it...it would've been Teddy. Hands down."

"So...that's it? You just say the darkness reclaimed him, and that's that?"

"What the fuck else can I do? I have to go back to the center tonight and try to save the damaged souls I got right now. I can't dwell on the ones I've lost. I can't try to make sense where there is none."

Trying to hold back the sea.

Frank took a pull off his beer. The silence between them grew awkward.

"Where did Teddy get the gun?" Frank finally asked. "To your knowledge, did he own it?"

"He didn't have it at Reboot. We don't allow it. That's grounds for instant expulsion. I never saw him with any kind of weapon. He either already had it salted away some other place or he got hold of it when he moved out. I didn't look that closely at it today."

"It was a Smith & Wesson .38."

"Easy enough to come by, as guns go. I don't have to tell you that. But it doesn't make sense to me that he would have kept a gun."

"Salted away. Maybe back in his dark days he got one, when he wasn't thinking straight. Maybe he already had it hidden away?"

"I don't know, Frank. That's one possibility. None of it fits with the guy I thought I knew." Wilde lapsed into another uncomfortable silence before continuing.

"So…you still trying to pin that crime on Teddy?"

"No. He was just trying to…I don't know, get attention. It was the same thing he did last time. I was just following up on a crank letter, like we often get when there are a series of serious crimes happening. I just wanted to clear that."

"Back when that woman got killed on the street…"

"Ronnie Rackham."

"Yeah. Back when that happened…you were really looking at Teddy for that, weren't you?"

"Did he tell you that?"

"He had his suspicions. Of course he was pretty paranoid when he first walked in."

"When I first tracked him down, all I had was the letter he'd sent us. So maybe for a minute, yeah. Then I talked with him, and I found out about the other letters he'd sent, and found a more logical suspect. And everything fell into place. I was satisfied Teddy couldn't be my guy by then. That's when I brought him to you."

"We talked a lot about that, the thing with the Rackham woman. He didn't have anything to do with that. Maybe you were never one hundred percent sure, but I am. He didn't know her. He never met her. He was nowhere near her."

"What I don't understand is why he sent us that letter…why did he send all those letters? The whole thing with 'There will be more.' What was that all about?"

"Teddy wasn't firing on all his cylinders back then. I don't know that he'd ever have been able to articulate it. He tried in group sessions. I'm sure he tried in his sessions with the shrink at the VA. Do you know anything about his service experience?"

"Not really, no."

"He saw some pretty heavy shit in the Middle East. I get it. It all takes on the feeling of senselessness and some people process it more successfully than others. The impression he would give me was, it was as if God had come down to talk to him personally, only this wasn't a loving God, this was an abusive parent who delighted in tormenting his children. He thought that God had taunted him, 'Teddy boy, you think it's bad now, it's only gonna get worse.' Of course that was when Teddy was in the depths of his sickness."

Wilde paused to sip his club soda and shrug. "Best I can make of it, that was where he was coming from. He felt whenever something bad happened, he should let people know it was gonna get worse. Because he had been told that directly by the mother fucking Almighty himself. And that's pretty much all I got on that."

"But he got better. He didn't exhibit those paranoid delusions anymore."

"Better living through chemistry, Frank. He came back to earth. Now back to what I need to be clear on: do you think he had anything to do with the crime you're investigating now?"

"As I said. No. No, I don't."

"Because I get the impression you went to some trouble to track him down. Why was that?"

Frank didn't know if he could articulate his feelings to Wilde any better than Teddy had done with his. He wasn't sure he could sort it out even in his own mind. And even if he had been able to, he wasn't sure it would have been advisable to share it. He'd felt he might have let something get by him, and he felt some guilt over it. But it was water under the bridge and there was nothing he could do about it now.

Frank thought back a couple of hours to the conversation with Castillo they'd had upon returning to the unit, before he went looking for Wilde. The Lou had asked a few simple questions:

"Is there any doubt that Ralski's death was a suicide?"

"No," Frank had answered. "That's pretty cut and dried."

"Okay. Is there any compelling evidence that he might have been involved in your case?"

"No to that one as well, Lou."

"Then I can't have you wasting any more time on it. You're already jammed up and I need some kind of break on this Creep case. That's your priority. Sign off on the suicide and don't pursue it any further."

"There are questions, though, Lou."

"Do they have relevance to any of your open investigations at this time?"

"No, but…"

"Then leave them. You can't always answer every question. Sign off on the suicide."

The door was about to close on Teddy Ralski.

Frank broke his reverie and drank some more from his bottle. "No trouble. I was just crossing all the T's and dotting all the I's. I like to be thorough. Teddy's letter was just out of the blue. He had absolutely nothing to do with my case."

8.

It was an odd dream from which Frank found himself being pulled by the chime of his phone: the Lattimers' gardener and Collis Westermark were chasing him through a subway tunnel on vivid magenta-purple HUMM scooters. It turned into the interior of Kerrie's Bar and Teddy Ralski was pouring him a drink, winking knowingly at him as the glass overflowed. He rang the "Last Call" bell behind the bar and the bell blended into the sound of his alarm.

Frank looked at the time on his phone: 5:35.

It was never a good thing to be awakened by an early phone call.

The daylight was still new when Frank arrived, yawning and chilly in his sport jacket, at the crime scene.

Athena had already arrived, as had the Scientific Investigation Division team in their blue coveralls and the coroner, the venerable Mickey Kendrick, in his usual Coroner jacket.

The knot of people filled the small pocket park behind the Public Library, which was being cordoned off by uniformed officers with skeins of the usual yellow police-line tape. Mickey and Athena were squatting over the body that lay on the ground, partially covered by a plastic sheet. They looked up in unison as he approached.

Frank stopped a few short steps before the body. The prone victim's head was turned to one side, mouth agape, eyes vacantly staring out. Frank had the eerie feeling the young man on the walkway was gazing directly at him. His arms were spread at awkward angles and the ground beneath him was stained blood dark.

He had close-cropped black hair and a scruffy patch of chin hair. The sheet covered his lower body but Frank could see the bulky sweater that had been gray before being saturated with dark red blood.

"He's just a kid! What is he, nineteen?"

"Multiple stab wounds," intoned Kendrick, never losing his trademark monotone voice and bloodhound scowl. "All to the back. Might have been taken by surprise. I see no evidence of defense wounds. Opening estimate, he was killed around midnight last night. Your Creep again?"

"Sure looks like it. Who found the body?"

Frank looked around and saw nobody who looked like a witness.

"It was called in anonymously around four, I'm told. In Spanish."

"Excuse me, Mickey."

Athena, already wearing the requisite gloves, reached under the sheet and probed for the victim's pants pocket. After some difficulty, she brought out a shoddy wallet that looked as if it had been made out of silver ducting tape.

"Driver's license says he's Raymond Luczon, age twenty," she said. "His address isn't far from here. Not much else in here. A few dollars. No credit cards, no other ID."

"No library card?" asked Frank. "Wonder what he was doing here behind the library in the middle of the night. Not returning a book."

Athena just stared at him. By now she knew his macabre sense of humor… as well as his recurring jokes that millennials didn't read.

The body lay next to a park bench that had seen better days. The mini-park was overgrown with bushes; like many municipal parks, these days it was mainly a hangout for people with nowhere else to go.

"Nobody sleeping here last night?"

Athena shook her head. She stood up and handed Frank the wallet. "Not when the unis got here. Anybody bedded down here got scared away…but might still have decided to call it in."

Frank browsed through it. "The interval just got a lot smaller between our guy's murders. Riemer's attack was, what, four days ago?"

"So much for our cyclical speculations. This guy has picked up the pace drastically."

"But for what it's worth, the victims are still getting progressively younger."

Mickey gingerly lifted the sheet. "Do you detectives want to see anything else before we all get to work?"

There were no other items in the victim's pockets: no phone, keys, or any other personal articles. No watch and no jewelry.

No phone? Someone his age?

The park was crisscrossed with cement walks; it was likely there would be no footprints. The Creep had not as yet left any fingerprints or other evidence at any of his crime scenes; they presumed that would be the case here as well, though the SID would do their due diligence.

Frank and Athena took photos of the victim and his surroundings, looked around a bit more, and decided there was nothing else they could do there at the moment.

"Why don't we walk over to Luczon's place?" said Frank. "There may be family."

Athena frowned. "Second time in twenty-four hours we have to break the bad news to loved ones. This is going to be the thing I hate most about this job."

"Take it from me: it always will be. It'll never get any easier and you'll never get used to it."

* * * *

The address on Luczon's license was a three-story brownstone that had once been a single-family dwelling but now had been subdivided into three apartments. The block was part of an older working-class neighborhood that was beginning to be gentrified. A number of younger renters and buyers were already moving in, and the pool-table bars and bodegas were beginning to be supplanted by a sprinkling of coffee houses, art galleries, pet groomers, and doughnut shops.

It was a study in contrasts. Young upscale-looking people were taking their dogs on morning walks, while a few individuals lay sleeping curled up in the doorways of storefronts that looked as if they had recently been vacated. There were a few HUMM scooters lined up in drop off racks on two corners.

Frank and Athena were halfway up the stairs of the building when the front door popped open and a distracted-looking young woman in a long coat and knit beret stepped out. It took her a moment to register that there were people on the stairs in front of her, and she came to an abrupt halt, her eyes suddenly wide.

Frank had his badge and ID out and held them up. "Do you live here, Miss?"

"Y…yes. Yes, I do. What's going on?"

"Would you happen to know Raymond Luczon?" Athena asked, trying to be a bit softer in tone than Frank's unintentional gruffness.

"Sure I know him; he's my roommate! What's going on? Is he in some sort of trouble?"

"When did you last see him?"

"I don't know…sometime yesterday morning? He was gone when I came home from work and he never came back last night as far as I can tell. What's up? Has something happened to him?"

"Can we come in and talk to you?" Frank asked, this time more gently.

"I have to get to work. Is this serious or can it wait? Has Ray done something stupid or what?"

"Just…please, can we come in?"

* * * *

"My God, I can't believe it. I just can't…oh my God!"

Brittany Weinberg had invited them into the tiny cramped apartment and now sat across from them in one of three mismatched chairs in what passed for a living room. She had removed her beret and let her bright blue-tipped brunette hair spill down, then listened as Frank and Athena had informed her of the fate of Raymond Luczon. She confirmed that the photo they had was indeed of her roommate.

From that moment on she'd sat stunned, repeating that same mantra over and over. "I can't believe it, I just can't…"

They waited patiently until she began to compose herself. Finally something came back into her eyes, and she looked up at them and sniffed, "What happened to him?"

"That's what we're going to find out, Ms. Weinberg," said Athena. She spied a box of tissues on a nearby table and handed it to the young woman. "I know this is a terrible moment for you but can we ask you some questions that might help us?"

Weinberg nodded her head as she blew her nose. "I guess so. If it will help…."

"First," asked Frank, "what's your relationship to Mr. Luczon? May we presume you were, uh, significant others?"

"Ray and me? Oh God no!"

The idea seemed to both shock and amuse her.

"It was like yin and yang, him and me, total opposites. We were friends. Roommates. Neither of us could afford a place by ourselves, so we went in together. It worked out pretty well because I work all day and he works through the night, so we slept at different times. There were days we didn't even see each other. That's why I wasn't particularly concerned when he wasn't here this morning."

She looked back and forth at the two detectives. "I'm a waitress, at the Urban Fern vegan restaurant on Goff, and sometimes I work a second job as a counterperson at the bakery up the street, Nutz for Dough. They make bagels and doughnuts and artisanal ice cream and…"

She stopped, still looking back and forth at them. "I'm…I'm babbling, aren't I? I'm kinda still in shock."

"It's perfectly understandable," smiled Athena. She had instinctively taken the seat closer to Weinberg, and now she reached over and placed a reassuring hand on the woman's arm.

"Take your time and tell us in whatever way is comfortable. So Raymond worked nights. What did he do?"

"Oh, he was a blogger. Total computer nerd. He loved gaming. Spent hours playing all sorts of games and then he found a way to monetize it, as he called it. He created a website and reviewed games and apps."

Frank and Athena exchanged glances.

"He used to be a busboy and a waiter at the Fern. That's how I first met him and after a while we decided to share a place since we were both broke. He'd work his shift and then come home and game and blog all night. Then he somehow started making some money so he quit the Fern. He said he was finally being *monetized,* so I guess he was selling ads on his site or something. At least he paid his share of the rent and utilities regularly, and he always seemed to have food in the house."

Weinberg pointed to a small room with no door off the living room, hardly bigger than a large closet. Frank suspected it had actually been a walk-in closet once, back when this building had been a spacious house.

"That's his workspace," she said. "He's got his computer and everything else set up in there. He'd unroll his futon and sleep on the floor."

"Let's come back to that in a moment. Does Raymond have any family or close friends nearby whom we can contact?"

"I don't think so. His mother died a couple of years ago, and there are no brothers or sisters. Whatever other family is in the Philippines and they must be distant. He only mentioned them once or twice in passing; I think they were estranged. He didn't socialize very much; he was pretty much a loner. I don't even know of any close friends he might have had. He never brought anybody here that I ever saw."

"Any romantic connections that you know of?"

"He'd been spending time with someone. I got that impression from a couple cryptic remarks he made here and there. But I don't know anything about who it might be."

"Woman or man?" asked Athena.

"I'd presume a woman, from what I know of Ray. But I couldn't tell you for sure."

"Did he leave any information about people to notify in the event of an emergency? Next of kin? Anyone like that?"

Weinberg shook her head. "No. Nothing like that. You have to understand... I don't mean any disrespect to Ray or anything like that... but he was kind of irresponsible, a bit of a flake. I mean, he was a really smart guy, but he did a lot of crazy things. He let a lot of things get by him. I was pretty surprised when he seemed to be taking care of his business lately. You know, talking about the future and planning and stuff like that? Until fairly recently, I used to kid him that he didn't know what the future *was.* He made some mysterious references to finding a motherlode, a real treasure…if he could just work for it."

"So…a good prospect of some kind. Could it have had anything to do with this clandestine significant other?"

"You mean like get a job and settle down? Be a *citizen*, as Ray called it? Dubious. More likely he thought he was going to strike it rich in some enterprise. Maybe he'd found some girl who believed his dreams and was tagging along for the benefits. Some internet guys are like that. They want to spend the rest of their lives working in pajamas in their bedrooms and figure they'll become overnight millionaires, with hot girlfriends."

Weinberg sniffed again. "Oh my God, I shouldn't be saying things like that. Ray's *dead*, for Pete's sake."

"It's okay. You're being honest."

As Athena continued her questions, Frank confined himself for the moment to taking notes in his pad.

He couldn't help reflecting on how she just kept amazing him. She was sensitive and tactful, and he wasn't necessarily sure he had it in him at the moment to do as well. He wondered if he'd ever been able to do it that well.

"Tell us more about this…enterprise of his. You say he ran a blog on apps and games and things like that?"

Weinberg nodded. "He'd been spending a *lot* of time on it lately. He told me he was trying to teach himself lots more about code so he could become a developer himself. His goal was to open his own gaming company. In the meantime he'd made connections with people in game development. He said he'd been able to start selling advertising on his site and to get investments from various people. He said he was becoming an influencer, as he called it. He even created an online identity. He joked he was a superhero, with his own secret identity."

Frank and Athena once again exchanged looks. Could it possibly be?

No, he heard himself thinking. *No, don't let it be.*

He didn't even look up, just put a hand to his brow as he asked, "Do you happen to know what his 'secret identity,' this online persona, was called?"

"Oh sure. It was a takeoff on his own name. He called his site the Ultimate Zone, and he called himself Luc Zone."

* * * *

The remainder of the interview went awkwardly, though Weinberg seemed completely willing to help them as much as possible. The workspace she'd pointed out to them contained a collapsible table set up for a laptop computer, but there was no computer. There was a free-standing floor lamp that Frank switched on.

"He must have had a laptop, right?" asked Frank.

"Sure. He was, like, attached to it. He…he didn't have it with him? I mean, when …you know, you…found him…?"

"No, he had nothing. No bag, no laptop, not even a phone."

"He didn't have that old courier bag he always carried? He didn't seem to go anywhere without that slung over his shoulder."

The room held almost nothing in terms of personal effects, just a jar of loose change and a few odds and ends on the table. No files, no papers, no documents. Apparently any records pertaining to Ultimate Zone and anything else in his sparse life had been kept digitally, on his missing computer.

They found nothing in the way of keepsakes, photos, or anything else tangible. There was a small plastic three-drawer dresser with his clothes, mostly jeans, sweaters and T shirts, and a futon rolled up behind it alongside a pair of tennis shoes.

They asked Weinberg if it was possible that Luczon had been spending time somewhere else, where he might have left more of his belongings. She shrugged; it was possible, but she had no idea.

There was no phone among the belongings. Weinberg confirmed that of course Luczon had one, and as with most people his age, it was pretty much regarded as an extra appendage.

Frank made a mental note to request Luczon's phone records and asked Weinberg to bring up the number on her own phone for him. It was the same number where he had called the witness, Lucas Zone, on Monday.

They showed her photos of the prior victims of the Creep, and asked if their faces or their names seemed familiar—had she ever seen them with Raymond? She said definitely not, but reiterated that she wasn't all that close to him and that they were seldom both in the same place for any length of time.

She agreed to leave everything of Raymond's untouched and to allow an SID team to come in as soon as possible. As the interview concluded, she decided she'd call in to skip work. Athena and Frank told her that was probably a good idea. They left her their business cards and departed.

* * * *

There had been a long thoughtful silence in the car returning to the unit before Athena finally opened her mouth.

"This is totally crazy."

"Tell me about it."

"What do you make of it, Frank?"

"It's hard for me to swallow it as a massive coincidence. I don't believe in such a thing. There's a connection."

"I'm not sure where we start looking for it."

"Me neither, but I don't buy that they're not related…any more than you're willing to allow the Creep's victims are random."

"I know…but you always tell me that we have to find the evidence to back up hunches, or they can lead us off in the wrong direction. That's why I've spent so long looking for something tangible."

She stirred restlessly in the car seat, crossing her arms. "I don't see how Luczon has any connection with the rest of the killer's vics. Maybe the guy *is* just killing opportunistically."

"The problem with thinking that way," mused Frank, "is where to go from there? If the assaults are totally random, how do you find the assailant, or how do you predict where he'll strike next? Because it's a good bet he *will* keep killing."

"One thing's odd. Mickey said there were, what, four stab wounds on Luczon? That's breaking the pattern. Up until now each attack seemed more intense than the previous one. Blanche Liwicki was stabbed six times. Ephraim Coates was stabbed nine times. And Natalie Riemer received at least a dozen stab wounds. For me that confirmed these are personal attacks and that the killer's rage is growing."

"Riemer did escape him initially and was trying to run away. That could account for the increased number of stab wounds in her case. He was jabbing blindly at her at the end."

"I thought about that. It was still consistent with my theory. Now I'm not sure. Mickey said Luczon had no defense wounds. All three of the other vics had some evidence of trying to defend themselves. Maybe the Creep is changing his approach, getting stealthier. And…well, just possibly the choice of victims is random after all."

"You just called him the Creep. That's the first time I've ever heard you do that."

Athena sighed. "Maybe I'm changing my mind. Maybe this guy really is a damned creep after all."

9.

"Thanks for the coffee, Mr. Coates. I'm really sorry to be bothering you again."

Ephram Coates, Junior, was only twenty-two. He and his wife had recently bought a small house and were raising two baby daughters. At the moment, he sat at his kitchen table, bouncing the older one, two year old Kelly, on his knee. The younger, nine-month old Violet, napped in a nearby crib.

Somehow people went on despite the hole in their hearts after a close loved one had been wrenched from them.

"I'm glad you could come by, Detective Pardo. We appreciate the efforts you and your partner are making to find my dad's killer. You're always welcome here."

"How are you holding up?"

"I'm not going to lie to you; it's been hard. But we're staying strong."

They made small talk for a short time before Athena turned to business. "I know we've been through some of this, but I'm still hoping to find some connection in these killings. Can I show you more photos and go over the names again?"

"Of course. Whatever you think might help."

Blanche Liwicki, and now Natalie Riemer, still drew blanks for him. He had never seen them nor heard his father mention them.

"Maybe if we go over your dad's background again, just in general. Maybe there's something there."

"Well, as I've told you, Dad was a straight arrow from the git-go. Grew up in a working class community in Michigan with parents who gave him a solid work ethic. Played three sports in school. Served in the Marines, mostly at Camp Lejeune in North Carolina…worked his way up to Staff Sergeant. By then he had a family, and when he was discharged from the service he went to work for Clips. About six years ago we moved here and he became regional warehouse supervisor for their distribution center."

"And as I recall, he didn't usually have contact with customers."

"No, he was almost never in any of the Clips office supply stores. He only dealt with the personnel of the warehouse and with higher-ups."

"By the time of that move, you were a teenager."

"Yeah."

Coates shook his head and smiled at a flood of memories. "It wasn't always easy. New school, had to make all new friends, and Dad insisted I go out for sports and keep real busy so I wouldn't get in trouble. He expected me to keep my grades up and the new school was tough. He was strict. My Mom would try to get him to lighten up on me but he insisted it was important I learn responsibility. I mean, we used to have arguments about everything. He wanted me to register to vote as soon as I turned eighteen. Said it was my civic duty. I would tell him, 'I won't make a difference but then they can call me for jury duty.'

"Can you believe we had a fight when I was eighteen over jury duty? He said I should never think that way, that I didn't make a difference. In fact he used to volunteer every year for jury duty, said it was his responsibility and privilege. Sometimes he'd be on a case that went so long he wouldn't be getting paid at work for it. But it was important. That was the kind of guy he was. It was all important."

Coates put his hand on his forehead. Little Kelly giggled at him. "Hey, sorry, I get caught up reminiscing about my Dad. You're looking for information, not my family memories."

"As a matter of fact," Athena said, "that's pretty interesting. Keep talking. You just never know when you might say something that means something."

By the time she left, she thought he had indeed said something that meant something.

At least two more calls remained to confirm what she now suspected. As Athena walked back to her car outside the Coates residence, she pulled out her phone to start.

"Mr. Liwicki? This is Detective Pardo, you may remember me…yes, I'm fine, thank you…we're working on it, sir. That's why I'm calling. Forgive me for being abrupt at the moment, but this could be important. This may seem like a strange question but could you tell me…."

* * * *

"Are you telling me, Frank, that your killer murdered my witness? What are the odds?"

"In a word, Russ, yes—that's what I'm telling you."

Frank looked up and down the street as he talked into his phone. The person on whom he was waiting had yet to make an appearance.

"Now why in the world would he do that?"

"That's what I'm trying to find out."

"Now see, that's a big reason I'm glad I left the PD. In Metro Transit we tend to deal in straightforward accidents, not messy murders. Everything's clean and simple…well, at least simple. It's a different kind of dead."

Russ Payne chuckled dryly. "This's a crazy development. And this Zone guy's real name is, what, you said Luczon?"

"Raymond Luczon, that's right. Lucas Zone was his alter ego online. For some reason he gave witness accounts under his pseudonym."

"Yeah, well, not the first time a wit's done that, is it? Everybody's got something to hide."

"You don't find any of this strange, that he turns up murdered two nights after he's the sole witness in a fatality?"

"Like that Freud guy said, sometimes a coincidence is just a coincidence. You're right, it's weird, but I'm not sure what bearing it might have on my case. Lattimer's an open and shut accidental death."

"So you're ready to close the book on it, huh?"

"Absolutely. I've even reviewed the video footage in the station. Brutal stuff, I tell you…but there's nothing to indicate it was anything but a boneheaded accident."

"Russ, are you sure that Lattimer wasn't carrying anything when he died? A briefcase, a courier bag, a folder of papers, anything?"

"Like I told you, Frank, there were no personal effects anywhere around. Nothing. Not even a phone."

"By the way," Frank said wearily, "I think Freud actually made that comment about a cigar."

"Yeah? Well, I've given up smoking so don't talk to me about cigars. Let me know if you hear any more about Zone's death, willya, Frank? Or better yet, never mind."

Frank ended the call, shaking his head. Somehow talking with Russ made him very tired.

He realized that Russ had used the same expression he'd encountered recently in a very disparate context: a different kind of dead.

He pocketed his phone and continued to look up and down the street from his vantage point in a storefront doorway.

Sharon Brooks came out of the door of Humbletech headquarters, wrapping her scarf around her neck against the breeze that was blowing dust down Goff Boulevard, looking both ways to navigate her way into the crush of people bustling to get home as it grew dark.

Frank, directly across the street, caught sight of her and moved to the crosswalk. The light changed and he calculated a path to intersect with her almost directly in front of a plaza with benches and statuary, sidestepping two people on HUMM scooters buzzing down the street against the light. Head down, rushing distractedly forward, she didn't see him until she almost collided with him. She drew herself up with a start.

"Oh! Detective Vandegraf!"

"Ms. Brooks. How are you doing?"

"I'm...I'm fine, thanks. Sorry for running into you like that. My mind is kind of far away."

"I can imagine. Must be pretty hectic at work right now since you've taken over Orrin Lattimer's responsibilities for the interim."

"Yes, it's totally nuts. I probably shouldn't have left this early but I've been working around the clock and I have personal matters to take care of."

Frank nodded. He pulled up the collar of his coat against the wind. "Have you got a minute to talk?"

"I'm sorry, but I'm really in a hurry right now. Can it wait?"

"If you don't mind my saying so, you look particularly distressed. When I talked to you the other day you were cool, collected and competent. I think something's happened."

"Of course something's happened! Orrin is dead! It's thrown the entire company into chaos! And then there's office politics that you don't need to hear about. Really, I have to go."

Frank didn't budge, and that stopped her from moving on.

"Ms. Brooks, I think there are lots worse things going on at Humbletech than what you call 'office politics.' I think you've found yourself in the eye of a storm. Maybe you even feel personally unsafe. And I think it's connected to the murder of Orrin Lattimer."

"Murder? Orrin? What do you mean?"

"Just give me a few minutes to put it together for you. I think you can help me. I really need to find Meryl Lattimer. I think she's a key to both your problems and mine."

Brooks exhaled heavily and considered for almost a minute before she replied, "All right, but not here."

Looking around nervously, she gave him the address of a coffee shop several blocks away and hustled off.

* * * *

Sharon Brooks sat at the small table, quivering hands wrapped around her cup as if they needed warming and steadying, staring down at the rippling beige *latte*. Frank sat across from her, ignoring his own coffee.

"You looked pretty anxious coming out of work."

"I was...distracted. Things are happening. Way, way too fast." She spoke very softly, as if afraid someone else might overhear.

"What kinds of things?"

Sharon thought for a minute before speaking, considering if she should start telling tales out of school.

A careful and deliberate soul, Frank reflected.

"You used the word murder before. Did you mean it?"

Frank nodded, never breaking eye contact.

"And you think it could have to do with internal issues at Humbletech?"

"I don't know. But I get the feeling something especially serious is going on, and maybe it's all connected, maybe it's not. But you look like you could use someone to talk to, so maybe we can help each other."

Frank rode out another long pause fraught with cautious deliberation before she finally spoke.

"It's Collis. She's making a push to take over the company. She's trying to get control of Orrin's share of everything. I think she wants to do it before Lane returns. She's been pressuring me to hand over Innovation and Development to her. She's trying to get hold of Orrin's ideas…and his patents. Those are the real treasures of the company."

"The patents are Orrin's?"

She took a deep breath, realizing she was going to have to fill Frank in on a lot of background.

"Yes. He's the patent holder on dozens of items, including the special technology behind the HUMM scooters. Most of the company is just what anybody can do, basically put together the parts. The intellectual property is the real company."

"And Orrin owned a big hunk of Humbletech, did he not?"

"Absolutely. He, Collis and Lane are the main shareholders by far."

"Since Orrin's death, who now holds his shares of the company, and his patents, and so forth?"

"That would have to be his wife, Meryl."

"So how would Collis be able to get hold of them?"

Sharon stared levelly at Frank. "It might not be that hard. She'd offer to buy Meryl out. Collis can raise a lot of money. Orrin, on the other hand, was overextended."

"You don't think Meryl would have any interest in taking over her husband's place at the table, then? The patents alone have got to represent a huge windfall, if everything I've heard about Humbletech is going to come true."

"Oh, the company *could* do quite well. And if they do, it's going to be on the basis of Orrin's work."

"I was under the impression that Lane Dembeau was the driving wheel behind the company. You even said so."

She pursed her lips, considering whether to be candid. She made her decision quickly.

"That's what we sell. He's the front man. He puts out the energy, has the eloquence, and makes the contacts. He's got an engineering degree and he likes to call himself the Lead Designer but the fact is, he couldn't design a basic prototype if his life depended on it. Lane's not a nuts and bolts man;

he's totally blue sky. He can sell any outrageous idea without any substance behind it. He's always been the perfect corporate face."

"Apparently he put up a lot of Humbletech money as well."

"Lane's well-to-do but not exactly filthy rich. He did invest most of his own money in the startup, but Humbletech wouldn't have gotten anywhere without Collis. Of the three original founders, she put up most of the seed money. She and her consortium: she brought in several friends as silent partners to back her as well."

"Sounds as if she might be financially beholden to a few people then."

"Altogether possible. She still controls the interest, though. Rumor is that she wants to bring someone in to take over the tech side, possibly one of her allies."

"What about Orrin? You said he was in bad financial straits?"

"I don't know specifically, but in recent times he was clearly worried. He's pretty heavily leveraged in the company. He took home significant money but he's been treading water. His wife doesn't work anymore; she's been home schooling their daughter for several years now."

"So…Orrin was the brains, Lane was the PR, and Collis the purse. And they were all working without binding contracts. Seems like a pretty wacky company."

"Nothing is done 'normally' around Humbletech. It's an eccentric place of business. You get used to it."

Frank shifted gears. "Orrin's house is up in the hills. But he was getting on a train miles away from there. Was he staying somewhere else recently?"

"He didn't talk about it around the office. I think he was staying in an apartment off of Goff, not far from the company."

"Were there marital problems? He and his wife seem to have been apart for a few weeks now. Or was he afraid of something?"

"I…I don't know," she said. Frank didn't buy it.

He also didn't buy that she didn't know where he'd been staying.

"Sharon, the night Orrin died, he was on his way to talk to a reporter. He said he had confidential information that would be a bombshell. What was he talking about?"

"What? This is all news to me. I suppose…Orrin might have known something improper connected with Collis's power play, or one on the part of Lane. I don't really trust either Lane or Collis, to tell you the truth. They're both scary, unpredictable characters, and they've both been making some kind of *sub rosa* maneuvers, and the rest of us are caught in the middle of their chess game. I think it's all coming to a head, whatever it is."

"So, the manure has hit the fan, so to speak, with Orrin's death, and now you're involved in it."

"Yeah, and I think my imagination has been running overtime as a result. For a while, I had this weird idea I was being followed. At one point, I had to go out of town, and I actually did some roundabout maneuvers until I was sure there was nobody on the highway behind me. Silly stuff. I decided my mind was playing tricks on me because I'm so worried."

"What are you so scared about? I don't think it's just about losing your job."

"I love my job. A lot of us in I&D do. As I said, there's a rumor that Collis wants to bring in her own person to run the tech side of things, somebody I've never even heard of. Once or twice I heard the name Reed or Mead or something. That would make a mass purge of the department altogether possible."

"I think you're worried about more than that. You strike me as someone impressively competent, who could land on her feet easily."

Sharon's eyes widened. "Collis wants to find Meryl. She's putting some pretty substantial pressure on me. She's threatening not only to have me dismissed for cause but to insure I can't get another job after I leave."

"How's she planning to do that? Does she have something on you, some indiscretion?"

Sharon was silent.

"You and Orrin?"

She stared back down into the coffee cup that trembled in her hands. Finally she spoke again.

"It wasn't any big deal. It was over before it started. I admire Orrin greatly. He is…I mean, he was…a great man. And a sweet one. He loved his family. He was never going to leave. But Collis found, let's say, damning evidence. She can make it seem a lot worse than it was."

"Are you sure there isn't more than that? No physical threats or anything like that?"

"This is a hell of a lot, Detective! This could ruin my entire life! And I don't know if I could live with the kind of shame it would bring on Orrin's memory…or to Meryl. I know her and I like her very much. Collis is insistent that I tell her where to find Meryl. I keep telling her, over and over, that I don't have any idea where Meryl and Kyra went."

Frank nodded. "But you do know, don't you?"

* * * *

The evening shift had already come on and things were reasonably quiet when Frank got off the elevator at Personal Crimes.

Athena quite literally ran down the hall to him and accompanied him back to his desk.

Frank looked at the wall clock. "Got your text to meet you here," he said. "What's so important that wouldn't keep until morning, Athena?"

"I've figured it out," she said. "...the connection."

She swept aside the papers on Frank's desk, opened a manila folder tucked under her arm, and laid three Xeroxed photographs on the desk.

"These were taken at the manslaughter trial of Nathan Trenier nine months ago."

She bent over the desk and pointed to the first sheet. "Blanche Liwicki, Juror Number Seven."

Next she pointed to the second sheet. "Ephraim Coates, Juror Number Four."

Finally she stabbed her finger at the third sheet. "Natalie Riemer. Juror Number Twelve."

Frank stared at the three images, the exact same ones that Athena had created earlier in the week and that had hung, until recently, on a board for them to pore over.

He finally realized his mouth was gaping.

"Trenier was acquitted on a hung jury, nine to three," Athena said breathlessly. "I'll bet it was these three."

She looked up at Frank. "He's had a purpose all along. He's been after the jurors."

Frank listened, his eyes flying over the photos of the victims, as Athena described the path she had taken to get to the conclusion.

"Something Ephraim Coates' son said set me to thinking. Then I called Charles Liwicki and Thalia Riemer and learned that both Blanche and Natalie had done jury duty around the same time as Coates, nine months ago. They both mentioned a rather lengthy jury experience. It all fit. A little time in court records pulled up the details."

"I'll be damned," muttered Frank. Then, louder, "This is great work, Athena. It's got to be what connects them. But what about Raymond Luczon? Do you think he might be connected with this court case as well?"

"No. Not that I've been able to figure out. My phone calls to Brittany Weinberg went to voice mail; she might not know anything anyway. The records of the Trenier case don't seem to have any mention of Luczon as a juror or witness or anything else. But there may be something I'm not seeing yet."

"Tell me about the case."

"Vehicular manslaughter. Nathan Trenier hit and killed a young woman, Mary McBroom, who was crossing the street on a bicycle one evening. He claimed she sped into the intersection in front of his car and that he had no chance to stop. There were allegations that Trenier was speeding at the time, and the prosecutor tried to introduce evidence that in fact he was trying to get away from a botched store break-in that had just occurred nearby."

"Sounds as if the case didn't go smoothly."

"Trenier apparently had a good defense lawyer who succeeded in getting anything relating to 'prejudicial reflections on Trenier's character' excluded. He couldn't be connected to the burglary; there were no witnesses and nobody was identified or arrested at the time of the trial. Trenier hadn't been drinking. The lawyer argued that the girl recklessly rode into his client's path, that he was driving safely, and that there was no way he could have stopped. And he cast sufficient doubt on the two witnesses to the accident, it would seem…at least as far as some of the jurors were concerned."

"Who was the lawyer?"

Athena checked her notes. "His name is Harlan Bledsoe."

"Oh yeah. Those of us who've been around a while know him. He's a tough nut. Trenier somehow lucked out to get him. So they were hopelessly deadlocked at nine to three?"

"The judge finally declared a mistrial. The prosecutor, after consideration, declined to pursue the matter and there was no subsequent retrial."

"Trenier went free."

"Uh huh."

"So the Creep might be pursuing a vendetta. He's somehow connected to the victim and has decided to act as a vigilante?"

"It's certainly possible."

"Could he be going after anyone else involved in the mistrial? Maybe Trenier himself? And how does Luczon fit into this equation?"

"I guess those are the next questions for us to chase for answers. I'm going to talk to the foreman of that jury tomorrow, and then whomever else I can find…what's the matter?"

"You just said *whomever*."

"So, what if I speak correctly? That's how I was raised!"

"Are you sure that's correct?"

"Frank…take my word for it."

"I'm delighted to have a partner who's not only a murder cop but a grammar cop. Anyway, we'll have to talk to Weinberg again and give her apartment a more thorough looking-over. As soon as I get back tomorrow, we'll do that."

"Get back? Where are you going?"

"A short trip up north. Shouldn't take me more than a few hours."

10.

"Oh yeah. Hard to forget that experience."

Leonard Killian shook his head with a wry, tight smile. He was stocky, with glasses, a balding head and a thin mustache, draped back in a huge chair behind a cluttered desk in his study. He was clearly a hobbyist; various models, memorabilia and collectible items filled the small room around them. It all made for a crowded space.

Athena was already finding the atmosphere rather oppressive; the fact Killian kept the room temperature at something like seventy-nine degrees didn't help much.

"My one and only jury experience," he rasped, "and let me tell you, it changed my viewpoint. I'd long hoped I'd get to serve on an actual jury, and then I even got to be foreman. Now that I've seen it up close and personal, I'll be sure next time to find any excuse to get out of it."

He shook his head again, looking down at his pudgy fingers. "It was like herding cats. People can sure be a pain."

"How is it you got to be the jury foreman, exactly?"

"Well, it's kind of a default. When the jury goes into deliberation, the first thing they're told to do is elect a foreperson. In our case, it was like that old joke about the Army sergeant asking for a volunteer so everybody in the line except one clueless guy takes one step back. Everybody just sort of turned to look at me and I shrugged and said, sure, I'll do it. It's not a complicated job. You serve as the spokesperson for the group, communicate with the court when necessary…and sometimes, serve as a human wrangler."

"By that I suppose you mean you preside over the deliberations, keep them on track and civil?"

"Exactly. It started easy enough. For most of us, it seemed the prosecution had a clear case against the guy. He struck and killed a twenty-two-year-old girl. The evidence, including two witnesses, showed that he was driving too fast at the time. He might also have been trying to evade capture for a crime that had just been committed, although that was a little more amorphous. As the members were polled and began to speak, that seemed to be the preponderance of opinion, that he was guilty."

"But clearly it wasn't everyone's opinion."

"No." Killian removed his thick glasses and began meticulously wiping them with a small piece of cloth. "No, it was not. There were several who didn't see it that way. Two of the jurors were on the fence, but they ultimately came around to the majority way of thinking. But three other individuals did not."

"Liwicki, Coates, and Riemer."

Killian thought about that for a moment, then nodded his head. "That's right. Yeah. Nothing could budge them. All three believed that the prosecution had not made a case. They felt that the accused was being railroaded, that the death of the girl was a tragic, unavoidable accident."

The last words were heavy with sarcasm. Killian replaced his glasses and stared at Athena. "The discussion turned highly emotional. Tempers began to flare. We deliberated for two days before informing the judge we didn't think we could come to an agreement. She sent us back to keep trying. At the end of the week, I again informed the court that we were hopelessly deadlocked, nine to three. She declared a mistrial and sent us all home."

"Including Nathan Trenier."

"Yes. He was free to go. The decision to seek a retrial, I was given to understand, ultimately went all the way up to the District Attorney himself, and he declined it."

"You say emotions ran high."

"Oh, did they ever. I felt like a grade school teacher or a recess monitor at times. Like I said, herding cats."

"You seem to remember the details of the case quite well, Mr. Killian."

He tapped his skull. "Burned into my brain. I remember everybody and everything: the jury members, the judge, the attorneys, the witnesses."

"How about the parents of the dead girl?"

"Edward and Moira McBroom. Yes, I remember them well."

"They must have been upset at the verdict."

"They broke down sobbing, both of them, when a mistrial was announced."

"To go back to the jury…were there any members that were particularly upset by the fact you came to a deadlock?"

"Many of us were, to differing degrees. The two undecided jurors didn't seem to care all that much. I suspect they came around to the majority viewpoint just to speed things up. They just wanted to see the case ended so they could go home by the weekend and not have to come back the next week."

"That left seven of you who were pretty convinced of Trenier's guilt. You all saw the last three jurors as, well, being intransigent?"

"Yes, I'd say so. He was guilty and they just couldn't see reason. In the end we threw our hands up and declared we were irreconcilably incompatible."

Killiam threw his own hands up, once again smiling mirthlessly. "Not unlike my former wife and me some years ago."

"Mr. Killian, you seem to have remarkable recall."

"I pride myself on it. Practically eidetic memory."

"But you didn't notice that the recent murder victims were all on your jury?"

He waved a hand. "Had I seen the full names, I'd probably have made the connection. But your mentioning them was the first time I've learned them. I don't really pay attention to the news. Don't watch TV and seldom read a newspaper or go online that much. To tell you the truth, I doubt any of the other jurors have noticed it either. I've learned that the average person doesn't pay attention in the least. They probably forgot each other the day after the trial."

So far, Athena thought, that apparently was exactly what had happened.

"You don't think any of them held a grudge?"

"It was more an annoyance. We all went back to our lives and chalked it up to a momentary unpleasant experience."

"Do you recall the name Raymond Luczon in any aspect of the trial? Or perhaps the name Lucas Zone?"

Killian pondered, then shook his head. "No, those mean nothing to me. I remember the names of all the witnesses, the legal teams...even the bailiff and the court stenographer. I never heard either of those names."

"He was a young man, Filipino, about twenty, dark hair, possibly cut short?"

Killian shook his head. "There was nobody like that in the courtroom. Guaranteed."

* * * *

Pelican Point was less than fifty miles from the city but over half the trip required Frank to leave the main highway, traversing winding roads through a national forest and then up the coast. He got a very early start, estimating it would take around two hours to reach his destination.

Partway en route he decided to try reaching the medical examiner, Mickey Kendrick, and turned on his phone's speaker. He lucked out; Kendrick was at work. His delivery was as dry as ever.

"Frank, I'm afraid I don't have anything to tell you yet on your stabbing victim. They're stacking up here. I probably won't get to him until later today."

"Actually, Mickey, I'm calling about another of your clientele. Orrin Lattimer, the guy from the train platform Sunday night."

"The accident? That's a Metro case. I didn't know you'd have any interest in that."

"You did perform an autopsy on him, didn't you?"

"What was left of him. Standard operating procedure in such cases. Not very pretty."

"Did you find anything in your examination that might indicate it wasn't an accident?"

"Do you mean like was he pushed off the platform? There's really very little I could glean that would tell me that. Now, if he had been shot or stabbed or clubbed over the head, sure. Those things leave marks. Everything I saw was totally consistent with it being accidental."

"Did the victim have any personal effects with him? Was there, like, a briefcase, anything?"

"Nothing like that, no."

"Was he carrying any papers or documents in a pocket?"

"Nope. A wallet, a set of keys. Nothing else. So what's up with this?"

"I'm not sure, Mick."

"Sorry, didn't get that. You seem to be fading in and out."

"Yeah. Not great cell reception along here. I'm driving up the coast. Thanks."

He broke the connection. It didn't look as if he was going to be making phone calls in this neck of the woods.

The last half hour of the drive was along roughly-paved roads through a thick pine forest. It was beautiful country, and desolate. A lovely place for a vacation cabin…or a hiding place.

Frank finally arrived at a high chain-link fence and a gate, with two cameras. He stopped his car and reached out of the window to hit the intercom. A woman's voice crackled, "Who is it?"

"Mrs. Lattimer, my name is Frank Vandegraf. I'm a police detective. I need to speak with you, if I might?"

"Hold your ID up to the camera."

Frank dug around and pulled out his badge and ID and held them open, waiting for a long time.

"Someone will come down and open the gate for you."

The temperature had dropped. The air was moist and heady with the morning mist and forest aromas still lingering. He sat in his car, chilly despite the jacket he was wearing.

It was a good ten minutes before he saw a figure in a hooded sweatshirt trudging down the gravel road towards him. A teenager. Kyra Lattimer, he figured.

She got to the gate, never taking her eyes off him, and called out, "Can you bring me your identification, please."

Frank got out of his car, stepped up to the gate, and again held up badge and ID card. The girl perused them carefully for quite a while before she nodded and said, "Okay. I'll open the gate."

She pointed behind her. "Keep driving on up the road here. You'll see the cabin. My mom will be there to meet you."

She took a key from her sweatshirt pocket and began to unlock several padlocks on the gate, then pulled the gate inward.

"Would you like a lift back?" Frank asked as he returned to the driver's side.

"No thanks. I'll walk."

She never stopped watching Frank the whole time he drove through and then she closed and relocked the gate. He saw her in his rearview mirror as his car bounced along the road; she was still staring at him when he turned a bend and lost sight of her.

The two-story "cabin" was large and modern, with big gleaming windows contrasting with rich wooden beams; he couldn't have missed it.

As promised, Meryl Lattimer awaited his arrival, standing with her hands thrust into the pockets of her plaid coat. She was a tall, lean woman, in jeans and boots, with long ashen hair tucked under a woolen watch cap. She had the same intent suspicious stare as her daughter.

Frank parked his car a few feet in front of her and stepped out, walking up to her with a nod.

"Mrs. Lattimer, I assume?"

"What do you want, Detective? And how did you find us?"

"May I come in and talk to you? Then I can explain exactly why I'm here."

She stared him up and down. "You did come a long way. I suppose I can at least offer you a cup of tea."

She turned around and started back to the cabin without another word. Frank followed.

The property was on a pine forest bluff overlooking the shore far below. They sat in a high-ceilinged, sunny room with large picture windows affording a breathtaking vista of the sea. Not long after Meryl had brought them each a mug of tea and sat down across from him, Frank heard the front door open and slam shut, and Kyra walked briskly through the room and ran up a flight of polished wood stairs. He heard another door open and slam. Clearly she wasn't eager for visitors.

Meryl wasn't any more welcoming. The silence was awkward and heavy in the room. She held her mug in two hands and sipped from it and just stared at Frank. He got the feeling she'd be perfectly okay with his silently finishing his tea, getting up, saying, "Thanks, I'll be on my way now," and leaving.

"My condolences on your husband," he started. "I'm very sorry for your loss."

"Thank you."

"Mrs. Lattimer, I'll come right to the point. I have reason to believe Orrin's death was not accidental. He may have been involved in some things that proved dangerous."

"You're saying someone *killed* my husband?"

"This can't be a totally alien idea to you. You and your daughter moved up here away from everything for a reason, didn't you?"

"You have no concept, Detective, of the things that Orrin was caught up in. I hadn't considered any of them could get him *killed*...but I suppose it's not unthinkable."

"He was on his way to meet a reporter the night he died. Were you aware of that?"

"No. Orrin hadn't communicated with us in a few days. He planned to come up to meet us as soon as he got a few things out of the way."

She sighed and looked around the airy room. "He loved this place. We found it one time when he was looking for a sanctuary. That was what he called it...a respite from the world of his work. It was getting crazier and more demanding by the week. We'd come up here and he'd just sit quietly, for hours...looking out at the ocean, just as you're doing now."

"You've been here, what, a couple of weeks now? Did he send you and Kyra up here? Was he worried something could happen to you in the city?"

"He said there was a lot of static in the company—he liked to use terms like that, *static* and *white noise,* to describe chaotic behavior—and his plan was to get away from it for a while. He said it'd be better for us if we weren't around while he went through some kind of senseless infighting at work."

"You just pulled Kyra out of school?"

"She's homeschooled; I used to be a teacher. She never felt comfortable in any of the schools out here she attended. She's a hell of a lot smarter and more well-read than most of the kids that used to be her classmates. And like her parents, she prefers to keep her own counsel much of the time. She actually likes it here."

"Not one of those kids who's on her phone all day, huh?"

"We don't even *have* phones up here. No landlines, no cell reception. Not even a television. We have to go into the town down the road to make a telephone call or to access the internet."

She put her mug on the table in front of her and stared at Frank. "Why do you think Orrin was murdered? Do you think it had to do with this meeting with the reporter you say he had set up?"

"I think so. But wait a minute. You have no phone, no TV, apparently no contact with the outside world. Somebody had to inform you of your husband's death."

"There's someone who knows where we are, who makes trips here, brings us the mail from the house and such, and contacts us by way of the general store in town. I'm guessing it's the same person who sent you here."

Frank nodded but said nothing. It had to be Sharon Brooks.

On a trip out of town, she thought someone had been following her...

He wondered if Meryl knew the full extent of Orrin's relationship to his assistant, but it wasn't something he could diplomatically ask.

"Are you hiding from someone here, Mrs. Lattimer?"

"That's a dramatic word. Let's say avoiding, perhaps. From what I've been hearing, there are people who are trying to get me involved in their little intrigues, and it's best for all concerned if they don't succeed."

"You're going to have to go back at some point to settle Orrin's estate. What happens to his share in Humbletech...does all that pass to you?"

"Yes. I'm now automatically the invested partner. When we go back for Orrin's services, and to deal with all of that, they'll undoubtedly latch on to me to discuss it all. I'm sure there's going to be a struggle between Lane and Collis, the other stakeholders. I presume you're familiar with both of them? Orrin's share is going to be crucial."

"Not to mention the patents, right? All these mysterious projects he was developing...aren't those the real plums everybody's after?"

"Without Orrin's research and development, there's no Humbletech. Those dumb scooters? Toys. There are other companies with those. They're just the foot in the door. Orrin had ideas *so* far beyond that."

"I've heard cryptic references, but nobody will tell me anything specific. They're proprietary secrets."

"The hell with their *proprietary secrets* and *intellectual properties* and *non-disclosure agreements*. I really don't care. That nonsense ruined his life and, accident or not, apparently got him killed. He had dozens of plans, even working prototypes, for sustainable urban transportation: small tech, cheap and easy, that would be affordable and accessible to the average person. Individual mass transit modules, running on solar batteries. Skyways, magnetic monorails. Even moving platforms."

Frank thought of Ben's joke about smart skateboards. Maybe he hadn't been far off.

"He showed you all these?"

"All his roughs, all the time. He had this enormous enthusiasm for everything. His brain was always on overdrive, creating, conceiving. At first I was just as jazzed as he was. I don't know if I really give a damn about the tech anymore. In the end the real world sapped him of all his spirit."

"It sounds as if you're considering selling Orrin's interests in the company."

"It was his crusade, not mine. I have no appetite for the personal detritus that comes with it all."

"I'm still trying to figure out who would have wanted Orrin dead. You're telling me he was caught up in intrigues and conflicts at Humbletech? And you have no idea what the issues were…why he would have thought an investigative reporter would be interested in the information he had?"

"He never talked to me in detail about the nuts and bolts of company politics, only about his ideas. He was nebulous about the company culture. But it's clear that in recent weeks he was…distracted? There seemed to be something brewing between Collis and Lane and I got the impression he and others were being asked to choose a side. Not surprising. Both of them are wild-cards and barracudas."

"Has anybody from any other company tried to contact you about Orrin's patents, or anything else?"

"No. Nothing like that."

"Is there any chance that Orrin was considering jumping to another company if he was unhappy with how things were going at Humbletech?"

"Absolutely not. You'd have to have known Orrin. He identified with Humbletech. It was like his alter ego."

"And yet he was apparently unhappy there in recent times. Something had gone wrong."

"But you have to understand: Orrin would never have gone to work for someone else. He might have ultimately tried to start up a new company…."

"He'd need investment capital to do that. What if someone offered him that?"

"He'd have talked to me about that. He wouldn't have made a serious financial decision that affected us without discussing it."

"Forgive me, but I've heard there were financial problems?"

"With us? Well, we were *stretched*. Orrin had invested deeply in the company and we have the two homes; we didn't have disposable income as such. We certainly weren't rich, not by the standards of an authentically wealthy person. But we weren't desperate. Why would you think any of that?"

"There are those who seem to think it."

"Then they're only believing what they want to believe, for whatever reason. It's nonsense. Why the questions about Orrin's leaving the company?"

"It's been suggested that Lane Dembeau thought Orrin was about to jump ship for somewhere else."

"Oh, Lord. Lane Dembeau is delusional. Have you ever read any of his posts or texts on social media?"

"Uh, no. I don't do stuff like that. I've read newspaper stories about them though."

Frank may have come a long way into the new millennium but there were still things that made no sense to him, and one of them was how people publicly lived the most private parts of their lives in the digital fishbowl. It was perverse.

"He does seem to live large in that world," he said.

"He's the most dangerous kind of nutjob, Detective. He's a nutjob who can convince people that he's actually a visionary and can coax their money and their loyalty from them. His insanity is what's made Humbletech a success, and what does that tell you about the standards the company is built on?"

"What about Collis Westermark?"

"She's a different kind of dangerous. She's totally sane but without a moral compass, quite the manipulator. Collis is the real money behind the company; she divorced two years ago and her ex made her pretty cushy, and she has well-heeled associates. She likes to play the personable, blithe free spirit, but she's a chess player, and a grand master at that. She came on board with a long range plan, I have no doubt."

"How did Orrin get involved with these people, anyway?"

"After his doctoral work at Princeton, he was offered research work out here at the University. We moved when Kyra was eight. He met Lane in the bar at some conference or other. They hit it off; Orrin always had far-reaching ideas but no practical way to implement them. Lane was always looking for ideas he could sell, the more outrageous the better. And he needed someone capable of bringing them to life. He also realized they'd need capital. Lane knew Collis and was aware she ran in moneyed circles and could solve that problem if he could attract her. So he brought her in as an equal partner and they started to hatch the idea of Humbletech."

She made a raspberry noise through her lips that surprised Frank. "It all seemed so bright. He was so excited that he could finally bring his concepts to fruition. He had no idea what a hornet's nest he was entering…not until the company began to flesh out with personnel and the maneuvers began. He once commented it was like when he was a kid and they would choose up teams to play softball."

Frank sat back in the comfortable chair and sighed deeply. He had come here looking for answers but he was beginning to wonder if he would ultimately leave with more questions.

"Did you ever hear the name Raymond Luczon? Or Lucas Zone?"

She thought for a time. "No, neither of them."

"Twenty-something guy, soul patch?"

"Detective, that describes a lot of the males in Humbletech's lower echelon."

"From the Philippines? Very interested in gaming?"

She thought for a moment and shook her head. "No, I don't believe I ever encountered him."

Meryl Lattimer seemed to thaw a little from their conversation. Maybe Frank had succeeded, not so much in gaining her trust as in lowering her level of mistrust. They continued to talk for another ten minutes. He learned a little more about the workings of Humbletech, at least as far as Meryl knew of them, and somewhat more about her and Orrin's life together, but very little that afforded any deeper insights into who might have wanted him dead.

Finally she obviously reached the limit of her strained hospitality and Frank rose, thanking her for her time. He left his card and said that he'd keep her informed of anything he learned. He also promised that her whereabouts would remain confidential, something she was clearly glad to hear.

"If it does turn out that somebody killed Orrin," Meryl said as she saw him to the door, "I hope you find them and they rot in hell."

"If they did, be assured I'm going to do my best to find them. I'm afraid I can't help you on the rotting in hell part."

11.

Frank was descending out of the national forest before he saw his phone was restored to full connectivity. He put it back on speaker in his dashboard holder and directed a call to Athena.

"Frank! Where the hell have you been? I haven't been able to get through to you for hours now! I left you, like, two voice mails and four text messages!"

"I've been out of phone service. What's up?"

She told him about her conversation with Leonard Killian.

"I followed up on the other principals in the trial, too. Nathan Trenier packed up and moved away a while ago. There was apparently no shortage of ill will being generated against him in the neighborhood. He left no forwarding address and nobody seems to know where he went. The McBrooms are still in the city. I figure they should be the first ones we take a look at."

Frank thought for a moment. Athena could be onto something here. He considered the pros and cons of going right to them, or trying to keep watch without spooking them. The former felt better.

"All right, I'll be back in town within the hour. Where shall I meet you?"

Frank arrived earlier than planned at the address given him by Athena. It was a residential neighborhood of single family homes and duplexes, and he parked around the corner.

As he sat in his car, his phone started in with its infernal chiming. He made a mental note to figure out how to change that tone soon.

"Detective, it's Mickey Kendrick. I wanted to get back to you after we were summarily interrupted earlier."

"Sorry about that, Mickey. I was in cellular hell."

"Well, welcome back to purgatory. I've just completed my examination of your victim and you seemed anxious to hear the results."

"I greatly appreciate it, Mick. I assume we're talking about Raymond Luczon."

"I'm sending over the preliminary report for you. He suffered four discrete stab wounds in the upper back with what looks to be a long slender blade, possibly a letter opener."

"Wait a minute. That's different from the earlier attacks."

"Yes it is. I took the time to look back at them to be sure. Obviously the non-fatal case hasn't involved an autopsy but I was able to access sufficient medical information for comparison. All three earlier attacks were perpetrated by an assailant using a larger, broader blade—such as a fishing or hunting knife."

Frank's brain spun as he tried to recall the details from the Creep assaults.

"How did the penetration depth of the wounds compare in this case?"

"The earlier ones were deeper, with considerably more force applied. You'll get all the details of this case, but I wanted to see if there was anything you needed to know immediately."

"That'll be fine, Mickey. Thanks again."

He disconnected the call and sat in thought. No sign of Athena yet.

He opened a text and clumsily index-fingered out a message. CAN YOU TLK?

Moments later the reply came from Ben Martinez: GIVE ME FIVE, I'LL CALL YOU.

Frank's phone chimed in three minutes.

"What's up, Frank? You actually find anything?"

"Nothing that would prove anything other than accidental death. I was tempted to tell you I was giving up on it, to be honest."

"I'm hearing a 'but' in there."

"There's a connection with a case I'm working. It might all be a weird coincidence. I just wanted to go over something with you real quick. I've only got a minute."

"Okay, what?"

"You said Lattimer was bringing you something tangible, something potent, right?"

"That was the impression he gave me. He knew I'd need something substantial. He just wouldn't tell me what it was he was bringing me."

"So you'd think he'd have a briefcase or bag with him, something to carry documents or photos in, wouldn't he? There's no indication he had anything like that with him…."

Ben was chuckling on the other end of the line.

"What?"

"Frank, you are a dinosaur, aren't you?"

"What do you mean?"

"It's a tech company. You're thinking he opened up a file cabinet, pulled out a stack of manila folders, ran papers through a photocopier, and packed up a batch them for me in an attaché case? Welcome to the new millennium, Detective. I'm guessing he downloaded whatever he was bringing to show me."

Frank slapped his forehead. "Downloads. Sure. Of course. You mean like on a disc?"

"Well, now at least you've pulled yourself into the 90s. It was more likely on a flash drive. You know what those are, right? Hell, he might have just had snapshots or screenshots on his phone! Or maybe it was on a recording of some sort. In any case, whatever he had would have likely been in his pocket. He didn't need to be carrying anything."

"But in that case, why wouldn't he just email it to you?"

"I think he wanted to establish trust first, not to mention to get it to me securely. You can't be sure of emails or texts. Or even shared cloud files. You know what they are, right?"

Frank saw Athena up the street, walking briskly towards him.

"Right. Got it. Thanks. Look, I gotta go, Ben. I'll check back with you later."

He stepped out of the car and joined her on the sidewalk.

She jerked a thumb back towards the corner. "The McBrooms should still be in the same house. When I walked by, it looked as if there are people at home."

"Okay. Let's take a walk around the block and catch up."

They each filled the other in on their interviews and conversations, Frank finishing with his short call from Mickey Kendrick.

"I'm beginning to wonder about the Raymond Luczon murder," Frank said. "Everything else is fitting together except for him. Even the murder weapon was different."

"He's definitely the odd man out."

"You know, when I talked with Russ Payne, he used a strange expression: he said that Orrin Lattimer was a different kind of dead."

"That's cute."

"Yeah, Russ is a real cutie."

"That sounds familiar somehow."

"Teddy Ralski used the expression in his suicide note. He said to continue living would just be another kind of dead."

"Damn, you're right, Frank."

"Anyway, I'm beginning to think that Raymond Luczon is a different kind of dead."

"By that you mean a copycat killing?"

"When you think about it that way, it starts to make more sense, doesn't it?"

They had reached the McBroom house, set back from the street by a browning front lawn that needed mowing and tending.

"Which means we can't discount that Luczon's death is related to Orrin Lattimer, and not to the Creep."

"Which, in turn, suggests that Lattimer's death was not accidental."

"Even though I have yet to find anything solid that backs that up, yeah."

They took the short walkway and the three stairs to the small porch of the house and rang the bell. It took some time before the door finally opened and they were being stared at by a large, unfriendly-looking woman of about seventy. They both already had their badges out in front of them and Frank made introductions, saying they were looking for Edward and Moira McBroom.

The woman scowled at them. "Mr. McBroom does not live here." Her voice was clipped, with just a trace of an Irish brogue. "Mrs. McBroom does, but I don't know if she'll want to see you."

"Please," said Athena softly, "could you see if she'll speak with us for just a few minutes? It's important. It has to do with her daughter."

"Wait here."

The self-appointed sentry closed the door on them. The detectives looked at each other.

Shortly thereafter, the door reopened and the woman motioned for them to come in and follow her. She led them through a musty parlor into a large back room.

"I'll ask you not to tax her for very long," she said. "She doesn't have a lot of energy these days."

The spacious room had large windows but they were all covered with thick drapes. The only light was an amber glow from two floor lamps. Moira McBroom sat on a sofa, a knitted comforter over her lap. Athena knew from her research that the woman was forty-eight. She looked twenty years older than that.

But she noticeably brightened as the detectives were ushered into the room.

She smiled and slowly struggled to stand up, putting aside the comforter. Her companion began to protest, but she waved a hand and said, "Oh, it's all right, Bridey. You're from the police, is that right?"

She reached out and took Athena's hand, and then Frank's. Her fingers were bony but her grip was firm. The guardian angel named Bridey huffed and left the room.

"We're very sorry to bother you, Mrs. McBroom, but we hoped we could have a few minutes of your time to ask you some questions. Please, can we all sit down?"

"You told Bridey this is about Mary?"

Her eyes showed excitement as she settled back down on the couch. "Is there new information?"

"New information, ma'am?" replied Athena. "I don't understand."

"Have you finally proven that he did it?" She sighed deeply. The spark in her eyes began to die; they could see her shoulders visibly sag.

"No. I don't suppose that's why you're here. Even if it was, it wouldn't solve anything, would it? It wouldn't bring our Mary back. But it might help Eddie. It might bring him back."

It was clear she was beginning to drift. She didn't pursue the question as to why they had come, but sat in silence.

"Where is Mr. McBroom right now?" asked Frank, leaning forward in his chair, fingers laced, forearms on his knees.

Moira McBroom stared down at the floor and slowly shook her head. "He's not here. He hasn't been here in some time."

"Where is he? Do you know where we can find him?"

"Thank God for my cousin Bridey. She came to take care of me after Eddie left. I don't think he could deal with me anymore."

Tears welled up in her eyes and she grimaced as if in pain. "You keep thinking it's going to get better and it never does. Mary was the light of our lives. She was a beautiful young girl. She was barely twenty-two."

Athena, who was sitting next to her on the sofa, reached over and took her hand gently. "How long ago did Eddie leave, Mrs. McBroom?"

"I don't know. It seems a long time ago."

She raised her head and looked around the room. "She used to play in this room. We called it the sun room. The curtains were always open and the morning sun just poured in. It was radiant! It was always cluttered with Mary's things…first her toys, then as she got older, her books and her music. When she was no longer here, it's as if she took the sun with her. We couldn't stand it. Eddie locked up all her belongings and we pulled the drapes shut."

"Mrs. McBroom, please, where can we find Eddie? It's important we find him."

"I don't know." She sobbed, trembling. "We didn't know each other after that. We were never able to reach around her to each other. Not ever again."

She seemed to slide into her own reality, whispering to herself.

"I think," came the brogue-tinged voice behind them, soft but unmistakably firm, "it's time you should go now."

Bridey had returned to the room. "She can't help you. This is just upsetting her."

Frank and Athena exchanged a glance. They both nodded slightly. There was nothing more they were going to get from Moira McBroom; not today. She didn't even seem to notice they were there as they stood up.

Bridey sullenly led them back to the front door. She turned to them as she opened it.

"I don't know why you're here; there's nothing she can tell you. She's likely already forgotten you were even here."

"Has she been like this since the death of her daughter?" asked Athena.

"It's gotten progressively worse, especially since the trial. She comes and goes. Sometimes she's sharp and clear for a while. The most merciful times are when she's not able to remember. Perhaps the Lord is being kind to her by making her forget so much."

"What's happened to Mr. McBroom?"

"He couldn't deal with her falling into that abyss. One day he called me and asked if I could stay with Moira for a few days while he took care of some business or other. Well, that was a story. The few days turned into weeks. I doubt he'll be coming back."

The lady's expression was stern but her voice remained soft. "Mary's death destroyed this family. Neither of them is a particularly strong sort under this type of duress, I fear, and Eddie, he was always a bit adrift. She was kind of an anchor for him, until this happened, and *she* needed *him*."

She shifted her gaze slowly back and forth between them. "I have no idea where he's gone."

"How long ago was it that he left?"

"It's hard for me to forget, being that was the day I moved in here to this haunted house with Moira. It was seventy-six days ago, just under three months." Her shoulders heaved in a massive exhalation. "Though to tell you the truth, it feels like a year."

"Can you describe Mr. McBroom? Better yet, do you have any pictures of him?"

"Wait here a minute." She walked through a swinging door into the kitchen. There was a sound of rummaging through drawers, and then she returned. She handed two photographs to Athena.

"They're old. Nobody takes actual pictures anymore. But that's how he looked."

In one photo, Edward McBroom was standing with a somewhat younger and happier looking Moira, and a young girl with a beaming smile was between them. They had their arms around one another. They were in front of what looked like a lake and they were holding fishing poles. The other photo of him seemed to have been taken in what Moira had called the Sun Room, on the same sofa, but now the window shades were opened and sun filled the room. He was shirtless, grinning and holding a bottle of beer.

"He's a big man," Athena remarked.

"Six foot four, I'd say. Always liked his beer and his pretzels. Probably weighed well over two hundred."

"They were fishing in this picture. Was he an outdoor type?"

"He did some fishing. That one was a rare occasion when they went on a vacation; he tried to teach them how to angle. I don't know that he did much in recent years. He was more the couch potato."

"May we keep these? We'll make sure they're returned."

"You might as well keep them. She's got plenty of pictures of Mary and herself. I'd rather she didn't see anything to remind her of Eddie."

"Please," Frank said," do you have any idea, anything at all, that can help us locate Edward McBroom?"

"He used to go to the poolroom. I think it's called the Cue and Mug, on Sadler Avenue. Otherwise, I don't know. I've never run into him around here since he left and I hope I never do."

She snorted, crossing her arms. "He was a weak man, a terribly weak man. Fell apart when his wife needed him the most."

They both handed her their business cards and asked her to contact them if she found out anything that could help them locate Edward McBroom. The woman's eyes were a burning mixture of anger and sadness as she nodded and closed the door behind them.

Athena looked again at the photos as they walked. "He's big. And I can see he could be creepy. Fits the description."

"Uh huh. And there's a case for vengeance. The daughter's death destroyed their lives."

"He disappeared not all that long before the first murder."

"We have to find this guy, Athena."

"Do you think he might go after anyone else? The other jurors? The defense attorney?"

"You said Trenier has vanished?"

"Yeah, he went into hiding about three months ago. He might be the safest of the bunch."

"Let's talk to the defense attorney. But right now, let's take a walk over to the Cue and Mug. Sadler's only two blocks away."

* * * *

As luck would have it, the proprietor of the Cue and Mug was on the premises. His name was Otis and he remembered Edward McBroom quite well.

"Eddie used to come in here all the time, shot a few games of pool, had a few beers, and maybe watched a game on the TV. He laughed and joked a lot. That was before the bad thing. You know about that, right?

"A few days after that, he came in and just sat at the bar and drank. He was usually a beer drinker but that time he ordered boilermakers…a shot of rye with a mug of beer. He didn't talk to anybody, accepted everybody's condolences with a nod and just kept drinking. As far as I know he never came back after that."

Otis shook his head sadly. "Eddie was a really sweet guy, you know? Always friendly and courteous. I don't know that anybody here was particularly close friends with him, but they all liked him."

"I understand he was a fisherman."

"Come to think of it, he did talk about that now and then. Sounded like he had quite a bit of gear he was proud of."

"So there's nobody that comes here that would have known him, kept in touch with him?" Frank asked.

"I doubt it. Now and then his name comes up and somebody asks 'What became of Eddie?' and nobody ever has a clue. I don't think anybody here is going to be able to help you, Detective, but leave me your card and if anything comes up, I'll let you know."

As Frank and Athena turned to leave, Otis asked, "Is Eddie in some kinda trouble?"

"We hope not. We just need to talk to him."

Otis nodded gravely. "I got the feeling nobody's gonna hear from him. I hope he's all right."

Outside the bar, Frank checked his watch. It was about 1:30. "We've got our work cut out for us this afternoon."

"I've got the info for Bledsoe, Trenier's attorney. I'll call to find a time we can go talk to him."

"Okay. And I'll see if there's a time tonight we can go by and check out Raymond Luczon's apartment again. Now that I've had some time to think about it, it occurs to me that he might have left some things there that we didn't find."

His call to Brittany Weinberg was picked up almost immediately.

"Ms. Weinberg. It's Detective Vandegraf. How are you doing?"

"I'm still pretty freaked out. But I went to work. I figure I need to keep busy, to help me from thinking about it all."

"So you're at the restaurant right now?"

"Yeah. I'm on my break. What's up?"

"My partner and I would like to come by and look through Raymond's things again, when you're home tonight?"

"Uh…sure. I'm on the early dinner shift and I'll be getting off about 8, so I can be back there any time after 8:30 tonight. Is that okay?"

"That would be fine. I'll call you when we're on our way."

"Hey, it's a weird thing, but I just got a call from Ray's girlfriend, Susan. Like five minutes ago. She wanted to come by tonight as well. She's very distraught about Ray. He went out late in a hurry the other night to pick up something from the market. He had a craving for a snack or something. When he didn't come back she figured he just got sidetracked. Ray was like that. But when he hadn't returned by the next morning, she started calling around, making inquiries, and that's how she finally found out he'd been—you know.

"She says there are some mementos that she'd like to have, stuff she gave him to remember her by. Looks like the mystery girlfriend really exists after all, huh? I told her what I told you, that I'd be home after 8:30."

"I'd be very interested in talking to her as well. Can I get her number?"

"That's the really weird part of this."

"Uh…I'm sorry?"

"The really weird thing is, she called me on Ray's phone! So I guess that solves that mystery too, of what happened to it, right?"

"Wait a minute. Did I hear that right? She called you on Ray's phone?"

"Yeah! Ray's number popped up on my screen when she called. She told me he had accidentally forgotten it the other night when he rushed out and never came back. Hey listen, my break's ending and I have to get back to work."

"Thank you, Ms. Weinberg. Listen, it's extremely important that *nothing* gets taken out of your apartment before we get there, understood? If she gets there before us, do *not* let her take anything."

"Okay. Whatever you say."

A thought occurred to Frank. "I have one more question. Do you know the company Humbletech?"

"They make the scooters. Sure."

"Do you know if Raymond ever had anything to do with them?"

"I know he went there when they first opened last year, in a brief moment when he thought about getting an actual job or maybe some work as an independent contractor.

"But lots of people I knew went there; it was big news. I even applied, seeing if they had, like, a receptionist position or something like that. But there was just too much competition. Hey, they need me up front. Gotta run. See you tonight."

Frank let the call disconnect.

This mysterious Susan had Luczon's phone?

Did she also have his keys?

She knew that the apartment would be empty until at least 8:30….

Athena was also ending her own conversation. "Bledsoe's in court right now but they expect him back around three. His office isn't far from the courthouse."

"I might not be able to join you for that. I think that Luczon's girlfriend is on her way over to let herself into his apartment."

"Wait, wait, wait…his *girlfriend?* Let herself in? What…?"

Frank filled her in rapidly. "I've got to get over there. Send me the attorney's address and I'll try to meet you there."

"Okay. Harlan Bledsoe. His office is on King Boulevard. I'll text you all the info."

She had to shout all that. Frank was already on his way, hustling back to his car.

* * * *

Frank lucked out and found a parking space almost across the street from Brittany Weinberg's apartment house, where he had a good view of the front. He yawned; it had already been a long day.

He'd thought about stopping to pick up coffee but he knew he had to get into position quickly. He had a hunch that this Susan, whoever she was, didn't just have Luczon's missing phone, but his missing keys as well, and would make an attempt to get into the apartment while it was empty. If she was going to do that, it might be soon.

Frank hoped if she did try to gain access, she'd hurry up and do it. He felt a twinge of guilt at having left Athena to interview Bledsoe herself.

He'd begun to think that he hadn't been doing a proper job of shepherding her in her early months as a detective. Her probationary period had finally ended, and she was a fast study, but still, he worried if he was leaving her hung out to dry way too much. She had incredible skills and instincts, but there was a difference between chasing down information on the computer and dealing with people on the street.

He had to remind himself that she had been a highly accomplished uniformed officer; she was no stranger to the ways of the streets. But, still. Detective work was *different*….

Maybe this was a waste of time. Was he just desperate because there didn't seem to be any solid leads on Luczon? He realized there was neither rhyme nor reason to any of this. He was chasing his tail….

He yawned again and realized he was drowsy. Better get out of the car and stretch his legs. He needed to stay alert. It was a nice cool and breezy day and it was too warm and comfortable in the car….

He realized he'd be a little easier to spot on the street but there were other cars, storefronts, streetlight posts and even trees to use casually as cover. With a little luck he could stay inconspicuous while moving around.

It wasn't long after that when he saw the woman, in a long coat and a wide maroon felt hat, turn and walk up the steps to the apartment house. At the front door she dug into her coat pocket while furtively looking around. She seemed to struggle with the front lock but finally got it open.

By that time, Frank had crossed the street and was rapidly moving up the steps toward her. She turned to look over her shoulder at him.

It was a tossup who was more surprised.

"Well, hello," Frank said, recovering first. "Fancy meeting you here!"

* * * *

"This news is very unsettling, Detective Pardo."

Harlan Bledsoe, Athena noted, looked very unsettled indeed, sitting back in a padded chair behind his desk, fingers tented in front of his face.

"I've no doubt it is, sir. That's why I'm here."

"I was of course aware of those dreadful slayings, but I never put together the identities of the victims. I have to admit, the names of the jurors don't often stay with me."

Athena reflected that he undoubtedly spent some time learning details about a jury before his case would begin, but it made sense to her that he'd forget them immediately afterward, when they were no longer important and a new pool had arisen on which to gather intel.

He didn't strike her as a warm "people person," exactly. Bledsoe was slick and officious, and she could see how that could inspire antipathy in some quarters, certainly, she had learned, among some members of law enforcement.

She sincerely hoped that he hadn't had that effect on Edward McBroom, who she increasingly suspected was the Creep.

"As you can understand, my partner and I are concerned that there might be threats against other figures in the trial. We'd like to keep you all safe until we can resolve this."

"By 'resolve,' I assume you mean apprehend the killer. I'm all for that."

"We'll arrange for police protection, of course."

Bledsoe waved his hand. "That's very nice of you, but I have access to private security. I'll have them on the case before end of day. No offense, but considering my reputation as a defense attorney, I'm not sure a police guard would be all that...devoted."

He leveled a stare at her. "It's that crazy father, am I right?"

"You surely know I can't comment on an ongoing investigation. We're looking at a number of people."

"You seem very young for a detective. Been doing this long?"

"Long enough."

"Who's your partner in this case and why isn't he here with you?"

"My partner is Detective Vandegraf. He's following up another aspect of this case and may or may not be able to join us."

Bledsoe nodded. "Vandegraf. I know the name. Good man. Thorough. Tough on the stand. Don't think he cares for me all that much, does he?"

Athena steered the conversation back on track.

"Mr. Bledsoe, do you happen to know how we can locate Nathan Trenier? We have to consider that he's a target as well."

Bledsoe spread his hands. "He won't be found. Nathan Trenier was being unduly harassed night and day after the trial. His home was vandalized numerous times. There were countless personal threats made against him. Every measure he took to maintain his privacy was stymied. His life had been basically ruined. His only resort was to leave the area and tell nobody where he was going. Nobody, including me. "

"He has no family, nobody close he would have informed of his whereabouts? That's hard to believe."

"Detective, Nathan Trenier marched to his own drum. He had some bad luck early in life, some crumby excuses for parents, and spent some time in prison. Because of that, he had two strikes against him wherever he went and learned to distrust everybody. His wife divorced him while he was incarcerated and took their children; he's had no contact with them since. He's got no other family and isn't the kind of person to make close friends. He's been what you would likely call a loner. I can guarantee you he had 'nobody close' when he decided to leave, and that he covered his tracks quite well. He's likely taken on a new identity somewhere. If you're worried somebody is going to find him, I'm telling you it would be next to impossible."

"I'm just curious, sir, how is it that such a loner and a loser got to be represented by someone such as yourself?"

"He looked me up in the book. And he paid me."

"Forgive me, that couldn't have been cheap."

"He had some savings—from where was not my concern—and I was willing to give him a substantial break, since I saw the case as a challenge. I'm always ready to slam dunk one over the police."

He made a thin smile. "Nothing personal, no offense I hope."

Athena let it pass. "Interesting, considering Mr. Trenier hit and killed a young girl while allegedly fleeing from the scene of a crime."

"It was a tragic accident. She rode her bike in front of him; he had no chance to stop. He wasn't going that fast, not even ten miles over the limit. People speed like that all the time. And he had nothing to do with that burglary; it was all set up to make him look bad. This is exactly the kind of case I love to take on, an attempted railroad. You're apparently not aware that a few weeks after the trial, the real perpetrators of that crime were apprehended. They confessed, and specifically stated they didn't know Mr. Trenier and that he had no connection to them."

"For someone who says the deck was stacked against him, you certainly did a good job of getting your client off."

"I simply pointed out the facts to the jury. I'm good at that. It's called reasonable doubt, Detective. And it's the foundation of the legal system."

"And you truly have no idea where we might find Mr. Trenier? If he was going to tell anybody, it would stand to reason it would be you."

"We didn't have much to do with each other after the trial, once the prosecutor decided to drop everything. It's not like we became best buds. Personally, I think he made the right move, taking off and not telling anybody. They were making his life hell. The system isn't supposed to work like that. But, well, people are people, and sometimes they stink."

Athena leveled a stare at Bledsoe, keeping her expression neutral. "I can't disagree with you on that, sir."

* * * *

It was well past four before Athena left the offices of Harlan Bledsoe, Esq. Where the hell was Frank? As she stood on King Boulevard deciding her next move, her phone started buzzing.

"Frank! Where…?"

"Athena, meet me at the station as soon as you can. You're not going to believe this…."

12.

Athena didn't wait for the elevator, but bolted up the stairs to the unit. She was still catching her breath when she opened the door to the interview room. Two seated people both looked up at her.

"Athena," Frank said, holding up a mug of coffee as if in a toast. "Perfect timing. You remember Ms. Westermark?"

Collis Westermark, who had shed her coat and hat onto a nearby chair, maintained her characteristic poise, but couldn't totally hide her disquietude. She nodded to Athena with a slight scowl and sat a cup of what looked like tea back down on the table.

"We were just about to get started," Frank smiled.

He took a large gulp out of his coffee. Athena noted that this time, he had gone to the trouble to find actual ceramic mugs for them both.

She pulled up a chair, giving Frank a bewildered look. He raised his eyebrows back at her.

"As I was telling Detective Vandegraf," Westermark said, a bit testily, "I've done nothing wrong. There's a perfectly reasonable explanation for why I was at that building."

"And I was telling Ms. Westermark that I appreciated her coming in voluntarily with me, and right now she isn't under arrest."

Frank turned back to Collis. "But you do need to explain to us just why you were letting yourself into the apartment building of a recent murder victim, and why you had these items of his in your possession."

He pointed to two plastic bags sitting on the table, one of which held a set of keys and the other a cell phone.

"It's quite simple." She looked down at her crossed hands. "Raymond gave them to me."

"And…just when did he do that?"

"The evening he died. He left his phone and his keys with me and went out and…that was the last time I ever saw him."

"You're saying you were in a relationship with Raymond Luczon?"

"Yes."

She looked up at both of them, eyes wide. "Yes, that is what I'm saying. Is that difficult to understand?"

"It's…a surprise."

"What part is hardest for you, exactly? That I'm somewhat older than he? That we inhabit different social strata? You're a very old-fashioned man, aren't you?"

"How did you two come to know each other?" Athena jumped in.

"We met when Humbletech opened and he applied for a position. I was his interviewer."

"A head of the company?"

"It was 'all hands on deck' for interviews. We only had a startup crew and there were *waves* of applicants, believe me. Every ambitious millennial in the city, not to mention a variety of individuals who were just in need of a job, showed up. At first he didn't impress me: just another of the herd coming through the doors from morning to night. But he persisted and he began to shall we say, catch my imagination."

"What did he do that was so special?"

"He said he didn't want to be a full-time employee but a contractor, and proposed proprietary internet services he could set up for us. Oh, I was unimpressed by the specifics of what he described to me, but I *was* impressed by the confident grasp he displayed of his material once he got into his subject.

"It was as if he came to life, became a very different person from the lackluster young man who had walked in nervously for a job interview. I could see his potential to fit in to many of the plans I was already forming for the company and beyond. I began to see possibilities in him."

She smiled at both of them. "It turned out that he really wasn't a very good fit professionally, but as we spent time together, we began to hit it off in other ways."

"He fit into your plans 'and beyond'?" Athena said. "In other words, this was a clandestine relationship from the beginning because you were already developing and recruiting people for outside projects? Is that right?"

Westermark held a steely gaze and that slight smile.

"Possibly…it's always important to find people who show the potential to be personally loyal to you…come what may. I certainly wasn't the only one in the company with that in mind."

"And when this relationship evolved into, well, something considerably different, you still felt the need to keep it…discreet?"

"I insisted on it."

"We understand that Raymond had a regular source of income in recent months," Frank said. "May we assume that was thanks to you?"

"Oh yes. He was very interested in getting his own enterprise off the ground but his grasp of the realities of business was, to be kind, naïve. He needed an extensive education in a hurry. He had that silly gaming blog. I explained to him the advantages of starting his own actual company, how he could develop in many different directions, and that was what he was working toward. He was a bit of an adolescent in many ways—I actually found that rather charming, that ingenuous energy—but I'd like to think I was helping him to become more of an adult."

"So you and he were carrying on a surreptitious relationship for…how long?"

"You make it sound so seamy, Detective. The word your partner used earlier was discreet. We were discreet. We'd been together for a few months."

"You didn't want to be seen together publicly, and so you couldn't live together."

"Essentially correct."

"What happened the night he was killed?"

"We were together at my place. He told me he had to go out to meet someone: something about a disagreement over something on his blog. It seemed to upset him, but he downplayed that and said it wouldn't take long. He threw on his sweatshirt and grabbed his bag and left. It was shortly thereafter that I noticed he had left his phone and his keys behind. I don't know whether that was intentional or not. He of course never returned that night; I was terribly worried and went looking for him the next day. That's when I learned what had happened. He apparently had the terrible luck to be apprehended by that serial killer you haven't been able to catch yet."

She let that barb settle in before continuing. "Naturally, I finally realized I needed to turn in his keys and phone to you. I was on my way to do just that, but first I felt I needed to make a stop en route, where you and I happened to meet up."

"At his apartment. Why were you going there?"

"There were certain…keepsakes I had given him. Little gifts. Very personal ones. Potentially embarrassing. I didn't want anybody else finding them."

"So you called his roommate and asked when you could come by."

"Yes. Her number was on his phone. So I used that. I just lost someone close to me. I haven't exactly been thinking straight. Perhaps that's understandable to you."

"You misrepresented yourself to her when you called."

"Not at all. I said I was his girlfriend. That was quite correct. I may have fudged the details of when I had last seen him, but that was hardly consequential. Basically I told the truth."

"I believe you used the name Susan?"

"That in fact happens to be my middle name: Collis Susan Westermark. I told her no lies."

"Except that your plan was never to wait until Brittany Weinberg came home, was it?"

"Well...no, you've got me there. As I said, the articles were highly personal, possibly compromising, and our relationship had to remain confidential. I saw no harm in letting myself in, finding items that were after all basically mine, and leaving everything else alone. Granted, I wasn't showing the best judgment, but given my aggrieved state of mind right now, it made sense at the time."

"It's a potential evidentiary scene under police investigation," Frank said. "Had you actually opened the door and walked in there, you would have been in a lot of trouble."

"Then I suppose I'm fortunate we met on the doorstep, when we did." She gazed guilelessly at Frank. "Have I committed any crime?"

Athena picked up the questioning.

"There's a remarkable coincidence here, Ms. Westermark. Raymond Luczon was the sole witness to the accidental death of Orrin Lattimer. Were you aware of that?"

She waited a long beat before answering. "Yes. Yes, I was."

"Can you explain that?"

"I'm afraid I can. I suppose it's time to lay all the cards on the table in the interest of transparency. I asked Raymond to follow Orrin that night."

"What?" Frank had started to take a sip from his coffee and swallowed loudly.

"I told you the other day that Lane had been harboring odd suspicions about Orrin. I didn't agree with him, but Orrin had been acting strangely distracted. I heard a rumor...just idle talk...that he had moved out of his house to a location he was keeping secret, and was behaving rather surreptitiously. I began to be concerned that maybe Lane was *almost* on to something.

"Obviously, there was no way I could personally keep an eye on Orrin. But Raymond was ideal. He was nondescript, anonymous, and had plenty of free time. So I asked him to keep tabs on Orrin when he was away from Humbletech. It struck Raymond as kind of exciting, like being in a spy movie. He waited outside on Goff Boulevard and followed him that night.

"He later told me that Orrin took a circuitous route around town, peering around as though he worried about being followed. But Raymond had no problem keeping up with him. So he was right behind Orrin entering the subway station and saw him slip and fall. It was horrifying to him, absolutely traumatic. He called me in a panic and asked me what he should do. I helped him compose himself and tell me exactly what had happened. I instructed him to wait and tell the story to the police, without explaining himself any more than he needed to, and then get out."

"Was it your idea for him to use his Lucas Zone identity?"

"Yes. And to monitor all his incoming calls from that point on, and to call back anyone who needed his witness story."

She shook her head sadly. "The poor boy. He needed a good deal of comfort and attention after that. He was ready to come apart."

"You never told us any of this," Frank said.

"No. I didn't."

"You withheld evidence," Athena added, leveling a gaze of her own at Westermark.

"I didn't see that it did any harm. What *evidence?* It was an accidental death. Raymond provided a complete account to everyone who asked for it...including you, Detective Vandegraf, if I'm not mistaken? It's my understanding that Metro Transit is satisfied with his account and ready to pronounce this a simple accidental death. How have I in any way impeded any investigation?"

"You had Raymond Luczon's phone. And his keys."

"And I told you: I was on my way to turn them in. If it took me a day to do so, well, you should certainly understand I haven't been at my best for the past two days. Someone I care about was brutally murdered! It's been terribly traumatizing for me."

"Would you excuse us for a moment?" Frank motioned Athena out of the room into the hall, closing the door behind them.

"Do we set her free?" Athena asked. "Or do we hold her?"

"Hold her on what, exactly?"

"Are you buying this cockamamie story with her tear-filled innocent goo-goo eyes?"

"Listen to you. Where'd you learn a word like 'cockamamie'?"

"Clint Eastwood used it in an old movie the other night on TV. Don't change the subject."

"No, Athena, I don't totally buy the cockamamie story. But what are we going to hold her on? The evidence thing won't stand. She'll have an expensive lawyer down here springing her five minutes after she dials the phone. We might do better letting her go and keeping an eye on her."

"Do you think any part of that story is true?"

"I can believe she got the poor kid involved so she could use him for something. She offered him fame, money, his own company, and a worldly, attractive girlfriend in the mix. For him it was like having a magic lamp that gave wishes; there had to be something she was getting back in the deal. Do I think she killed him? Damn, I don't know. There's nothing to prove that right now. We got nothing."

Athena heaved a sigh. "Alright...it's your call."

They returned to the interview room and Frank said, "Thank you, Ms. Westermark; you're free to go. Your cooperation is appreciated. We can arrange for an officer to drive you home if you'd like."

"That won't be necessary," she said, standing up and reaching for her coat and hat. "The company has accounts with two ride services. Just until we have our own service up and running, of course."

"Thank you for bringing in Raymond Luczon's effects," Athena said. "By any chance, did Raymond leave anything else at your home? Any clothes, perhaps, or personal property?"

Westermark's smile was wistful. "No. He kept nothing at my place. Discretion, Detective."

"Of course. Thank you again."

"I'll be on my way, then. I've got hectic days ahead of me. As far as I know, Raymond had no surviving family, so I'll likely be the one to handle his…final services. Hopefully his body can be released to me by the coroner. On top of that, the company's in turmoil and Lane returns tomorrow evening."

She sighed dramatically. "But if I can be of any further help to you, of course let me know. Oh, and…please do me a favor, Detective Vandegraf?"

"What's that, Ms. Westermark?"

"If you find those private items--and I believe you'll know them if you do—please try to keep them discreet?"

She sauntered through the open door and down the hall toward the elevator.

"That woman really makes me tired," Frank sighed.

"She's still playing to you, for whatever reason. This time it's as the grieving lover."

"Yeah, well, it's not working."

Athena pursed her lips. "There's something about her characterization of the relationship that bothers me."

"What's that?"

"Suppose you're a mature, sophisticated businesswoman and you decide to have a fling with a much younger man…?"

"You find something objectionable about that? I'm surprised at you."

"No, that's not what I'm getting at. You have an affair with a younger man from a considerably different social and economic world from yourself. For whatever reason, you find him attractive—there's a lot of plausible reasons, they're not important. But he's kind of a slacker and, well, dresses and looks like a vagrant. Logically, what's one of the very first things you'd think to do?"

"Well, since I never have been a successful upper-class businesswoman…."

"Frank, would you just play along with me here and not be obtuse? You'd want to make him presentable. Even if you're carrying on a clandestine relationship—maybe especially because you are—you don't want him to stand out when you're together. And you don't want to hang around with a slob. Whatever dubious charms you find in the guy, you're going to work on his appearance. You're going to get him to trim his hair, at least neaten up his beard, and you are definitely going to buy him better clothes."

"You're right."

"So…where are the clothes? Or maybe a better question is…what was the *real* relationship between Collis and Raymond?"

"I think we both know there's something she's not telling us. Maybe more will be revealed."

Frank yawned and looked at his watch. "I'm going to go find an empty room where I can catch a nap. I've got to do some overtime tonight. No need for you to go graveyard shift with me."

"Actually, I've got a commitment this evening, but I admire your dedication."

"It's more like I got nothing better this evening. I'm fine handling it myself."

"Are you going back to check out Luczon's apartment?"

"Uh huh. Now more than ever, I have to believe there's something there worth looking for."

* * * *

At nine o'clock, Frank was let into Brittany Weinberg's apartment, apologizing for the inconvenience.

"Glad to help," she said, "but I gotta tell you, it's been a long day. Can this be quick?"

"Hopefully very quick," said Frank, pulling on a pair of disposable gloves as he considered his own long day. "That small room was Raymond's personal area, right? Is there any place else he might have kept anything of his?"

"Well, the kitchen. We each keep our own food. The living room, if you can call it that, was a common area. Now and then he'd fall asleep on the couch watching TV."

"How about your own bedroom? Forgive me, but did he ever have reason to leave things there?"

"No. We had a strict rule. I didn't go into his personal space and he didn't go into mine. My room's not all that much bigger than his to begin with."

Frank walked into the converted closet that had been Raymond Luczon's combined bedroom/workspace. He reached over to switch on the old floor lamp and swept his eyes over the area for several minutes.

There was the work table with the small jar of loose change, the three-drawer plastic dresser, the futon and the shoes. He spilled the coins out on the table, making sure there was nothing hidden among them, and poured them back into the jar. He carefully opened each drawer, laying the articles on the floor, and going through the rolled-up articles of clothing. There was nothing in the pockets or stuffed inside. He pulled the dresser away and then the table. All that was left lying against the wall was the futon and the shoes.

It appeared that when Luczon had wanted to sleep, he simply cleared the space on the floor and unrolled the futon then rolled it back up in the morning. Frank opened it; it was worn and musty. There was nothing rolled up inside of the thin mattress.

He pondered what could be the appeal of a slacker without even a bed or decent change of clothes to a mature, wealthy, worldly woman. He still figured it wasn't a love attraction. It felt completely wrong. Athena's point, that Collis should have insisted on at least a minimal wardrobe upgrade, especially struck him as right on.

If Collis Westermark had really expected him to find hot photos or love letters or the like, she would have been disappointed. But Frank was convinced she'd wanted him to find something else.

When he pulled the bedroll away, he heard a slight rattle from the wall behind it. He bent down and began to inspect the wood paneling that ran from the ceiling, a bare seven feet high, to the floorboards.

There was an almost imperceptible crack in the wood.

A closet was hidden within the closet.

He had a penknife in his pocket, and he used it to gently pry the board away from the wall at the break. When he found the right purchase point, it easily pulled off.

Behind the panel was a cubbyhole, about four feet high, wide and deep. Inside was a pile of items covered with a blanket. He slid everything out carefully and lifted the blanket.

"Is this Raymond's laptop?" he asked Weinberg, who had been watching from the living room. He held up the computer.

"Sure looks like it. Yes. He put that sticker on it. It was one of his favorite games."

Frank opened the laptop and turned it on. As he figured, it was password protected and he couldn't get past the opening screen. He closed it again.

"I don't suppose you'd know his password?"

"Are you kidding?"

There was a plastic box of what looked to be external hard drives…and a cell phone. He held the phone up.

"Did he have more than one phone?"

"Not that I knew. That's a pretty nice one. Looks like those newest and biggest ones. Ray had a slightly older model. He'd talked about getting an upgrade but hadn't gotten around to it."

Frank turned it on and it still had a small charge, but it was password protected. Just the other day, Athena had taught him a trick that worked on many models, even when locked. Turning so Weinberg could not see what he was doing, he held the phone close to his mouth and spoke to activate the digital voice assistant: "Whose phone is this?"

A name popped up on the screen. It was what he'd figured.

Frank had come prepared. He had several plastic evidence bags folded up in his pocket, and he pulled three of them out.

"I want you to watch that I'm bagging these items. I'm going to take them with me. I'll give you a receipt for them and will need you to sign my copy saying you witnessed what I took with me."

"Okay."

He probed the rest of the room and, deciding there was nothing else to be found, he went to replace the wall panel. That's when he saw what he'd missed the first time around, stuck into the far dark corner of the little space that had been hidden by the other items he had pulled out.

He had to bend down and reach in to get to it.

It was a brand-new black leather tote bag and, while Frank was no expert on such things, it looked pricey.

He slid it out into the light and unzipped it. It was jammed full of carefully packed clothing. Frank removed the first few items: two expensive shirts still pinned and never unfolded; two pairs of what looked like very nice dark slacks' and a casual light sweater. There were even several pairs of socks. Nothing looked as if it had ever been actually worn. Everything had been crammed in so tightly that many items were creased.

At the very bottom of the bag were a pair of sleek shoes and a smooth black billfold-style wallet in an open-faced box that bore the name of a high-end purveyor.

He held up a shirt to Weinberg. "Did Raymond recently buy a new wardrobe?"

She squinted at the silky pearl-grey shirt. "Nice shirt! Wow, is that a Bartiromo? Those are *not* cheap!"

"Ever seen him wear stuff like this?" He held up another shirt, this one a deep maroon.

"My God, I can't imagine him wearing anything like that! He would have snorted about looking like a Silicon Valley tycoon wannabe or something. Where'd that come from?"

He gestured at the tote bag. "That seems to be full of new clothes." He removed one of the shoes to take a closer look.

"Those couldn't be designer shoes! And let me see that bag! Wow, that's gorgeous!" She reached for it but Frank held out his hand.

"Please, don't touch anything."

"Can you hold up the tag for me? Yeah! That's a Strazza, an imported Italian leather bag! It's gotta cost a couple hundred dollars!"

"And you've never seen Raymond using it?"

"I've never seen that bag before! In fact I've never seen him with anything but the beat-up old courier bag that he always carried. Ray without his old bag was unthinkable!"

"And this?" Frank held up the wallet.

"Are you kidding? Ray had this old homemade wallet. It was a fad among his friends to make them out of, like, gaffer's tape, like the lighting guys use in the movies. I constantly kidded him about it."

"He had this stuff squirreled away. Think he was planning on a makeover?"

Weintraub smirked. "You have no idea how impossible it is to imagine that! It's just not him! I never saw Ray in anything but a ratty T-shirt or pullover and jeans! He had scroungy put-together stuff like his duct-tape wallet. It was a point of pride with him to be a tech rat!"

"Appears he was planning to adopt a secret identity," Frank mused, returning the clothing to the bag and carefully zipping it up. He considered for a moment the best way to bring the bag with him.

"Might you have a large trash bag I could have?" he asked.

"Sure. I've got a whole box of them. I'll get you one."

"If you can bring out the box and let me be the one to pull a bag out that would be helpful. Thanks!"

Once he had knotted up the bagged tote and was convinced there was nothing else to be found in the wall space, he replaced the wall panel and returned everything to their original locations. He placed the bagged laptop, drives, and phone in a neat group on the floor next to the big garbage bag and asked if he could now take a look in the kitchen, and if she'd also stay with him while he did so.

She showed him the cabinet that was reserved for Raymond's groceries, and he pulled various boxes and cans off the shelf, laying them on the counter next to the sink in the cramped kitchen. A typical single young man's food supply: cereal, crackers, beans, rice, bags of cookies and chips.

It seemed as if everything had been taken down, but he reached up and stuck his hand back on the upper shelf, sliding his hand along it. There was something pushed all the way back in the cabinet. It took him a minute or two, and a few muttered curses, but he finally was able to roll it forward until he could grab hold of it.

It looked like a flashlight, but Frank recognized it as something else.

He began to have a hunch of exactly what might have happened at the station.

His search revealed nothing else, so he replaced the food articles, bagged the implement, stripped off the gloves, filled out the receipts, obtained Weinberg's signature, and thanked her for her time.

"Thank God," she sighed wearily as she let him out the door, "that this day is finally over."

Frank could only think, *if only you knew, sister.* His own very long day was also finally over.

13.

"For someone who worked late, you're certainly in early, Frank."

"I could say the same for you." Frank was scrutinizing the bagged items spread over his desk as Athena walked towards him. "Big night last night?"

"Nothing like that. Family stuff. Birthday on the Greek side of my family, so I definitely overate."

"Lucky you. I grabbed a sandwich on the way home."

"You definitely have to start eating better." Athena perused the desk full of material. "Looks as if you had some luck last night?"

Frank filled her in on his find. "I was about to go in and ask the Lou for his help in expediting these through SID's Computer Forensics." He held up the bagged laptop and phone. "And someone from the Crime Lab is also coming over to pick up this other stuff.

In the meantime, I'm going to make a couple of phone calls and inquire about some other things. Then let's go see Russ over at Metro Transit, with a quick stop en route. I think you're going to find all this quite interesting."

"A quick stop where exactly?"

Frank smiled slyly. "An electronics store...."

* * * *

"Frank, I'm not quite sure what you expect to do here. You guys at Personal Crimes can waste your own time all you want, but now you're wasting mine."

"Nice to see you too, Russ. Thanks for indulging me."

He had introduced Athena to Russ, under the gaze of a dour tech who sat behind a console beneath a wall of monitors. The introduction hadn't seemed all that engaging to either man...nor for that matter...had it to Athena.

They were in the nerve center of Metro Transit's Surveillance Room, the access point to literally thousands of video cameras throughout the Metro stations that viewed the parking lots, entrances, ticket machines, and the platforms themselves.

Frank had asked the tech to bring up the videos from the Northcote platform on the evening of Orrin Lattimer's death.

"Frank," sighed Russ as if the weight of worlds were upon his shoulders, "I've gone over all this footage. You're not going to find anything."

"Please, bear with me." He turned to the tech. "Would you, please?"

There were nine video cams on the specific platform itself, affording a wide set of views, all displayed simultaneously.

"This is when Lattimer came down the stairs to the platform. There."

Frank pointed to several of the monitors showing different angles of a figure stepping into view, holding what looked to be a phone in his right hand, as if he were reading the screen. The rest of the platform seemed deserted.

"No phone, you said? What's that he's got there?"

Russ paused a moment, almost seeming chastened before he regained his attitude. "You can't be sure that's a phone. That could be anything in his hand."

"And look, there's Luczon, coming down the stairs behind him."

As they watched, one of the monitors began to blink crazily, then another.

"Why are those cameras flashing?" Frank asked, pointing to them on the wall.

"Glitches," said Russ. "They happen all the time. They last maybe a few seconds. There are still seven views of the platform."

"Except all of a sudden Lattimer and Luczon are behind that big pillar and you can't see them on any of the live cameras. Look, here comes the train into the station."

A few seconds later, the image of Lattimer reappeared from behind the pillar as he hurtled in front of the oncoming train.

The fluttering screens came back online, showing the train as the driver jammed on the brakes.

Now they could see Luczon, standing frozen, and much farther up the platform, two other people reacting as they suddenly became aware of what had just happened.

"So you're saying, Russ, that what we just witnessed squares perfectly with the witness's story?"

"I don't see anything there that suggests otherwise."

Frank pulled something out of his pocket and held it up. "I picked this up today on the way over here. Do you know what this is?"

"Looks like a big laser pointer."

"In fact it's in a particularly large power rating of lasers, Three-B to be exact, that's a little more specialized. It's sometimes misused to disrupt video cameras."

"Sure," said the tech. "Now and then somebody, some kid usually, beams one into one of our cameras. It messes them up for a while but then they come back on again. We're constantly monitoring real-time to be on the look for those. But the problem is, our cameras also go out all on their own sporadically, and it's difficult to tell the difference between a glitch and a deliberate disruption. Usually it's a matter of how long it lasts before we send out an alert."

"So you're saying these glitches…" Frank pointed to the two monitors that had briefly gone out. "…these didn't last long enough to raise any red flags?"

"At the time, I guess not. Monitoring personnel may not have even noticed. They're toggling around to thousands of cameras at any given moment. It's a big system."

"Okay." Frank heaved a deep sigh in exasperation. "But once your investigation opened, you had to go back and look. Russ, two cameras blinked out at the exact moment a man fell onto the tracks and you didn't think it warranted a further look?"

"I had everything I needed. I still don't see…."

Frank turned to the tech. "Could you go back to the moment when Luczon is coming down the stairs again and freeze it?"

When he had the right frame, Frank pointed to the figure of Raymond Luczon in one of the cameras before it began to blink. "He's got that courier bag I'm told he always carried. And he seems to be reaching into it, see? Now if you advance the frame…he steps out of view and…boom, it starts fluttering."

He pointed to another monitor. "Same thing happened there. By an odd coincidence, they are the only two cameras that would have given us an unobstructed view of Lattimer at the moment he fell onto the tracks."

"Frank, I think you're concocting a conspiracy theory here. You gotta go with that, whattayacall it, Gillette's Razor theory. The simplest explanation that explains the most is still that it's an accident."

"I think you mean Occam's Razor. Okay. I'd like to look at one more thing, if I could…the point-of-view video from the driver's cabin?"

The tech nodded, worked at his keyboard for a moment, and pointed to a screen.

"Can you start it at the point where the train is just entering the station?"

The Northcote station was the point where the aboveground train went underground into the more heavily congested part of the city. They watched as the view from the front window of the train moved along the track and descended into a tunnel. The screen blackened for a second before the camera acclimated. They could see a line of green lights sweeping by, then the track took a left turn and the lights of the station came into view.

Now the train was entering the station, and suddenly the figure of Orrin Lattimer hurtled into the scene. Everybody watching the screen involuntarily flinched at what they saw next.

Even Russ Payne groaned loudly and then said, "Was that really necessary to go through again?"

What must it have been like for the motorman to have watched that as it transpired? Frank had learned that the operator had not yet returned to work. Probably Metro Transit would be sending him for mandatory counseling. As a cop he had seen lots of things, violent things, but this experience was of a different nature altogether.

He wondered how long it took to deal with something like that.

"Okay, stop it there, can you back up and halt that? There."

The blurry figure of Orrin Lattimer was frozen eerily in the spotlight of the train. He was facing the train and his arms and legs were spread out, his right foot still on the platform.

Even blurred, it was easy to see that the fingers of both his hands were spread wide and empty.

"Where's the phone—or whatever you want to say it was—-that he just had in his right hand?" Frank asked. "And why is he facing the train? If he had slipped, wouldn't he have gone headfirst onto the tracks?"

He turned to Russ. "I'll tell you what happened. Someone grabbed the phone out of his hand and pushed him into the path of the train: the only other person there, who had just zapped the video cams. Someone who, as the sole witness to it all, would have had a plausible story ready to explain what had happened..

"Raymond Luczon…or as you knew him, Lucas Zone."

* * * *

One thing remained: requesting officers to pick up a suspect. Outside Metro Transit headquarters, Frank made the call as Athena just smiled and shook her head.

"Well, I must say Frank…that was impressive. Do you think Russ Payne is ever going to speak to you again?"

"Who knows? If he didn't…would that be a bad thing or a good thing?"

"He sure dropped the ball on this one. Kinda lazy, isn't he?"

"Russ and his different kind of dead…."

"It's ironic, but in a sense he was right. Lattimer *was* a different kind of dead."

Athena's phone began to sing. She answered it, spoke tersely and rang off.

"The hospital's on the way back to the unit, right? That was Thalia. Natalie Riemer started to wake up early this morning."

* * * *

"I must instruct you to only spend a minute or two with her and to not stress her. I wish the family had not contacted you at all; she's still very weak."

The neurologist, Dr. Sara Guarani, was a surprisingly young woman who clearly took her job very seriously. She stepped aside, arms folded, to allow Frank and Athena to approach the bedside.

Natalie Riemer's eyes were closed and she wore an oxygen mask but she was no longer intubated and was breathing on her own.

Athena laid a hand gently on Natalie's arm.

"Ms. Riemer? Ms. Riemer, this is Detective Pardo. Can you hear me?"

Her eyes shot open, wide with alarm. Her body seemed to go rigid. She turned and looked at Athena. She spoke in a bare hoarse whisper through the mask.

Athena bent lower, saying softly, "I'm sorry, I didn't get that. What did you say?"

"He…was…here."

Athena stared and waited. The words came slowly, weakly, but with clear urgency.

"He…was…here. Man."

The detectives traded looks.

"Which man? Do you mean the man who attacked you?"

She nodded, tears starting to well in her widening eyes.

"When? When was he here?"

"Now."

Frank turned to Natalie's mother and sister, standing in the corner of the hospital room. "How long ago did she first open her eyes?"

"Not very long. An hour ago, maybe less."

"He's here in the hospital. McBroom." Frank stepped away from the bed and turned towards the door. Athena followed him.

"How is that possible?" Athena whispered. "She was dreaming. She's not completely coherent yet."

"We can't take that chance." Frank was out the door, his phone in hand.

Athena turned to Thalia.

"At any time was Natalie left alone in here? I mean, did you both step out for a break or anything?"

"Only for very short times…just to walk up and down the corridor or get a cup of coffee. There was always a nurse here when we did…and of course the officer."

Dr. Guarani stepped in. "That's enough. I have to insist that you leave her alone now. You can perhaps come back and speak with her later. She can be exhausted very easily. *Please.*"

She pulled her stethoscope up to her ears and motioned them all back, pulling the curtain around the bed. They stepped into the hall.

Frank hustled down the corridor, speaking rapidly into his phone, requesting police presence at the hospital. When he reached the nurse station, he showed his badge and asked to be put through to hospital security with whom he requested a hospital-wide alert, giving the description of Edward McBroom.

If somehow McBroom had gained access to the hospital and to Natalie's room, *if* Natalie Riemer had actually seen him, then it was possible he was still in the building, awaiting his chance to finish her off.

Maybe it had only been a fevered dream of hers, but no matter how implausible, he had to act on it.

"Where's the stairwell?" he asked the nurse behind the counter.

Meanwhile, Athena gathered the Riemers and the officer on guard and asked who had entered the room in the past hour. The uniform, a grave young patrolman, listed a handful of nurses, doctors, and techs, all of whom wore the proper badges and none of whom met the description he had been given of Edward McBroom.

Aside from that, he said, there had only been the family and friends.

"Friends?" Athena asked, turning to the Riemers. "Has Natalie had visitors today?"

"Oh yes," said her mother, Helen. "People are constantly coming by for short courtesy visits, just to let us know they are thinking of Natalie. Of course she was unconscious, but they'd often lean over and just speak to her."

"Who's been here today?"

"One of her fellow nurses was here. And there was that nice man who knew her from the jury duty."

"Jury…? Who was he and when was he here?"

"He was very sweet. He said he only knew her from serving on the jury with her but he said she'd made a lasting impression and he just wanted to look in on her. He stayed less than a minute, just before she started stirring and coming back to consciousness."

"What was his name? Who was he?"

"He was a rather portly man, like a big friendly bear. He said his name was Lawrence. Lawrence Gillman, I believe?"

She turned to Thalia.

"Killian, Mom. His name was Killian. And his first name was Leonard."

Athena had her phone out, hitting the contact for Frank.

Frank was halfway down the stairs when his phone buzzed.

"Frank, it was Killian, the jury foreman! He was here! That's who Natalie saw!"

"What? What's this guy look like?"

"He's pretty heavyset…with a mustache and glasses. And he's balding."

"Call it in with his description. Tell them this is related to the request for backup I just made. Then do the same with hospital security."

"Roger that."

"I'm almost at ground level. If he's still here, he's got to go out the front door unless he sets off an emergency door alarm. When the unis arrive I'll send them to you."

"Okay, Frank. As soon as I can get them underway, I'll come down to the ground floor."

There were only two flights to the main floor, but Frank was huffing and puffing nonetheless as he scrambled down the stairway. He burst out into the lobby just as several members of hospital security were converging at the reception desk. He held his badge out as he ran to join them.

According to the receptionist, nobody meeting Killian's description had left through the front door in the past half hour.

"How many other ways are there to exit this building?" he asked one of the security people.

"For the public, at this time of day, this is it. There's an employee/service exit and a maintenance and delivery port, but they're guarded or require a badge to unlock. And there are emergency exits that trigger an alarm."

"Can you get people at all of the exits?"

"Right away," he said. He lifted his walkie-talkie and barked orders into it. "Who are we looking for?"

Frank named Leonard Killian and repeated the description. The security man added the information and dispatched his team across the hospital.

Three police patrol cars arrived shortly thereafter, including a sergeant who was authorized to direct operations.

Frank filled her in on the situation and she began to direct the unis to sweep the building, working their way up and down from Riemer's floor. Once he was satisfied they were on their way, Frank decided to begin his own survey of the perimeter of the ground floor.

He wished that he and Athena were carrying their own portable radios—what were commonly termed "Rovers" by some departments—but those were checked out by detectives when there was a need foreseen, and this day had started with the expectancy of routine.

Generally they were able when necessary to communicate by their phones, but now, when he tried to call her and open a channel to stay in touch as to what each was doing she didn't pick up. Possibly she was onto something upstairs. Maybe she had actually encountered Killian. He suppressed his annoyance at the inability to get through and hoped she'd get back to him quickly.

There were patrol officers covering the building now and Athena could take care of herself, but he couldn't help feeling a tinge of concern for her. There was nothing he could do but carry out his original objective to check the service exit and see if there were any other possible means of egress that the security guard had neglected to mention.

He strode quickly around the front of the building, checking first one side and then the other. It was free-standing, separated by landscaped walkways from other medical center related buildings to either side of it. There did not appear to be a way someone inside the structure could pass through to another building from within. If Killian was in there and was going to try to leave, it would have to be from one of this building's ground floor exits.

Why wasn't Athena calling him back?

Not breaking his stride, he made a second call to her, which also went immediately to voicemail. He broke the connection and pocketed the phone.

He turned down a concrete walkway running along the north side of the building, lined with tall shrubs, and saw what he was looking for. About thirty feet down the walk was a short paved turn-in that led to a pair of double doors, with a uniformed security man standing outside, hands on hips.

Frank had just reached the corner to the walk when the doors flew open. A figure in scrubs and mask, with a pair of thick glasses sticking out under a paper hair cap, pushed what looked like a linen cart out the doors. The security guard gave the newcomer the once-over and waved the person through.

Frank picked up his speed. As he got closer, the attendant pushing the cart reached the walkway and turned to look back at the closing automatic doors. Some commotion seemed to be happening. The security guard looked as if he was trying to hear what someone inside the door was yelling to him.

The scrubs-wearer pushed the linen cart to the side, practically tipping it over, and turned toward Frank, head down, hustling away from the entrance. Frank could now see it was a large man in tightly-fitting scrubs that looked to be, almost comically, two sizes too small. He finally raised his head, saw Frank coming, and hesitated.

The doors slammed open. A figure dashed out: Athena Pardo. She pointed towards them and hollered.

"That's him! That's Killian!"

Killian only paused for a moment then barreled at Frank.

Frank for some reason flashed back to his mercifully short football career in high school when he was, inexplicably, a one hundred seventy pound lineman defending against two hundred pound defensive rushers from the bigger schools. He fleetingly considered bracing himself to try to hold the oncoming "big friendly bear" and actually began to assume the stance.

Both men prepared for the inevitable impact, and the outcome didn't seem to be in doubt for either of them.

Frank was going to get creamed by Killian.

Then common sense flashed. At the last second, Frank sidestepped, leaving only his foot planted. Killian hadn't anticipated the move and hurtled past, his foot stumbling against Frank's.

As Killian swept by, Frank slapped his hand on his back and shoved. Killian gave a frustrated holler and sprawled to the ground, face first, with the crack of falling glasses and then the unpleasant smacking sound of nose on pavement.

It wasn't elegant, and it wasn't Police Academy book, but it had the intended effect.

Athena Pardo was right behind him, running, her service weapon held pointed skyward with both hands.

Killian was struggling to get to his feet when she yelled, "Hold it!" and assumed the absolutely correct position: legs apart, elbows locked, two-handed grip aiming her police issue Glock directly at his body mass.

Despite himself, Frank had to admire her form. He was never as good as that.

* * * *

"It would have been too much to expect he had the knife on him," Athena was saying, sitting on the corner of Frank's desk.

They had returned to the unit after turning their prisoner over to the uniforms for delivery. He now sat handcuffed down the hall, awaiting them.

"He must have realized he couldn't get it past hospital security," she said. "Hopefully we'll find it stashed in that cluttered apartment of his. I'm not sure what he planned to do, exactly. He didn't have any weapon, as such, in his possession."

"Maybe he was just doing a reconnaissance mission, to see if she was going to make it, planning to improvise if need be."

"Lucky thing you happened upon him right there and then."

"And it was just luck. I was heading for the elevator and I saw the door closing on him bursting out of those scrubs and mask. It was pretty ridiculous, and I was pretty sure it looked like him. It was that owlish stare he had, magnified by those glasses, when I interviewed him. I saw the car was heading down to the ground floor and then took off down the stairs. It was better luck that you happened to be right outside to stop him."

"Sometimes the luck runs our way."

Athena's phone buzzed. She pulled it out and thumbed through to the new text that had come in.

"It's Thalia. Natalie's fully conscious and looks to be regaining strength. The doctor is cautiously optimistic that she's turned a corner."

"Good news for everybody," mused Frank, standing facing her, "except Killian. She'll probably be able to make a positive ID in a short time."

"Speaking of which…shall we?"

"Yeah. After you…."

They headed towards the interview room where their guest awaited.

Leonard Killian was handcuffed to the gray metal table, his molten glare magnified through his hairline-cracked lenses as they entered the cold sterile room.

Athena had already checked that the video equipment on the wall was running. The detectives took up chairs across the table from him.

"That was pretty bold, Leonard," Frank began. "Just had to go back and finish your work, didn't you?"

Killian said nothing, simply stared at them intensely.

He does sort of look like an owl, Frank thought. *A rather psychotic owl...*

"She's going to make it," Athena said. "She's already identified you. And we're going to get enough from the search of your place to match you to the other attacks. We might even find the murder weapon. I'm guessing it's a rather nice hunting knife. Did you keep it?"

Leonard Killian then surprised them both.

"They deserved it," he growled. "They all damn well deserved it."

"I understood you were frustrated debating with them over Trenier's guilt. I didn't realize *how* frustrated."

"He destroyed that family. He was guilty as sin. Anybody could see that."

"You don't think Trenier's lawyer made a convincing case for his innocence?"

"I don't blame the lawyer. That was his job, to twist the truth. Any halfway decent and intelligent person could have seen through it. Those three idiot bleeding hearts couldn't."

He shook his head. "I told you the experience turned me off to the whole system. But the system couldn't have worked so ineptly if the jurors weren't such imbeciles."

"So you took it upon yourself to track them down, one by one, and…. "

"...*exact retribution*. Yes. It wasn't hard. They had no idea they were being watched. I developed quite an effective system, in fact. And I knew I could count on nobody noticing the connection among them. I believe I mentioned that to you when we first talked, in fact...the average person doesn't pay attention beyond his own self. And this was definitely a jury of very very *average* sorts."

"What about Raymond Luczon? How did he fit into all this?"

"Who do you mean? You mentioned that name to me before. I've got no idea who you're talking about."

"He was your most recent victim...the man behind the library earlier this week."

"I don't know anything about that. That wasn't me. The Riemer woman was the last...the last one."

Frank and Athena looked at each other.

"I saved her for last. You want to know why? She and I had quite the donnybrook one day when I was reaching the end of my rope with her intransigence. She called me a big creep. More than once she called me creepy. Can you imagine?"

Man. Big. Creepy. Could it really be this simple?

"How about Trenier himself?" Frank asked. "Are you disappointed he got away from you?"

Killian smiled...a terrible, diabolical smile. "What makes you think he got away?"

14.

Frank and Athena left one interview room and, with a quick stop at Frank's desk, headed back to another.

"They brought her in about twenty minutes ago," Athena said as they walked. "Reportedly she's not very happy."

"I'm sure she's not," Frank sighed, the slightest smile curling up the corners of his mouth.

She clearly wasn't very happy. She sat next to a dour man in a dark suit, both with their arms folded, in the far more squalid chamber informally called the Fortress, complete with peeling ugly green paint.

There was no cup of tea on the table.

"Ms. Westermark," Frank said as they walked in and closed the door behind them. "My apologies for making you wait."

Collis Westermark had no charm for Frank this time; she glowered at him.

After Killian, Frank reflected, it couldn't match up in the "menacing baleful stare" category but it still had its own drama.

"That's not a problem, Detective, since I wouldn't have spoken to you before my attorney arrived, which he just did. What *is* a problem is how you are now harassing and seriously inconveniencing me. I was on my way to meet Lane Dembeau's plane when your officers detained me. This is going to have repercussions—for my business and for you and your department."

The old chairs grated loudly as they pulled them out and sat down across from Westermark and her lawyer.

"We were delayed because we just took the confession of the alleged killer of Raymond Luczon. That at least should make you happy."

"So you did one thing right today. Congratulations."

Athena sat back, content to let this be Frank's show. She looked forward to being entertained, in fact. He continued.

"I have some more good news for you. I believe I found what you were on your way to look for last night, at Raymond's apartment."

Her eyes narrowed but she said nothing. Frank held up a plastic bag containing a smart phone. He laid it on the table between them.

"This is what you were actually looking for, isn't it?"

The lawyer laid his hand on her arm and cautioned her to say nothing.

"That's fine," Frank continued. "You should by all means heed your attorney. Tell you what, why don't you just listen while we tell you a story? Raymond Luczon had this squirreled away very securely in his apartment, along with his own computer and data backup. And what a surprise to find out whose phone it is."

Frank bent over the phone, touched the screen right through the bag, and asked the voice assistant, "Whose phone is this?" A moment later it flashed on the screen.

ORRIN LATTIMER'S PHONE

"That's a nice feature on some newer phones that not everybody knows about. Well, at least tech dinosaurs like me don't always know about it. You still can't access anything on the phone if it's locked, but it *will* tell you whose phone it is, in case it gets misplaced. That in itself doesn't unlock the phone."

"Raymond had Orrin's phone?" Westermark said. "What's that got to do with me?"

"Collis, don't say anything," said the lawyer. He looked back at Frank. "But yes, what does that have to do with Ms. Westermark? Why is she here?"

Frank continued to speak directly to Westermark. "Let me tell you the story I promised."

He sat back in the chair, which made a creak.

"The way I figure it, Raymond was supposed to meet you Tuesday night and hand over Orrin's phone. But things didn't work out that way. He wanted to change the terms of your deal and you wound up killing him instead."

The attorney held out a hand. "That's quite a fantasy and totally preposterous. How did he get that phone to begin with and why do you think my client would go through all this to get it?"

"How did Raymond Luczon get Orrin Lattimer's phone, you ask? He snatched it away from Orrin a split second before shoving him onto the railway tracks in front of that train."

"This just keeps getting wilder and wilder. I'm not even going to try to dignify the ludicrous nature of these conjectures with a response. The question right now is, why have you decided to implicate Ms. Westermark in your harebrained theory?"

"I'm getting to that," Frank said. "Ms. Westermark has already been connected with Ray Luczon by her own admission. Just yesterday she told me she'd met him when he applied for a job at Humbletech, that she was impressed by his innovative know-how, and that they subsequently entered into a romantic relationship.

"But I think it all went down a little differently. There's nothing to indicate that Ray Luczon was even an above-average techie. I've seen his website; even a Luddite like me can see it's a mess. I think what Ms. Westermark actually saw in Ray was someone she could manipulate who knew his way around just enough to be of use. She planned to groom him to do her dirty work, as it were. For one thing, he was tailing Orrin Lattimer and Orrin's assistant, Sharon Brooks. I believe the potential was there for far more serious deeds, if and when they became necessary.

"In general, he made a good all-around errand boy who could go places she couldn't and not be noticed. In return, she could supply him with the money and know-how he might be missing and hook him up with her hot-shot connections. Then he could start the online company and become the high profile media influencer he so wanted to be. I think that was her main lure from the beginning."

Frank looked at her. "I don't mean to deny your considerable charm, Ms. Westermark. But perhaps this was a cynical business deal without the heart strings you tried to sell me on."

"This is all still utter supposition!" barked the attorney. "You're painting my client as a…a kind of predator on a young man, what, two decades her junior? On what do you base all this nonsense?"

"I'm glad you asked, counselor. Unbeknownst to anyone else—that's a nice word, isn't it, *unbeknownst,* very lawyerlike—Orrin Lattimer had been in touch with an investigative reporter and was on his way to meet him Sunday night with what he considered to be damning evidence of misconduct at Humbletech. He was paranoid…justifiably, as it turns out.

"Possibly Raymond wasn't as much of a ninja as he thought and Lattimer had spotted him at some point. Lattimer was afraid he was in mortal danger and so was his family. He needed to move cautiously, without being detected. That's why he had his wife and child leave town, why he'd been staying somewhere other than his own home, and why he had been taking circuitous routes around town that night…until he arrived at the Northcote train station."

"You're saying Raymond was planning to…to be an assassin?" Westermark blurted out. "That's insane!"

"*Collis!*" barked the lawyer.

Frank raised his hands. "He certainly didn't seem the type. But what if his objective was simply to locate Lattimer or his family? That information would be extremely valuable…and dangerous, if passed on to the right people."

"This is totally preposterous!" the attorney sputtered. "On what basis is any of this anything but an outrageous smear job on my client?"

Frank pointed to the bagged phone on the table. "Remember, I was able to determine the owner of the phone but that didn't unlock it. But, check this out...."

He opened up the bag and removed the phone.

"The bag's just a precaution. Earlier today when SID sent someone over to pick up several items, I asked if they could fingerprint and process the phone here, download a copy of the data, and then leave it."

He held his left hand out to block them from seeing and with his right, tapped in a password. The home screen opened.

"This stuff is like magic to me!" Frank tapped the screen a few more times. "Luckily I know someone who was able to provide me with his password, because there's a lot on here that began to make sense of things for me."

"Who would have had his password?" Westermark yelled. "Who would have given it to *you* of all people?"

"Collis," the attorney cautioned. "Please!" He was beginning to look a bit weary.

"I'll get back to that in a minute. Right now, I'd like you to hear this."

He pressed more icons on the phone and sat back, crossing his arms.

* * * *

"Orrin, I really need to get a solid commitment from you on this, before Lane gets back next week."

"Collis, this is nuts. You want to box Lane out?"

"You know as well as I that he's going over the deep end. They're picturing him as a lunatic in the media. Everything we've worked for is in danger of going up in smoke if he keeps it up."

"He's the face of the company," Orrin said. "Humbletech is more his vision than yours, mine, or anybody's."

"Orrin, he needs to go before we launch the IPO. Come on, you know this is true. He calls himself Lead Designer but we both know all the ideas are yours. He basically bloviates and presides over an assembly line. We can offer to keep him on in some figurehead status, which is all he's good for. But I doubt he'll go for that. It will have to be a clean break, a buyout. You and I together can do it."

"He's invested a substantial stake in the company, Collis. He won't go. And we need his support, in more ways than one."

"I'll take care of all that. He'll leave. I've got a new slate of directors ready to step in with us, and we can more than cover his share. I can guarantee you'll have the necessary funding for all your R&D needs for the foreseeable future. Keep your eyes on the finish line, Orrin."

"I have to wonder, where is all this magnificent funding coming from, exactly? Who are these mysterious benefactors you're bringing in?"

"Let me worry about that. I'm the financial side of the company. Believe me. I can keep the money flowing in without Lane in the picture."

"I *have* to worry about that. I've got an idea who some of your silent partners really are, and I don't like it."

"What are you talking about?"

"I know about the Meads. How did you get involved with them, Collis—organized crime and drug cartels? Are they looking to turn Humbletech into some kind of personal money laundry?"

There was a long silence before Westermark replied.

"How did you find out about them? Yes, the Meads are a part of the consortium. They're looking for legitimate investments. Money is money, and they've got plenty. Our development requires substantial capital. I'll take it wherever I can find it."

"If it's all so aboveboard, why are you keeping Andre and Philippe Mead's participation such a secret?"

"You know why. The media would have a field day with that. The crusaders in the legislature would jump on it as a vehicle to higher office. It would be an utter fiasco. We can't *conspicuously* take their money."

"So how much are your silent partners the Meads into us for?"

"Let's just say that if they pulled out, we'd be in major trouble... especially if we want to buy out Lane."

"So they've already got their hooks deep into Humbletech, thanks to you. They want Lane gone, don't they? So they can get a larger share of Humbletech before the IPO? Collis, they're the ones who are going to destroy the company."

"I don't see it that way, Orrin. I see them as giving us our shot at success beyond our wildest dreams. We're talking a *very* large influx of money to you as well. I know you're heavily leveraged in the company. Your worries will all go away, very quickly. You've just got to work with me here to outmaneuver Lane before he returns."

"It's a deal with the devil, Collis. I don't know."

"Make up your mind, Orrin. And don't take too long to do it. The clock is running. I can do this without you. You think your patents and your ideas are locked up but they're not. I'd rather have you with me, but I'm committed to moving forward."

"Threats, Collis? Really...?"

"No threats, my friend. Call them cautions to a dear and valued colleague."

* * * *

Frank stabbed the button on the phone and looked up at a clearly frazzled Collis Westermark.

"There's more, but you get the idea. Andre and Philippe Mead: we know them well around here. Forgive me the awkward metaphor, but they've got their fingers in a lot of pretty nasty pies: drugs, extortion, human trafficking, and murder. The list goes on. You're running in some particularly unsavory circles, Ms. Westermark."

"Don't say a word, Collis!" the lawyer said quietly.

"By all means, don't. But do keep listening."

Westermark folded her hands on the table and glared darkly. *If looks could kill,* Frank mused before continuing:

"You needed Orrin on your side to make your move against Lane Dembeau, and you'd been badgering him to come on board for some time. He realized he was being followed. He'd figured out your connection to the Meads—I'm thinking he was expert at following digital trails himself—and was sufficiently worried about them to move his family away and find a safe house of his own.

"Then he formulated his escape plan: get you to open up about everything and secretly record it. He was good, leading you to speak openly and making sure he named the relevant names. Maybe you didn't realize at the time that Orrin was recording your conversation, and you may not have known that it was his plan to go to a reporter with that recording, but you put it together quickly enough.

"It was Orrin's habit to come to work every single day, even Sundays. You enlisted Raymond Luczon to follow him when he left work that Sunday night. Now there was no other choice. He'd have to act.

"I think you instructed Luczon to eliminate Orrin; alternately, you just told him to get that phone away from him and the killing was Raymond's idea. Either way, you started everything in motion. Raymond tailed Orrin, and this time he apparently was pretty good at it, since Orrin had no idea his evasive tactics hadn't worked when he entered that train station.

"Shortly thereafter, Orrin was dead…and Raymond had his phone. He played the shocked witness to an accidental tragedy, which persuaded the officers on the scene and the investigating agent at Metro Transit. In some ways he really was a pretty smart kid. Maybe that's what you saw in him: he was stealthy and crafty in his own way. In the end, after a few small mistakes, he was turning into a decent henchman for your dark ops.

"You were going to be busy in the next few days before Lane Dembeau returned. The control situation of the company had gotten very complicated and urgent, if you were going to bring in your own slate of operators. Among other things, you needed to convince Meryl Lattimer to side with you. You also needed to harangue Sharon Brooks, who not only was the gatekeeper to Lattimer's department but probably knew where to find Meryl. You had Raymond follow her as well, but Sharon eluded him.

"When you got word that a homicide detective had spoken with Sharon, you figured it as a potential roadblock in your plans. You visited us as a pre-emptive strike, to throw us off by getting us on your side, planting some nonsense about Lane and wild rumors about Orrin bolting the company. You were subtle enough that you hoped it'd send me on a wild goose chase to find some tampering in the company, or that I'd start to suspect Lane as complicit in Orrin's death.

"Ideally, you'd just convince me the company was a hive of crazies that distracted Orrin enough to cause his accidental death. In any case, your goal was to confuse us, to have us think of you as a charmingly ditzy tech-world character that we shouldn't suspect of anything—and to some extent you succeeded with both scenarios.

"Then another unexpected problem arose when Raymond was supposed to deliver the phone to you and instead decided to renegotiate his deal. Whatever you promised him wasn't going to be enough once he realized just how high the stakes were in this game.

"I've heard you described as a chess player. You try to think ahead. You also stay well-informed. You were familiar with the assailant the media were calling the Creep. So you set up a meet with Raymond in a remote location similar to the ones where the assaults had taken place and you carried a suitable weapon in your bag…just in case.

"I'm thinking it was a letter opener you had; I'd like to imagine a very ornate and sharp one? Or maybe it *was* a knife. I wouldn't be surprised if you disposed of it in short order in any case. The point is, you did find it necessary to use it. You weren't about to be soaked for more money, or whatever he now demanded. So you figured to kill him, making him look like a new victim of the Creep, and take the phone at the same time.

"He didn't suspect in the least; maybe you pretended to go along with him. But the moment he turned his back on you, you stabbed him… four times."

Frank made stabbing motions with his hand into empty air.

"You said he left *his* phone and keys with you before he went out," he continued. "But actually they were in his trusty courier bag which you grabbed and ran off with.

"But you didn't get Orrin's phone which is what you really wanted. Raymond was a step ahead of you; he hadn't brought his major bargaining chip. He had hidden it away in his apartment…and you had killed him before you realized that.

"It's been just one problem after another for you this week, hasn't it?"

Frank smiled sadly at Westermark.

"You wanted us to believe that you and he were having an affair and that he was very taken with you. You played that to the hilt for us last night. In fact, however, this was a cynical business deal all along. What did you offer him—to underwrite his company and foot his bills? Were you going to turn him into a for-real star? For a hacker-slacker like him that must have been a pretty tempting offer. He just got too greedy."

Westermark suddenly rose and slammed her hands on the table. "That little son of a...."

"Collis!" bellowed the attorney, reaching out for her.

"I genuinely *cared* about that boy! The things I could have taught him...and all he cared about was how much he could get from me! I...."

"*Please!* That's enough!" The lawyer settled her back down and turned to Frank. "This is all quite a fairy tale, Detective, but tell me how any of this cock-and-bull story translates to real evidence that my client has committed a crime?"

Frank continued to direct his narrative directly to Westermark.

"You've been confident all along that you had the situation under control, Ms. Westermark. For instance, I think you really were intending to bring Raymond's phone to us with your story about how he left it and ran off on some mysterious meeting.

"Of course, first you made sure to delete his text conversations with you and clear his call history. Your story would explain to us your fingerprints on the phone and, you hoped, remove the evidence of your collusion with him.

"But I'm surprised that you didn't stop to think of the possibility that we already had requested the call records for his phone. It would stand to reason you'd been careful in other ways as well, such as disposing of the weapon with which you dispatched poor Raymond. But I'd venture you've got a streak of arrogance, a belief in your supreme cleverness that overrides your instinct for caution.

"Maybe Raymond's bag—along with that letter opener or stiletto or whatever that you used to kill him—is still in your apartment somewhere? Maybe there's just some trace of Raymond's blood somewhere? If it is, we'll find it."

Frank rummaged through the folder in front of him on the table and pulled out a piece of paper which he laid in front of Westermark and her attorney.

"This is a search warrant for your apartment. There are already officers there securing it, and my partner and I will personally oversee the search in just a little while. I wonder what we'll find that you didn't think you needed to get rid of?

"And oh, by the way, you asked how I was able to open Orrin's phone? It just so happens he confided in someone who had his back throughout this entire situation. I don't think I need to say who."

The attorney whose name they never did get continued to bluster and rant. They ignored him as they read their suspect her rights and informed her she was under arrest.

They couldn't tell if Collis Westermark was going to erupt in a fit of temper, or break out crying.

All they knew for sure was that something was about to explode.

15.

The evening shift was coming on and one by one the day crew was trickling out. What had been a hectic and bustling squad room had knocked down a notch or two.

"So here's what I'd like to know," Athena said, almost idly, as she began to power down her computer and clear her desk.

"What's that?" asked Frank, who had already pushed the piles of work on his desk into some semblance of order and was just sitting, looking quite fatigued, as if he needed to summon the energy to stand up and leave.

"Who was using who? Was Collis using Raymond, or vice versa?"

"Don't you mean *whom?*"

"Frank, I'm too tired to take any grief. Who was using *whom* then?"

"I'm thinking it went both ways. Raymond saw an opportunity to get a leg up in his world if he played along with Collis."

"And Collis was getting, what?—someone to do her dirty work? It had to be more than that," Athena said. "First she wanted us to believe that they were having an affair. Then, I'm not sure what she wanted us to think. And finally there was that little outburst at the end."

"I'd say finding those fancy clothes was the tipoff," Frank said. "Like you said, she wanted to make him presentable, to bring him into her culture… and, I suspect…her life. Raymond wasn't buying any of it. Maybe he finally let her down on that score. I'd say there was a definite emotional dimension to it all for her to do him in that violently."

"It's kind of ironic," she said. "When you come down to it…here we were presuming Raymond was being seduced, one way or the other, by the worldly, well-to-do older woman…"

"…and in the end, perhaps, he ended up taking her for a ride." Frank's beloved crime novels with the lurid cover burbs came to mind. "Too bad it was a one way trip."

"For both of them," said Athena, reaching for the leather jacket draped over her chair. "Been quite a day, huh?"

"Be quite a day again tomorrow. Heading off to have some fun tonight?"

"Believe it or not, I'm celebrating another birthday. This one's on my dad's side. We're having two kinds of mole, among other good stuff."

"Sounds like your family's full of good cooks."

She smiled. "We're Greek and Mexican, with great food traditions and fantastic chefs everywhere. Oughta be fun. And don't you dare make any jokes about my putting on weight."

He raised his hands innocently. "Cross my heart, never entered my mind."

"So what're you up to? Don't tell me you're stopping for a pastrami sandwich again."

"I might just order in a pizza. Now that I finally got streaming TV, there are a couple of good classic noir films I was going to catch tonight."

"Interesting. You spend all day consorting with the dark side and then you go home to watch it as entertainment, huh?"

"And read it. I got into the habit back when I was married. My wife, Muriel, loved mysteries and I loved debunking them."

"Why don't you at least go to one of the revival theaters around town and see something classic in black and white on a big screen?"

"What, by myself? Looks like Collis *is* out of the prospective dating pool now and I don't really have any other prospects lined up at the moment."

"Frank, we really need to get you back out into the world. You're not as old as you try to make yourself out to be."

"Appreciate the concern, partner, but if something's gonna happen, it's gonna happen. I'm content to live the serene life of the bachelor for right now."

"Alright then…enjoy your pizza. Maybe mix in a salad or some vegetables, okay?"

"I thought no jokes about putting on weight."

"I just want to keep you around long enough for that 'something' to happen for you. See you tomorrow, Frank."

As she headed for the stairs, Frank powered down his computer and prepared to head out as well. That was when his phone chimed.

"Frank, it's Cary Wilde."

"Hello, Cary. What can I do for you? I assume you're calling about Teddy Ralski. I haven't heard about whether the autopsy has been completed or if his body has been released to his uncle yet. I can find out for you."

"I'd appreciate that, but actually that's not what I'm calling about." Wilde's voice was grave.

"What's up?"

"I've been running things over and over in my head. Since we, you know, found Teddy. That was tough."

"Yes. It was."

"You see shit like that all the time, huh?"

"Way too often."

"I've seen people die. It never gets easy."

"No. It never does."

"And I bet you've seen a lot more than I have. This was a whole other level of serious. Like I said, I keep running it over and over in my head. It's like a movie I can't stop. A lot of the vets I deal with talk about that. They can't shut their heads off. Maybe that was how it felt for Teddy."

Frank was at a loss for words. He didn't know where Wilde was going with this, and he had no answer for him. "It should never end like that for anyone."

"Well, see, that's the thing. I can't help but think he didn't end it."

"What do you mean, Cary?"

"We both saw the note. We both saw the gun. We both saw the ink stains on his fingers."

"Yeah. We did."

"The gun was in his right hand. The fingers of his right hand were stained with ink."

"That's right."

"It finally dawned on me. Frank...Teddy was left handed."

There was a long, silent pause before Frank finally answered.

"Are you sure?"

"I'm positive. I spent a lot of time with him. He wrote left-handed. He threw a baseball and a football left-handed. I've even got a service photo he left pinned up on a bulletin board, of him holding a weapon. Left-handed."

All Frank could do was exhale heavily. His brain raced.

"You still there, Frank?"

"Uh huh. I'm still here."

"Still think he killed himself?"

"Suppose he didn't. Suppose someone else killed him. Any thoughts as to who that might be?"

"I've thought about that. No."

"He spent a long time at Reboot. Did he cross anybody there, mix it up with anyone?"

"That's the thing. He was pretty well-liked there. He went out of his way to help people. I think I mentioned that he just had a way with them."

"What about when he first arrived, when he was still...confused? Maybe he made an enemy early on that never forgot?"

"No. He was hearing the voices but they drove him inward, to isolate. You remember what he was like when you brought him to Reboot? He could hardly talk. He barely interacted with anybody whatsoever."

"Any chance he got involved in anything extracurricular? Hanging with the wrong kind of people he might have met at the center?"

"You mean shady stuff, like drugs? It just doesn't feel right with Teddy. Sure, we have our share of, let's call 'em marginal characters, even a few dangerous ones that have to be weeded out, but Teddy was smart enough to avoid 'em. He understood how fragile he was chemically. I can't see him getting involved in anything like that."

"He needed money. There are a lot of ways someone can get in trouble who needs money."

"No. Just…no. I can't see Teddy doing any of that kinda shit, stealing or hustling or whatever. You'd have to have known him. I get a pretty good sense of the guys who come through Reboot, I've seen all types. Teddy just wasn't that kind of guy."

"So… you don't think he killed himself, but you don't know who would have gone to the trouble to kill him?"

"Hey, you're the cop. None of this makes sense to me; does it make sense to you?"

"I'll have to think on this some more. You say there are photos?"

"I've got 'em right here."

"Any chance you can scan them and send them to me?"

"I can do that."

"All right, let me give you my email address. I'll look into some things and get back to you."

After ringing off, Frank took another deep breath and considered leaving it all for the morning.

He couldn't. He restarted his computer and sat back, thinking.

* * * *

Suicide was of course a familiar topic to every member of the Personal Crimes unit. Frank's own experience was that in self-inflicted injuries involving handguns, including fatalities, the victim tended to use their dominant hand to fire the weapon. He could still quote the textbook line because he had done so on numerous occasions to young detectives coming up:

"If it is found that fatal injuries were inflicted by the non-dominant hand, this gives rise to doubt that the manner of death is suicide…."

He still had the binder from the Ronnie Rackham case in his drawer. He pulled it out and flipped through to Teddy Ralski's block-lettered note. Then he walked to a nearby metal cabinet, pulled down the evidence book they had created for the Creep case, and brought it back to his desk. He found the plastic liner sheet that held the crank note they had decided had come from Teddy Ralski and laid it alongside the other.

They looked the same. In both, the capital R's were slightly squared off. He peered at each of them, back and forth. The letters leaned a bit to the right in both notes.

Were they the same? Was his imagination just starting to run away with him?

His memory of the note left beside Ralski's body was that the writing was similar, but he needed to see it to be sure. He dialed SID: they still had the suicide note found with Teddy. Nobody picked up. He'd have to try again in the morning.

There was a BING from his computer to indicate new email. Wilde hadn't wasted any time in getting the scanned photos to him. He must have had them handy, and had probably been looking them over just before he called Frank.

The first photo showed a group of men of various ages in tee shirts and jeans, on a baseball field. The backstop fence was clearly visible in the background. Frank decided it was a group of residents at some point in time from Reboot: he recognized Cary Wilde among them.

There was one figure that had been circled with a marker: Ralski. Frank zoomed in on it. He was wearing a weathered baseball glove, what looked like a classic first baseman's mitt. And it was on his right hand.

The second photo, likely staged, showed Ralski in profile, in combat fatigues, holding an automatic in a two-hand stance, dramatically grimacing. He held the pistol grip in his left hand, left index finger on the trigger, and braced it with his right.

Frank sat in silence, staring at the screen, for how long he wasn't sure. He finally came out of his reverie and switched off his computer once again. There was nothing else he could do tonight.

He wasn't sure how much attention he'd be able to give a crime film tonight, or how much of an appetite he'd have for that pizza.

Tonight he'd be dealing, mainly, with his renewed guilt over Teddy Ralski's death.

16.

"Well, you look ready to roll. Dressed for success, I see."

Frank hung up his phone and looked up at Athena. He was wearing jeans and a well-worn sweatshirt that still held some indeterminate shade of greyish-blue, appropriate for the anticipated morning activities. She saw he actually looked pretty worn out.

"Tough night?" she asked.

"Yeah. I didn't sleep too well. Something bugged me most of the night. I just got off the phone with the ME and SID. This whole thing…I'm trying to put it all together."

"What's *it*? What's so important?"

Frank related the conversation he'd had with Cary Wilde the previous evening.

Athena sat on the edge of her desk. "Damn. That changes things."

"Sure does."

"So…we're now looking at Ralski as a possible murder?"

"I'd say we have to. That's why I came in early and I've been on the phone this morning, to take care of some of this before I head out. We need to give the evidence a much closer look."

"The Lou's gonna love this."

"I already talked to him, too. Yeah, he was truly delighted."

"What'd Sela say about the examination of Ralski's body?"

"She gave me the short version over the phone. She estimates he'd been dead since the prior Saturday, so about four days before we found him. Everything is consistent with a self-inflicted contact gunshot to the head, using a Smith and Wesson .38 special. She found gunshot residue on the victim's hand."

"His right hand."

"Uh huh."

"And of course, ink on his fingers."

"Yeah. Made up of a permanent dye and an alcohol-based solvent. The same type of ink used in the marker found at the scene."

"But no GSR or any kind of marking or stain on his left hand?"

"No. The left fingers were clean. She's sending over a hard copy report. It should be here when we both get back today."

"What about SID, any insights from them?"

"They initiated a trace of the weapon. I can follow up on that. But you know how often that's of no help. Everything else they've got so far will be in the report they're sending over today."

"Still the old school guy with the paper reports, huh?"

"Hey, we can't do anything until we both do our thing today, anyway. We might as well get the hard copies."

"Speaking of which, Sandy's probably waiting on me. I better get going. You have fun today, partner."

"Yeah," Frank replied wryly.. "I can't wait. You have a good day, too. See you back here later."

* * * *

"That fancy tech exec in handcuffs. That must have been something." Sandy Kovetsky shook her head and smiled as they approached the library park from the sidewalk.

"Oh yeah," Athena agreed. "Frank played that interview just right. You should have seen him. It was quite a show. But I still need to luck out here this morning if we're going to make this stick."

Kovetsky motioned for them to stop as they reached the walkway.

"That's your guy right over there. He's a fixture; if anybody was here, it was him. Domingo's not a bad guy, but he spooks really easily. It's better if he doesn't see me. Good luck."

"Thanks, Sandy. Nice catching up with you."

She waved and waited for her uniformed colleague to disappear down the street before turning back towards the park. She peered at the bench where the figure lay huddled against the chilly wind of the morning, trying to sleep. His face was turned away. She hoped she could get close enough to talk to him before he got frightened, and that she didn't look too much like a police officer herself.

She stuck her hands into her leather jacket, her dark hair flying in the breeze, and walked quietly towards the bench.

He was wrapped in a tattered brown blanket, and his hair was disheveled. When she was still a few steps away, he turned his head, instincts kicking in, and bolted up to a sitting position. His eyes widened in alarm. She could see he was ready to run.

"*No tengas miedo, señor Domingo,*" she said softly in her perfect Spanish, smiling, pulling her hands out of her pockets slowly and opening them. "*No tiénes ningún problema. Necesito tu ayuda. Por favor....*"

She hoped that the fact she was a friendly, smiling young woman and not a hard-eyed, tough looking old male would at least give her a minute or two to try to gain his trust. He looked her up and down suspiciously, but didn't move. He never took his eyes off her as she slowly sat down next to him.

* * * *

At the same time, several miles away, at a sprawling automotive scrap yard, Frank and his colleagues assembled: two patrol officers happy to garner some overtime and two eager Police Academy cadets who, he reflected, would likely feel differently about volunteering soon enough in their careers.

He presented his warrant to a bored-looking manager who summoned a drowsy young underling. The kid appeared under-motivated, to say the least, but he lazily led them to the designated area. They followed him, lugging packs and toolboxes through the steel labyrinth of dismantled and corroding vehicles, some jammed side by side, some even piled one atop another, to all sides.

The kid finally stopped, waving an arm around him.

"If it was dumped here around the time you said, it'd be in this area. Aside from that, I can't really help you much."

Frank pursed his lips and nodded. That was why he'd brought help. "Thanks. We'll take it from here."

As the kid slouched back to his work station, they surveyed the detritus around them. They had all come dressed in coveralls, expecting to get dirty.

"Let's get to it," Frank said.

Over four hours later, sweaty and soiled, they found what they'd come for. It might have taken even longer, were it not for the smell they finally started noticing.

That led them exactly where they needed to go.

Frank got on his phone, first to the crime lab and the coroner. Then he rang Athena and told her to come join him.

The salvage yard was soon crawling with the usual crime scene personnel, along with some heavier equipment than usual, as it became necessary to move a few vehicles out of the way to provide access to the older model sedan that matched the description of Nathan Trenier's car.

Its back seat was filled with boxes and a suitcase, and in the trunk, jammed in with still more boxes, was a decaying body, wrapped in layers of blood-stained plastic sheeting.

There was little doubt it would turn out to be identified as Nathan Trenier. He had been stabbed multiple times before being encased in the plastic and wedged into the trunk of the sedan.

Frank and Athena both figured it wouldn't be all that difficult to reconstruct what had happened, especially once Mickey Kendrick had established an approximate time of death, and given what Leonard Killian had confessed to them earlier.

Killian had caught up with Trenier on the very night he was preparing to leave town, killed him right there on his own dark street, placed him in the trunk of his own car alongside the stuff that he'd packed, and driven him to the yard, which he knew was a place where wrecks could sit for months without being paid much attention.

Over time it would be piled among other wrecks, maybe compacted, and that would be that. He abandoned the car among the heaps and walked home.

Killian had described it as his "trial run" for his intended kills and he had decided it was "too crude," with too many elements to control. It worried him that a certain amount had been left to chance. He decided to "refine his technique" thereafter to a "more elegant solution."

As Athena watched Kendrick and his team unwrap what was left of the body of Nathan Trenier, Athena said quietly, "I'd say Killian was right about one thing."

"Huh? What's that?"

"This is anything but an elegant solution."

* * * *

They finally felt they could call it a day. Trenier had been taken away by the Coroner's van and the crime lab techs were ready to wrap things up.

Frank wearily peeled off his coverall and shoe covers and deposited them in the portable bin where the rest of his team had left theirs when he'd dismissed them earlier. He still looked grimy and ratty as he and Athena trudged back through the junkyard to their cars.

"I for one will be happy to get home to a long, hot shower tonight," he said.

"No doubt."

"So how did things go with your witness in the park?"

"Better than I expected. That guy Domingo? He finally admitted he was the one who phoned in Luczon's murder. He was sleeping behind the bushes where nobody could see him to bother him. According to what he told me, Collis's argument with Luczon woke him. He looked out and he saw her attack him. He said she went at him "like a man, a crazy man." That was how he described it. Frightened the daylights out of him; he just stayed frozen motionless there in the dark shrubbery while she stabbed Luczon, took his bag, and hurried off.

"When he decided it was safe, he lit out of there, terrified. He was panicked but he wanted to do the right thing, so after going back and forth about it for some time, he made the decision to call it in."

"Just his luck, I guess, to have change. And he was even luckier, to find an actual working pay phone."

"Yeah. By a good turn of events, the library still has a few of those in front. Go figure."

"Library patrons must include old farts like me, I guess."

"But I also got lucky with the timing," she said. "The whole thing spooked him enough that he'd stayed away from the park for several days. He'd pretty much just returned, thinking it was safe."

"Do you think his story will hold up?"

"I think we've got a good chance of that, yeah. Domingo's actually a pretty coherent guy, once you can get him to talk."

"And you seem to have been able to convince him to do just that. Good job."

"Sandy says he's a longtime street person with that intense wariness. But he doesn't strike her as a psycho, a druggie or a drinker. I got an assistant DA down to talk to him and the attorney seemed hopeful they could use his testimony. I'm going to see if I can get him someplace to stay for a while too."

"We've had a pretty good day, all in all. We caught some breaks."

"When you're hot, you're hot."

"Yeah, well…wish we could get hot on the Ralski thing. I'm not sure where we're going to go with that one."

"Oh yeah. The reports came in from SID and the ME. After handing Domingo over to talk to the ADA, I took some time to look through them. Ballistics confirmed the gun, not that we had much doubt about that. I also followed up on the gun trace that SID had initiated."

"Good. Anything?"

"Not much help. Last registry was with a guy in the Las Vegas area named Garth Swinton. He reported it stolen about a year ago."

Frank shook his head. He was too aware of how futile a gun trace could be. There were too many rabbit holes.

"Any other thoughts jump out at you from what you saw?"

"I spent some time looking at the photo of the suicide note. Comparing it to the other notes we have. They're similar, but I wouldn't call them identical."

"What do you mean?"

"It's the same kind of block letters, that slightly squared off R and things like that, but they lean slightly to the other direction, to the left. I'm no handwriting expert but I'd venture they were written by a right-hander."

"A right-handed person trying to imitate Ralski's printing, would be my guess. I'm impressed, Pardo."

"Maybe I'm right and maybe I'm wrong." Athena lapsed into silence as they walked. Finally she heaved a sigh.

"What's on your mind?"

"I'm trying to make some sense of why somebody would kill Ralski," she said. "There's no motive for robbery; the guy didn't have the proverbial pot to piss in. And from what we've been told, he wasn't involved in any kind of sketchy stuff like drugs or contraband. He didn't hang around with troublesome sorts, and he had no enemies.

"Ralski was an unqualified success story. He'd returned to some kind of sane existence. He got along with everybody. Everybody liked him. His life was all sweetness and light and all of a sudden he plunged back into darkness."

"Yeah," said Frank. "That's how Wilde and the uncle both put it. It was downright symbolic. He even went from his uncle's bright, sunny home into the dark…"

Now it was Frank's turn to lapse into silence.

"What. Frank?"

"There's something. Something maybe I should have picked up on earlier."

"What?"

"Maybe it doesn't mean anything, but…."

"*What?*" Athena exclaimed. "Are you going to tell me, already?"

They had reached the street and stopped near where they had both parked. He laid out what he was thinking. When he was finished, she nodded.

"You might have something there. I should've caught it as well."

"Let's look into this, first thing tomorrow morning." Frank yawned. "I definitely need some quality sleep."

"I hope you can put this stuff out of your mind long enough to sleep better tonight."

He smiled. "I think I'm so damned tired, I'll fall asleep the moment I get home no matter what. But I've suddenly got a good feeling about this. I think I can definitely sleep a little better tonight."

17.

"Frank Vandegraf! Rumors of your demise have been exaggerated!"

Frank, at his desk phone, sat back in his chair and looked across to Athena, who was totally absorbed in her computer monitor. It looked as if she just might have found what they'd hoped. Neither of them had let up since they had walked into work that morning and set up their course of action.

"How have you been, Sam? Enjoying LVPD?"

"Hey, it's a living. It could be a lot worse. And how are you?--still with Personal Crimes?"

"Yeah. In fact that's why I'm calling you."

Frank laid out what information he had about the last known registered owner of the Smith & Wesson that had been the instrument of Teddy Ralski's death.

"That's a pretty common story around here. Probably is everywhere. I'll tell you what I think *could* have happened. Guy needs some money so takes one or a couple of guns he's acquired by whatever means and quietly sells them. He's supposed to have them fill out the required background check and all that, but sometimes a few steps get missed, if you follow me. Then he reports the weapon as stolen. Whoops, I left it in my car, the car got broken into, or my house or whatever, what are the odds, officer? I'm shocked, shocked, I tell you! What's his name, this last known owner?"

"Garth Swinton. Does the name mean anything to you?"

"Damn, I've heard the name. I just can't place it. Tell you what, I'll look into this a little bit and call you back, how's that?"

"Greatly appreciate your help, Sam."

Frank hung up the phone.

"Sam just might have a lead on this Swinton guy," he said. " Let's keep our fingers crossed."

"How exactly do you know Sam?" Athena asked absently, never taking her eyes off the screen or her fingers off the mouse and the keyboard. She was clearly onto something.

"Sam Barnes? He used to work here, in Personal Crimes, then in Vice. He moved to Vegas a while back and wound up on LVPD. Good guy. We kept the channels open just in case, every so often, one of us might be able to help out the other. How's your search going?"

Athena had about three windows open on her screen and was tapping away like a world class stenographer. "I do believe you had something there, Frank. Come look at these public documents I was able to access."

Frank rose from his chair and crossed to her desk, looking over her shoulder at the monitor. She moved one particular window to the foreground and enlarged it, then slowly scrolled it while Frank read what she wanted him to read.

Finally Frank exhaled, subconsciously rubbing the back of his neck with his hand. Athena looked up at him.

"Bingo," she said.

"Uh huh," he replied.

She activated another window and pointed to the screen. "I'd say we need to talk to this guy, wouldn't you?"

"Morton Smollin, huh? I would say so."

"I'll track him down. In the meantime, what do you think about Dr. Audrey Chen...will we have any better luck with her this time?"

Frank had his phone back in his hand and he was dialing. "I would say she'll definitely be more helpful this time around."

She wouldn't be happy about it, but she might be a lot more helpful.

"Hello, Detective," Dr. Chen said. "If you're calling to tell me about Theodore Ralski, I have already been informed of his death."

"I'm sorry. I'm sure it was difficult to hear of it."

"That would be an understatement."

She was silent for a while, as if struggling to decide whether to continue.

"It's the first time a patient of mine took his or her own life. I think this is going to stay with me for some time. But if you're just calling to bring me up to speed, let me assure you, you can't make me feel any guiltier than I already do."

Frank thought back to their prior conversation when she had stonewalled him and claimed she wasn't worried about Teddy missing an appointment.

She thinks she could have prevented this if she'd just shown a little more concern.

It fell together for him as he sized up the situation. It wasn't all that different from what people faced in his own line of work. She's young, smart, dedicated. She's in a facility that's constantly overworked. She thought she had everything figured out, but she didn't.

None of us ever have.

Wozniak said that Teddy called her Audrey. Not Dr. Chen. Did she call him Teddy?

"Dr. Chen, I'm not calling to make you feel guilty. You aren't responsible for what happened to Teddy Ralski. But things were different from what you may have been led to believe."

"And what's that supposed to mean?"

"We're now looking at this death as a murder, not a suicide."

"What?"

"I can't tell you any more than that. It's an ongoing investigation. But I'm pretty sure that he did not die by his own hand."

There was another long pause on the other end of the line. "I…I don't know what to say to that. You're saying somebody killed him? And then made it look like suicide?"

"That's what we now believe."

"My God…but who would do such a thing? And why?"

"That's what we're trying to find out. Somebody has to speak for him… for the dead. That's our job. I'm hoping you might be able to help us."

There was still another thoughtful pause. Dr. Chen was a deliberate soul.

"What do you need from me?"

"Can you tell me what you know about his prescription? Is there any chance he stopped taking his medication?"

"I of course can't say definitively yes or no, but it wouldn't have made sense to me. He's maintained his regimen faithfully for the whole time he's been under my care, which is more than a year now. He seemed quite dedicated to his continued recovery. And he's refilled his prescription regularly. He gets two months' worth at a time and it's not due for a refill for another week or so."

"Forgive me, but…if I understand such things properly, wouldn't it be standard procedure for him to be monitored regularly for adverse side effects?"

"Of course, and originally he was watched quite carefully. But over time there seemed to be no problems, so it seemed reasonable to extend the period between routine monitoring for such things. By every criterion, he was doing very well in his daily practice."

There was another long pause and an audible sigh. "If there was a patient here for whom I would have predicted long term success, it would have been him."

Not the first person with that assessment, Frank reflected. By everyone's measure, it would seem, Teddy Ralski was an inexplicable tragedy.

"What medication was he on, precisely?"

"It was Fluphenazine. It's a common antipsychotic. To be taken PO twice a day. In his case it seemed to be working quite well."

Frank jotted the name down on his pad. He understood PO meant it was taken orally.

"What would be the effect if someone on this medication were to stop taking it all at once?"

"There's a strong danger their psychosis would return, among other things. What are you saying?"

"I'm not quite sure," Frank replied. "Not yet."

"He knew that," she said. "Teddy wouldn't have just stopped his medication. He would have talked to me if there were some kind of a problem like an unpleasant side effect. But he had absolutely no history of anything like that. The medication was working perfectly for him."

Chen paused again and when she continued, her voice held a new note of obvious apprehension. "I just don't understand. Why would somebody want to kill him? He was such a sweet and happy man."

"So…he never talked to you about anyone who, well, caused him any concern?"

"No…not at all. He often talked about his life at the Reboot center. He absolutely loved his time there. It would seem he had had no conflicts of any kind with anyone. And he spoke downright glowingly of Mr. Wilde who runs the center. He loved helping the other residents, and it would seem they liked him as well. And he was so appreciative of his uncle who had come to town to help him get on his own two feet again."

"What about before he went to Reboot, when he was still in his sickness? He must have talked about that with you."

"Oh yes, quite a bit. He had made almost no contact with anyone in those days. He was very isolated which only compounded his delusions at the time."

"Did he seem to think someone was out to get him back then?"

"That was clearly part of the delusions. He had long come to the realization that those 'people' he was writing letters and making phone calls about weren't after him at all. No…he had no real enemies, Detective. Not even you. It was you who brought him in for questioning back in those days, wasn't it?"

"Yes, it was."

"Well, he held no grudge against you. He had come to understand why you had done so, and he appreciated that you had, in fact, helped him. He saw how everything fit together."

Not everything, thought Frank. Not everything.

The rest of the conversation ended quickly. Frank asked a few more quick questions before deciding he had enough to proceed with his investigation. He ended the call by suggesting Chen might want to take some time off to process what had happened.

"The administration is trying to get me to do that," she admitted. "But there's so much to be done and I've got a huge workload of patients."

"I hope this isn't taken as speaking out of line, Doctor, but this event is something we see in my line of work too often. You can't take it all on yourself. If they're offering you leave to sort it out, please, take it. You'll come back better equipped to help your patients."

There was a very long silence on her end and Frank wasn't sure if she was getting ready to tell him where to shove his advice.

Finally she said quietly, "I'll think about it, Detective Vandegraf. I hope you find the person responsible for Teddy's death."

"I will," Frank said. "I can pretty much promise you that."

Athena hung up her own phone a while later, swiveled in her chair and flashed a thumbs' up signal to him.

"Success on Smollin," she said. "I asked him for some further info and he's emailing it to me. How'd you do with the good Doctor?"

Frank filled her in on his conversation. He picked up the pad he'd been scribbling on. "Would you mind doing a few quick internet searches for me on something?"

It was less than two hours later when Frank's phone rang again.

"Frank, we don't talk for ages and now twice in one day. What are the odds, as we say here in Vegas?"

"Sam…thanks for getting back to me so promptly. Might this mean good news?"

"As luck would have it, your Mr. Swinton is presently in the system here. One of my colleagues had a recent conversation with him on other matters. Let's just say that he's presently in a bit of a situation and could use some consideration from us. Turns out he was reasonably willing to volunteer a little information if it bought him some consideration in return."

"Sounds promising, but I hope you didn't have to waste a favor to help me out."

"It's no matter. Swinton's a little fish. If this helps you turn a murder, I'd rather have you beholden to me any day."

"Now you really make it sound promising."

"Turns out, like I figured, he sold a couple of his guns last year and filed a report that they'd been stolen in a break-in to his garage. We find some knucklehead doing that fairly regularly."

"It was just dumb luck you had my particular knucklehead in custody just now, I guess."

"Yeah, well, Mr. Swinton is often a guest of the city. He's fond of waltzing around the rules. Illicit property has a way of turning up in his shed, not to mention illicit substances. Anyway, after a short conversation, his memory improved remarkably on the topic of the guns he'd reported stolen. Turns out he was a little short of cash and certain people were strongly urging him to pay his debts to them, and the guns were a strong temptation for quick bank. One was a shotgun that went to a felon here in town. But the handgun…"

"Tell me it was a Smith & Wesson .38."

"As a matter of fact, it was."

"And tell me he remembers who he sold it to."

"Well, it's not like he asked for ID or filled out a receipt. He just happened to be at one of those sketchy unofficial 'gun shows' that crop up here and there, you know, where a guy who knew a guy who knew a guy..."

"Of course. But...?"

"He did, as it turns out, remember basically what the buyer looked and sounded like, because he wasn't your usual customer type...."

Athena overheard Frank's side of the conversation and had walked over to Frank's desk to listen raptly. When it was over, Frank once again held up the pad upon which he'd been jotting down notes.

"I think we got it," he said.

"How about I drive this time?"

* * * *

"Detectives! This is a surprise! Do you have some new information?" Phil Wozniak stared out through the partly-open door, his eyes wide behind his thick lenses.

"You might say that, Mr. Wozniak. And we also needed to ask you a few more questions to move things along. May we come in?"

"Um...certainly you may!" He opened the door and stepped back to let them enter. They surveyed the boxes stacked on the floor throughout the living room as he motioned to the chairs. There were no piles of books or magazines on them anymore. Likely most had already been boxed up. "I'm sorry. It's a bit of a mess. Please, sit anywhere."

"It looks as if you're getting ready to move?"

"Yes. I've decided to return to Lake Havasu City. There really won't be much to keep me here any longer."

"Oh. I'm surprised. I thought you had a lease here until the end of the year," said Athena, moving towards one of the chairs. "And that you had tenants leasing out your place there until the end of the year as well?"

"That's true. But I was able to negotiate my way out of both of those agreements. I really don't want to stay here any longer than I absolutely have to, what with all that's happened. I'm sure you understand."

"It must be hard, even for a short time, to have all your books boxed up like this. You seem to be quite the voracious reader."

"That's true. I don't have a television or even a computer. I like to spend my time reading."

"I couldn't help noticing last time we were here, how wide your interests are. You have books on all sorts of subjects. I even saw medical texts."

"Oh, you must mean the Netter anatomy books. I found them at a thrift store. They're very interesting, since I really don't know all that much about the subject."

"And the pharmacology book, the one with all the drugs and stuff? I remember seeing one of those when I was much younger. I remember being fascinated by all the different colored pills and capsules and things."

"Yes, I got that at the same time. I'm always interested in something new. You'd be amazed at the range of things one can find for just a couple of dollars at the second-hand shop."

Wozniak did not in the least seem bothered by Athena's comments: neither how she knew about the medical texts nor why she would ask about them. He must have figured it was small talk leading up to the real subject. They all sat and the conversation lapsed as he looked at them expectantly.

"I'm hoping that my nephew's body will be released to me soon," Wozniak continued. "...I mean after the autopsy has ended and all. This new information you need...will it help speed up that process?"

"It certainly could," answered Frank. "It will be up to the coroner's office to contact you when they can release your nephew."

"I hope they do so soon. I'd like to take Teddy's remains back with me to Havasu. There's a family plot there where he can be laid to rest. I don't think he'd have wanted to remain here. Now he can be with his family."

"Is that where your sister, Teddy's mother, is buried?" asked Athena.

"Yes. In fact, it's also the cemetery where my wife, Julia, is interred... and my brother-in-law, Teddy's father."

"If you don't mind my asking, sir, just how did Teddy's parents die?"

"My sister, Hilda, had cancer."

"I'm sorry."

Wozniak removed his glasses and wiped them with a piece of cloth, then paused before replacing them to wipe a gleam from the corner of his eye.

"It was, let me see, almost two years ago now. She fought a valiant fight against it. We all thought she had turned a corner and might beat it. But then her husband, Alex, suddenly died. He had a blood clot in his brain that hadn't been diagnosed and he just keeled over in the street one day. That seemed to take the fight out of her. Her cancer came roaring back a few weeks later. She lasted about another eight months and...well, that was it."

"How terrible. So you lost them both in less than a year. That must have been hard."

"It was very hard. I had just lost Julia only two years earlier."

"Had they had any contact with their son before they died?"

"They tried. Both Hilda and Alex went to some trouble to locate him and reach out, but he was in the depths of his sickness and simply lashed out at them every time. After a while they gave up."

Frank did some calculations in his head. It was about three years ago that Teddy had gotten into Reboot. Had his parents kept trying, they could have communicated with him and found a very different person. But they had apparently despaired of reaching him before that could happen.

"How did you find Teddy?"

"It was after Hilda's death. I had nobody left. I decided to go looking for Teddy. To be honest, it gave my life some meaning at a time it needed it. I knew he was somewhere in this city when he'd last contacted the family, so this was my starting point. It wasn't all that hard from there."

"So," said Athena, "you found he was at the Reboot recovery center and came here to be with him."

"Exactly. It was easy enough to rent out my condo and find this apartment, to be near him and hopefully to support him."

"It would seem you came at the perfect time. He was ready to leave the center and try living on his own again."

"Yes. I'd say I lucked out all around. I found this lovely place and reconnected with Teddy at just the right moment." He looked down at his lap gloomily. "And it was a good thing. I'd say I needed a spot of good luck at that point."

"I would say you did," Frank replied, a small, strange smile playing across his lips.

Wozniak looked up at them. "But please tell me, why did you come here? What do you need from me? What can you tell me?"

Frank leaned forward, his forearms resting on his knees, and gazed at Wozniak. "I believe you told me you had no personal contact with your nephew since he moved out of here, is that right?"

"That's right. He called me a couple of times but he never came to visit."

"And if I recall, you said you never visited him?"

"No...I tried a few times, but I never saw him."

"You didn't visit him, say, at work?"

"No...Never."

"And you didn't visit him in his new apartment?"

"No. No, I didn't."

"Surely you've seen it, though? Perhaps when he was first looking at it?"

"No. I've never set foot in it."

"I'm curious how you pictured it, in your mind." Frank looked around and gestured with his hands. "This apartment is so bright and cheerful. He seems to have been very happy here."

"Yes. Yes, he was. I did my best to make it all happy."

"Probably Teddy would have chosen some place like this. Lots of windows. Lots of sunshine."

"I...I don't know, Detective. What's the point of all this?"

"Do you remember the night we came to inform you of the death of your nephew, Mr. Wozniak?"

"Do I remember? What's that supposed to mean? How could I ever forget?"

"You made a comment to me that evening. You said something like, 'If only he hadn't gone to that dark apartment.' And his apartment really *was* dark. Depressingly so. If you'd never actually been in there, how could you have known that?"

"I...I couldn't have said that. You must be mistaken."

"No, sir," Athena said. "I was there too. I heard you say it as well."

Wozniak sat and just stared at them for a long, long time, his eyes magnified disturbingly through his Coke bottle lenses. Frank and Athena let the heavy silence do its work.

"I...suppose I just assumed. For some reason, it's how I envisioned it. Likely he told me about the apartment when we talked on the phone. I've never been near his place, as I told you."

Frank nodded and raised his hands. "Okay. That's certainly possible. The fact you said that to me doesn't necessarily mean anything in and of itself. But let me ask you something else: when your sister died, to your knowledge, did she leave a will?"

"A will? I suppose she did, yes. I know for a fact that she didn't leave me anything. I don't know that she had much to leave to anyone."

"Actually, sir," Athena said, "the Ralskis invested and saved quite well over their lifetimes. By the time Mrs. Ralski passed away, she was worth something like eight hundred thousand dollars. That's a lot of money. Maybe not as much as it once would have been, but a hefty sum nonetheless."

Wozniak looked at her, his lower lip quivering. "Is that right?"

"I believe you know Morton Smollin, don't you?" asked Frank. Wozniak's head bounced back to look at him again.

"What...who?"

"Morton Smollin is an attorney in the state of Arizona. He wrote the last will and testament of Hilda Ralski."

Athena had brought a small zipped case with her. She opened it and removed a file folder.

"Here it is. A copy of her will, certified by the registrar of Mohave County."

"I think you know exactly what it says," Frank continued. "I believe Mr. Smollin was in fact the one who read it to you. I assume we don't have to read it to you again; I'm guessing you know it verbatim, by heart."

Athena opened the file and flipped through the pages of the document. "She left everything to her son Theodore. But with certain conditions: The money was to be held in trust for him and to be used to support his care, until such time as he could acceptably demonstrate his capacity to act in a responsible manner. There are certain specific guidelines set down to define exactly what that meant: being under the care of responsible medical providers, holding regular employment, living on his own, demonstrating there was no substance abuse, and so on. Until such time, the money was to be kept and administered, keeping Mr. Smollin informed, by a certain designated trustee and guardian."

Athena looked up at Wozniak. "And guess who that designated guardian happens to be, Mr. Wozniak? And upon the death of Theodore, the money then reverts to the trustee... but you know that, too, don't you?"

The deathly stillness fell over them all again. Wozniak could only stare blankly in their direction, his mouth now agape. He couldn't say a word.

"Did Teddy ever actually know about this, Mr. Wozniak?" she finally asked. "Did he ever in fact learn that he was heir to almost a million dollars?"

Wozniak had no answer.

"By the way," Frank added, "if you're wondering how we knew about Morton Smollin...well, we had a conversation with him, just today, in fact. You were required to check in with him regularly about how you were spending Teddy's money. Somehow he never got the message that Teddy had moved out and was on his own."

"His situation was getting awfully close to the conditions stipulated in the will that would have turned the money over to him," Athena said quietly. "And where would that have left you?"

The words seemed to fight being expressed, and Wozniak seemed to be struggling to let every single one of them out. "I was...*going* to tell him! I was afraid for Teddy...I thought he'd relapse." He spread his hands to indicate the room in which they sat. "I needed to keep this place open for him...to be here for him! I just didn't think he'd make it! And I was right! You...you see what happened?"

"What exactly did happen, Mr. Wozniak?"

"Why, he gave up on his treatment! He stopped his medications! He slid back in to that awful insanity...."

"How do you know that? Didn't you just tell us you had almost no contact with him since he moved out?"

"He...he called and told me! Right after he moved out! That was probably why he wouldn't see me anymore. I tried to convince him to go back to the hospital and go back on his medication! That...that's when he started acting crazy!"

"How did you decide he started acting crazy?"

"You told me about the letters and everything when you first came to see me!"

"Mr. Wozniak," Frank said, gazing intently at the old man, "we've got a team going back to Teddy's apartment to fingerprint it extensively. Are we going to find any of your prints anywhere in that apartment?"

That gave him pause. His hands had begun to shake in his lap. "I was never in there. I told you."

"How about his medicine cabinet...were you in there?"

"I was never in there!"

"It's interesting to me that you think he stopped taking his medication. Because, you see, we found out earlier today that he'd been filling his prescriptions regularly up until only a couple of weeks ago. And there wasn't a trace of them in his apartment. You'd think there would have been at least a bottle, even an empty one?"

"I...I don't know! I can't answer questions like that! Teddy wasn't thinking straight! You expect that his actions would make sense? He shot himself, for God's sake! Sane people don't do that!" Wozniak's voice was beginning to break. It felt as if any moment he'd start sobbing.

Frank's voice remained calm, almost gentle. "You're right. But sometimes sane people kill other people."

"What? What do you mean by that?"

"You told us you didn't know where Teddy would have gotten that gun, didn't you?"

"No, I...I can't imagine!"

Frank was slowly removing a folded piece of paper from inside his sport coat as he spoke. He opened it up and handed it to Wozniak...a photograph printed off the internet.

"Mr. Wozniak, have you ever met this man?"

The elderly man squinted at the picture through his thick spectacles, scowling. "No. I have no idea who he is. Why are you showing me this?"

"His name is Garth Swinton. He lives near Las Vegas. That's not all that far from Lake Havasu City is it? Maybe a couple hours' drive or bus ride? Do you ever go to Las Vegas, sir?"

"Not...not very often. I've been there once or twice. There are package vacations for retirees. There are plenty of us in Havasu."

"Were you there, say, a year, a year and a half ago?"

"I—no, I don't remember, I don't think so. That's when I was getting ready to move here to take care of Teddy."

Frank quietly took the paper out of the trembling fingers of the old man. He held up the picture.

"Garth Swinton seems to remember meeting you. He has good reason to remember. He just told a Las Vegas detective that he sold someone a pistol, a Smith & Wesson .38 Special…the very same kind of gun that killed Teddy Ralski."

Frank lowered the picture and stared at Wozniak. "And he described the person in some detail. He especially remembered the glasses. It was you, Mr. Wozniak. So are you going to tell us about it?"

Wozniak began to reach a trembling hand out for the paper but then he dropped his face into both hands. His thick spectacles slid off his nose and past his fingers into his lap.

"It wasn't fair!" he sobbed. "It just wasn't fair!"

Then for the longest time, he cried, hard and bitterly, never removing his face from his hands. Frank and Athena just waited.

* * * *

Frank found Wilde at the end of the bar at Kerrie's, huddled over his glass. The stools to either side of him were vacant, as if the regulars knew to leave him alone. Frank, never one to take a hint, ordered a beer and slid onto the stool to his left. Wilde didn't react.

"When I called Reboot they told me I'd find you here."

Wilde continued to stare down at his glass. "Has not been a good day."

"Sorry to hear that. I suspect you have your share of those."

"One of my guys got himself killed in a car wreck. They asked me to ID the body…What was left of it. This is where I come after shit like that."

"I'm amazed you can come to a bar after shit like that and not drink. That is club soda, I assume."

Wilde did the thumb-and-finger shake of his glass. The ice cubes tinkled. "For some reason I'm just not tempted to do anything stronger. I'm not sure why. I wouldn't recommend this to any of my guys who are in recovery. I'd tell them it was plain stupid."

"Do as you say, not as you do?"

He replaced the glass on the bar, almost exactly on top of the water circle it had left when he picked it up. "Guess I was definitely done when I was done. Too bad tonight's my ex's night off. She could tell you some stories."

"You're not curious as to why I'm here?"

He looked sideways at Frank. "Okay, I'll bite. So why are you here?"

Frank paused while the scowling tattooed bartender, a guy slightly smaller than a four-bedroom house, brought his beer and departed.

He took a swig out of the bottle. "This is between you and me."

"Understood…."

"Teddy *didn't* kill himself. You were right. The old man did it and made it look like suicide. He wrote the note, put the gun in Teddy's hand, put it against his head and pulled the trigger."

"Damn. The uncle did it? You're shitting me."

"One and the same. He just signed a confession at the station."

"Never met the guy and still never liked him. He seemed to be too ready to help out. It's funny. I thought he was going to be too much of a support, that Teddy would grow too dependent on him. He needed to stand on his own two feet."

"Well, in a sense you were right. He did kind of set up Teddy to fail."

"Is he the one who got Teddy off his meds?"

Frank nodded grimly. "He mounted quite the campaign. He had something called a Physicians' Desk Reference…are you familiar with it?"

"I know what that is."

"Wozniak actually looked up Teddy's meds and went out and found over the counter drugs that looked reasonably similar. He'd visit Teddy regularly, slip into the bathroom, and substitute the useless drugs. Teddy apparently never noticed and just took them."

"Son of a bitch, are you shitting me?"

"Pretty ballsy of the old man…I have to give him that. He doesn't even have a computer. He had to page through that huge book until he found something similar that he could get easily his hands on. That still took some kind of application on his part. Generic drugs like Teddy was getting tend not to be fancy; sometimes they're just nondescript white things. He made the switch and then he waited.

"After a while, Teddy started to slip and began to believe his uncle's reassurance that he was doing fine and didn't really need the meds anymore. So finally he stopped taking them altogether. It wasn't all that long before the old voices started coming back, along with all the delusions. He even called Wozniak not long ago and told him he'd heard about the Creep killings. He was sure the same evil force that had killed Ronnie Rackham was back in action again and he needed to let people know."

"So, Teddy really did write that letter to you that set you on his trail?"

"Yeah. Wozniak confirmed it. It tipped him off that Teddy was close enough to the edge that he could finish him off and it would be believed as a suicide. He must have been delighted to see Teddy fall back down into the pit like that so he could carry out the rest of his plan."

"That evil scumbag. And what about the gun?"

"It was his, not Teddy's."

"Fuck. His uncle did it...his last family member...and why? Why would the man do something like that?"

"Did you know Teddy had an inheritance?"

Wilde's eyes widened as it slowly dawned on him.

"Well, fuck me. No!"

"Teddy never knew either. It was held in trust by the uncle. Once Teddy could demonstrate independence, it would go to him and the uncle would be out of the picture. But if for whatever reason Teddy were no longer around...."

He didn't have to finish the sentence.

"Was it a lot? I mean, how much are we talking about here?"

Frank told him. Wilde's jaw actually dropped, literally.

"You're shitting me."

"Some people will do some pretty terrible things when that kind of money is at issue. Phil Wozniak was one of them, I guess."

"Aw, hell." Wilde took a slow drink from his glass. "So...much...that just didn't have to be, you know?"

The two men sat in silence for the next few minutes, each slowly working on his drink. There wasn't much more that needed to be said.

It was Wilde who broke the hush.

"Appreciate you coming to tell me. At least you made the best of a bad situation."

Frank acknowledged him with a silent nod.

"I suppose now there's nobody to claim Teddy's body and arrange for service and burial and all that. Why don't I take care of that?"

"I hope that's not an undue burden on you or Reboot."

"It's what we're here for, Frank. Make sure I got all the info I need, would you?"

"I'll also get you in contact with the lawyer handling Hilda Ralski's will. His name is Morton Smollin. I figure the will goes into civil court now to disinherit Wozniak. I'm not sure how the disposition works after that but maybe there's some way some of the money can go to a nonprofit charity...like say, Reboot. At very least there might be provision to pay for the service and burial."

"That'd be something, even if it's a long shot. I'll look into it but I won't hold my breath. Just let me know what I need to know."

"You got it. Sorry to be the bearer of more depressing news on a day when you really didn't need it. I just needed to let you know we wouldn't have gotten him if you hadn't told me that Teddy was left-handed."

"No, Frank, this is *good* news. You made sure the motherfucker didn't get away with it. You stood up for Teddy. All things considered, this makes my day."

"Good way to look at it."

"You know, there's something we say at Reboot a lot, you're having a shit day, you can start it over anytime you choose. I think this is an optimal time for me to start right now."

"Good advice," Frank mused, thinking that he actually could look forward to a day off tomorrow, and it suddenly inspired a deep sense of relief.

But there was no reason he couldn't start over right now as well. "Mind if I sit with you a bit and finish my beer, maybe order a second?"

"No problem," said Wilde. "Long as you do it quietly, okay?"

They both grimly smiled and clinked bottle to glass. Neither one had a single thing to say for the remainder of the evening.

18.

It was, as the famed malapropist Yogi Berra once said, like déjà vu all over again. On the morning he returned to work, Frank stepped off the elevator to find Lieutenant Hank Castillo waiting for him, arms folded.

"What is this, Frank, are you being considered for Chairman of the Board or something?"

"What are you talking about, Lou?"

"You've got another high powered big wheel waiting for you in Interview Three."

"What? I didn't have anybody scheduled for this morning."

"He's a walk-in. He's with Pardo right now."

"Who the hell is *he,* Lou?"

Castillo smiled mysteriously. "Why don't you go see for yourself?"

As he entered the interview room, Frank recognized the visitor, though he had never met him in person and had a slightly different set of expectations about him. He was a short man with bristly dark hair wearing an expensive black suit and a white shirt open at the collar.

Before Athena could make introductions, he sprang from his seat across the table with a smile and extended his hand.

"Detective Vandegraf, I'm Lane Dembeau."

"Mr. Dembeau, this is a surprise. Please, sit down."

"I had to come by," Dembeau began as Frank pulled out a chair to join them, "to thank the both of you for your efforts."

His personal energy was scattershot but powerful. "It was sufficiently a surprise that you uncovered the murder of Orrin Lattimer, but it seems you may well have saved my own life in the process. And you've most definitely saved the life of Humbletech."

"I'm not quite sure how we did all that, sir, but I'm happy we were able to do our job."

Dembeau shook his head and pursed his lips. "I knew there was some friction developing with Collis, but I had no idea of the extent to which she had gone to undermine me. And those...*people* she brought in as silent investors..." he visibly shivered. "I had no idea of that either. She got so much by me."

"So you weren't worried that Lattimer was going to bolt your company?" Frank asked.

"Orrin? Bolt the company? What do you mean?"

Frank told him the story that Collis Westermark had related to them about the late-night meeting in which Dembeau had described Lattimer as a "mole" planning to leave Humbletech with its proprietary intellectual properties.

Dembeau looked totally nonplussed, not replying for several beats.

"That's crazy. No. I've never doubted Orrin for a moment! In fact Collis and I did have a conversation in which *she* expressed suspicions about Orrin. I dismissed them as nonsensical rumors. Orrin was always the most solid, essential member of our team."

He looked back and forth at Frank and Athena. "Things are beginning to come into focus now. It's making a little more sense. Collis was trying to poison the water, so to speak. To drive us apart, keep us off balance."

The man was a veritable font of metaphor, Frank mused.

"It would seem," Athena said, "that she was planning to take advantage of your absence to pull off her coup. By the time you returned...."

Dembeau nodded sadly. "...it would have been a *fait accompli.* Or so she hoped."

"I can't figure her out," Frank said. "She was probably the wealthiest person in the company, but it wasn't enough."

"No. You'd have to understand Collis. It would never be enough. I'm afraid I do understand, though. Many of us are driven by something and there will always have to be more. Believe me, I get that. With her, it happened to be the money."

"So," interjected Frank, "what's going to happen next to Humbletech?"

"There's definitely going to be a period of uncertainty, but I'm confident we'll pull ourselves out of it. Right now we have to address the publicity that's about to erupt. I suppose you'd call it spin control. But... perception is so much a part of success. Meanwhile, the truly important work is reorganizing the company, shoring up its resources and restoring capital. That's already underway. Luckily we have some highly capable people who have stepped up in the time of crisis, notably in our Innovation and Development department."

Sharon Brooks, thought Frank, but he said nothing.

"We may have to look inward for a short period," Dembeau continued, rising from his seat, "but I won't accept anything but full recovery. And speaking to that, I'm afraid I'm needed desperately right now, so I'll take my leave. But I wanted to personally give both of you my sincerest gratitude. Please let me know if there's anything I can ever do for either one of you."

"All in a day's work, Mr. Dembeau," said Frank as they shook hands. "Best of luck to you and to Humbletech."

"We're going to try to keep the HUMM scooters on the streets through this difficult time," Dembeau said as he shook hands with Athena. "If either one of you ever wants the use of one, just let us know."

When hell freezes over, thought Frank, once again remaining silent.

They walked Dembeau to the elevator, said their final farewells, and as the elevator door closed, Athena and Frank looked at one another.

Athena heaved a sigh of weariness, despite the early hour. "Does that end the parade of crazies?"

"Maybe the Humbletech parade. There's sure to be another procession before too long."

"Damn, this was quite the week. Even a couple days off didn't help me recover completely."

"Eating dolmas and tacos and scootering all over town, no doubt?"

"I had some fun and relaxed. I bet you spent the whole time watching noir films and eating pizza, huh?"

"Pretty much."

"Frank, you really need to expand your horizons, you know?"

"I don't know if I could handle my horizons if they were to get any wider."

* * * *

"It's kind of strange to be back here," Meryl Lattimer was saying, looking around her living room. "For a while, I wasn't sure I'd ever see this place again, and then I wasn't sure I ever wanted to."

"I'm sure it's difficult," Frank said. He and Athena were sitting with her in the sunny room. There was still that subtle smell and feel of a house that had been shut up for some time.

It made him think of another household, and he hoped that one day Moira McBroom would open her shades to re-admit the sun as well.

"Orrin did what he could to protect us. That horrible woman; I had no idea, the depths to which she'd sink. I'm happy she's behind bars."

"And I doubt she's going to be getting out. It was as I thought: she assumed she was too smart for us and made some careless mistakes."

Fortune had been on their side. Westermark had probably disposed of Luczon's bag, the murder weapon, and most of the clothing she wore when she killed him, but the SID team found Raymond's blood trace on one of her shoes.

Athena had established that Domingo, the homeless man behind the library, had indeed witnessed the murder from his sleeping place behind the bushes. He'd been the one who, in a panic, anonymously phoned it in; he was sufficiently frightened to stay away from the park for several days. He had seen enough, in grisly detail, to be able to identify Collis Westermark.

Their final stroke of luck had occurred when Computer Forensics had been able to access Luczon's computer. Collis may have been cautious in deleting all her emails and messages with him, but Ray had been somewhat less circumspect; in fact, it seemed he was covering himself by archiving their messages on his hard drives. There were several indirect but incriminating exchanges to add to the evidence trail.

"I assume she'll have a pricey defense team to fight it all," Meryl sighed. "She opened the door to those…*gangsters* to come in and take over the company. What was she thinking?"

"I don't think at first she realized with what kind of devil she was making a deal. Again, she was overconfident, convinced that she could handle them. Then, I believe, the reality of the situation dawned on her. She finally felt trapped and might have been scared for her own life."

"As well she probably should have been," Athena added.

"Speaking of which…I was contacted this week by a reporter," Meryl said. "Probably it was Orrin's reporter? He wanted to talk to me about what I might have known about the goings-on at Humbletech. I said that all I could tell him was what I heard from Orrin, but he still wants to see me. We're meeting tomorrow."

Frank nodded. Ben was on the job. Dominoes were beginning to fall and he was sure they wouldn't stop falling until the entire Humbletech story had come out.

Already there were inquiries being launched into the Meads, their organization, and their ties to Humbletech. And they knew that Lane Dembeau would be hyperactively busy with damage control---or more likely he had turned it over to his legal and PR personnel.

"Thank you for coming to the services for Orrin yesterday," Meryl continued. "I've got a lot to take care of in the next few days before Kyra and I can start to get our lives back to some kind of normal again. Just getting this house open and feeling like home again has been a challenge. I especially have to pay attention to Kyra to get her through this. She's still keeping everything bottled up. But first there's all this other legal and financial nonsense to be settled. "

"Have you decided what you're going to do with Orrin's patents and shares in the company?"

"I'm meeting with Lane tomorrow to discuss all that. He's lost both his co-principals and a scandal is breaking. It would be a lot for anybody to handle, but he wants to soldier on. I have no stomach for starting up a new venture with him or anyone. But there is someone who might be."

"You mean Sharon?"

"There's nobody who knows the ins and outs of the company better. She was an apt pupil of Orrin's, and the most loyal colleague he could have had. She watched out for us, took enormous amounts of her own personal time to look after Kyra and me. Orrin trusted her sufficiently that she was the only one who knew where he was staying or how to access his phone."

Frank and Athena said nothing. It still seemed the level of intimacy between Orrin and Sharon had been beyond ordinary. Meryl sensed the awkwardness.

"I know what you're thinking. And yes, for a moment, there was something between them. Orrin and I talked about it some time ago and worked our way through it."

She saw the hesitation in both their faces. "Surely, detectives, you realize that even smart people can do stupid things? I honestly believe it didn't last more than an evanescent second; they both came to their senses quickly. But it was enough to give Collis a toehold to threaten them both. I know it seems strange to you, but Sharon became my own confidante and supporter, perhaps partly out of guilt. She's given to us far beyond the call of duty…as that politician once said, one hundred and ten percent."

"She's the one who kept you in touch and tended to your affairs here in the city after Orrin was gone. And she did all that on top of keeping her department running."

Meryl nodded. "She's an amazing woman. Did you know she's got degrees in both engineering and business? She might be the smartest and most capable person in the company. She's certainly got the most guts and integrity. And nobody saw it in her but Orrin. I have a feeling Lane is going to need to depend on her a lot in coming days."

"Well, I hope you're able to come away from this with some financial security as well as doing the right thing."

"I've been talking with my own financial advisor. The patents are still the biggest and surest asset the company has. I think it's going to come out just fine."

* * * *

They also learned that Natalie Riemer was progressing well and was communicating. The trauma of her experience still remained, but she was beginning to come out of it gradually.

One morning Frank and Athena were informed by Thalia that her sister could be released in a matter of a few more days, and that they were welcome to visit. The next morning they spent a quiet but pleasant time with Natalie and her family.

They were walking to the parking garage when Athena asked Frank, "How are you holding up?"

"Better, with time. What is it that comedians say about comedy, that it's tragedy plus time?"

"I doubt we're going to ever laugh about the last few weeks, even if we give it years."

"No. I guess there's no place to go but up for the Riemers. And Meryl and Kyra Lattimer for that matter, as well."

Athena shook her head and looked down. "This job...I don't know if I'll ever get used to the depths of depravity."

"Let's hope you never will. You're the last stand against the darkness sometimes."

"It's you and me and the rest of us, huh?"

Frank shook his head. "I'm not so sure about me anymore. I'm thinking maybe it's time for me to get out of the game."

"What? You're thinking of retiring?"

"I've got the time put in. I could do it."

"But why in the love of heaven would you?"

Frank shrugged, composing his thoughts as they walked.

"It really struck home to me with these cases, how far behind I really am. I'm trying to drag myself into the new century but I think I'm physically slowing down and mentally not keeping up."

Athena stopped and grasped Frank's arm, staring at him gravely.

"That's crazy...Just crazy. You just cleared two major cases."

"You did most of the legwork. You figured out the connections with the victims. You put out energy 24-7 until you found the missing pieces. I don't know that I could have done that."

"Frank, maybe I can fly through cyberspace faster than you, but you bring something that I can't. I hope someday I can, but right now I don't possess the gut instinct and the understanding of human nature that you do.

"You figured out what happened to Orrin Lattimer when everybody else wanted to just let it go...even me."

A small tear actually began to form in the corner of Athena's eye. "I hope you're not serious about this, that this is just you talking out of exhaustion right now. You're the best mentor and the best partner I could have asked for. I don't want you to leave just yet. Not for the reasons you just gave me."

"And there's something else," Frank continued. "I think that the darkness is getting to me more than it used to. Some of the stuff that happened this past week...it's nothing new. Maybe I just can't handle it as well as I once could."

"And you just gave me the lecture about how we're the last stand against the darkness. How many times have you told me that we're not supposed to feel good about what we do, were just supposed to do it as well as we can no matter what kind of hits we end up taking? Does that sound familiar?"

"Hoisting me on my own petard, are you, Pardo? I guess I might have taught you a thing or two after all." Frank simply stared at his partner for a long time, then smiled and once again shrugged. "Maybe I'm just thinking out loud. I appreciate the vote of confidence, Athena. I'll give this a lot more thought."

They resumed walking side by side into the parking garage.

"I'm not letting you leave until I help you get your social life back on track, Vandegraf."

Frank laughed. "That remains to be seen. But I guarantee, you're not getting me on one of those damned scooters."

* * * *

Athena's internet skills once again paid off when, two days later, she discovered a female cousin of Raymond Luczon in Cebu, in the Philippines. Her family had had no contact with him in almost a decade but she expressed a willingness to come to make his final arrangements.

At least Raymond would not be laid to rest in what was once called a pauper's grave.

That same day, Frank answered his phone to a voice he didn't immediately place.

"Detective, this is Otis, the bartender at the Cue and Mug. You asked me to call if I heard any word on Eddie McBroom."

"We're not looking for him anymore, but what's up?"

"You're not gonna believe this; he walked in here this morning. I didn't even recognize him. He came in to settle a bar bill I didn't even remember he had. Something about making amends. He's in a rehab house, been sober nearly a month now. There's, like, this light in his eyes or something. His skin's actually lost that grayish yellow color. Who knew, the damn mick is actually kinda pink. He looks good."

"Really?"

"Yeah. He said he was on his way over to see his wife, Moira. Said he talked with her earlier and had a lot to try to make up with her. He sounded pretty guilty about leaving her and all. You know how it is. Your bartender turns out to be your father confessor and he wanted to tell me the whole story. I told him I hoped he could work it out and go home again."

"That's good news. I hope he can too."

"So you're not looking for him anymore? Whatever that was got taken care of?"

"Yes," replied Frank. "Yes, it did. But thanks for letting me know, Otis. I'll tell my partner."

"He's lost weight, too. It looked like a huge burden had been lifted off his back. It was nice to see. Being a bartender, you see a lot of the downside. It's nice to see the good side of things once in a while, if you know what I mean?"

Frank laughed to himself. The guy had no idea.

"Do I ever, Otis. Do I ever."

ABOUT THE AUTHOR

Tony Gleeson, an inveterate fan of jazz and classic mysteries, is a writer, illustrator and graphic designer. He lives with his wife Anne and their en cats, Django and Mingus, in Los Angeles, California.

Made in the USA
Monee, IL
25 April 2021

66318556R10105